Naomi’s Legacy

Rick Hardesty

illustrated by Elizabeth Rachael

ISBN-13 978-1-0986-2098-1

To my dear sweet bride Peggy. I am grateful for every year we were blessed to be together. You fought the good fight alongside me throughout all the challenges and victories of life. You have always been the best friend, helpmate, and example of Godly living. You finished the race before me.

Chapter 1

A police radio crackled as the occupants of the SUV listened. "We have eyes on the target, a male, female, and three children just arrived and entered our target residence."
FBI Special Agent, Sandra Boyd, then spoke into the radio, "We're rolling up to the residence now." A three-car convoy of dark SUV's quickly entered a quiet middle-class neighborhood subdivision and stopped at a plain, but well-manicured house on the block. Agent Boyd continued, "I want the surveillance units to hang back at the perimeter and bring in the two marked police units at each end of the block in case if we need them for security. Agent Wilbrink and I will make contact with the female now, standby..."

~~~~~~~

December 1941

The Manchester family gathered together for their annual Christmas dinner at their winter estate in Greenwich, Connecticut. It was just days after the attack on Pearl Harbor. The whole world seemed to be in chaos and now it was about to hit the Manchester family. Jack Emmerson Manchester was planning to tell his family that he was going to enlist in the United States Marine Corps, but that meant postponing his entrance into Yale. Jack felt it was his duty to serve in the war. Even though he was not eligible to become a commissioned officer without a college diploma, he didn't care. Jack being impatient, decided to enlist anyway.
~~~~~~~

He knew this would cause a great divide between him and his parents, as the Manchester's were a prominent family in oil, banking, and the railroad. A Manchester could never leave the family roadmap of success and prosperity. They were titans in finance for generations; they were old money. How could Jack desert such a golden family tradition and walk away from what was expected of a Manchester? It was absolutely unthinkable, he knew he might be disowned and even disinherited by his family if he chose to become like a commoner, a mere enlisted soldier.

Jack had often argued with his father and openly disagreed with him in both politics and business. He knew that today's news would be the final straw.

With all the friction between him and his father, he would never inherit the family business as he would lead it in a progressive and drastic new direction.

But to Jack his enlistment was more than a patriotic move; it was a social statement to his father that topped years of arguing with him about values, business philosophy, and social responsibility.

For too long now he had waited while this burning sensation trickled in his chest, and now he could no longer suppress this urge. He has a calling to follow his duty, and time was only making him more impatient. As he watched the seconds tick on the clock, it was like a hissing reminder to him of all the moments he was wasting, while somewhere out there, many were marching out into the battlefields of the world to fight for freedom and deliver the world from evil.

Jack entered the dining hall where everyone was seated. Jack's younger brother Reginald, sat next to him. Jack was closest to Reginald, growing up the two were inseparable.

Jack's grandfather, Thomas Manchester Sr., was seated on the other side of him. Jack's mother and father sat opposite the brothers. Jack knew he needed to reveal his secret soon before the servants brought out the food. He felt that the conversation would quickly be dominated by Thomas Sr. with their business plans for the next year and changes to the economy due to the war. Jack had one quick moment to make his announcement before the conversation was dominated by grandpa with his usual mundane talk of business plans and possible changes to the economy due to the war.

He glanced across the dining hall and saw the servants about to bring out their first course. Jack knew he had to act fast or he would lose all hope of getting his parents attention, especially with grandfather present.

"Mom, Dad, I have an important announcement which is going to change my future. I enlisted in the Marines."

"What?" Jack's father yelled out. "This is not a time to start an irritating family prank!"

"Dad, our country is at war. Manchester's have the same patriotic duty as any other American citizen. The war could be over by the time I graduate and finish college. I need to go now if I am going to be a part of this."

"Jack," his mother answered as she placed her cloth napkin into her lap, "fighting in a war is something the 'middle class' might engage in. You have a family heritage to think about. You can do so much more for our fighting men by helping out with the family business, being a leader in finance, someone who shapes our national political destiny."

"Mom, I can't do anything about that now. Men are shedding their blood, mine is no better than anyone else's. Besides, I signed the enlistment paperwork already. I ship out next week to boot camp."

Jack's father interrupted. It was obvious the inflection in his voice revealed he was trying very hard to hold in his intense anger. His cutting gaze pierced across the table as he spoke, "Jack is this really your choice?"

After a few tense moments of awkwardness with both father and son locking gazes at each other, Jack firmly answered, "Yes, I'm going."

"Then we're done with you. I'm tired of your endless shenanigans." He slammed his hand down hard onto the table shaking the silverware and dishes on it. "You walk away from this family now, and we sever all ties with you. That's the deal. We're not risking the family legacy with your foolish and hasty move".

Reginald jumped in his seat startled at his father's outbreak then stared caringly at Jack.

Thomas Sr., Jack's grandfather interrupted not moved by the latest explosion of emotion, "Gentlemen, we all know the real reason why Jack continues with these endless theatrics to ruin the family legacy. Jack come now, let's be reasonable. We know you are in support of the unionizing efforts with some of our companies. We can't allow you to stay involved in Manchester business if you are going show a sympathetic ear from the very top of our corporations."

"Grandpa, look, I don't believe in everything labor unions stand for, but they have done some good so far with creating 40-hour work weeks, and 8-hour work days. We can't just work people into the ground. Some union achievements are actually good for business. As for the military, I'm going Dad."

Jacks father stood up shouting, angrily pointing to the door, "Fine, get out and never come back! Your younger brother Reginald will be the sole heir to the entire Manchester family estate. He will lead the family name into future success. You, on the other hand, will go into obscurity and all your children after you will inherit poverty and meaningless existences. This is your own stubborn fault, Jack. Now get the hell out of my house!"

Jack turned to leave to the sound of his mother crying. His feelings were hurt that she didn't stand up for him at all. He felt alone in the family. Almost as if he wasn't part of the family anymore.

Reginald immediately got up to chase after his big brother. "Jack, please wait" he yelled out, as they left into the hallway outside the dining room. "I'm going to miss you. Its always been just us. What am I going to do brother? After all, 'We're all of us there are' he said affectionately to his brother. They invented the phrase due to the long hours spent alone together while their parents were off maintaining the mandatory business and social requirements of people in their status.

Jack turned back to Reginald, "Hey little brother, I have to go I will keep in touch with you as best I can. Don't ever forget that 'We are all of us there are'. You're my brother no matter what!"

Their discussion was interrupted by Jacks father, "Reginald get your ass back in here and don't go chasing after your brother he's a family traitor." The last of anything Jack heard of his family was his mom crying and his brother pleading for him to stay…

~~~~~~~

Present Day

Princess Charlotta Dorothea Katarina Maria Bergfalk checked her cell phone and realized the time. She disguised herself under a brunette wig and secondhand clothing she picked up last month at a church thrift shop when she toured the Monastery. She hoped nobody would question her at the time about why she would purchase such obscure items but luckily it went unnoticed. Princess Charlotta escaped out of the kitchen loading doors that opened to the rear of the palace. She carefully walked out the back and joined a tour group as they walked the gardens.
~~~~~~~

The Drottningholm Palace gardens were the most beautiful in all of Europe. Once the tour concluded, they exited the palace grounds. Charlotta discarded her phone and hailed a taxi, straight to the airport.

Charlotta had saved several thousand dollars over the last year in her preparation to leave her royal responsibilities in order to start a new life. 21-year old Charlotta was the next in line for the throne of Sweden. “Hey it’s the 21st century”, she thought to herself. It’s the modern era. The monarchy was a dead institution. She was tired of all the pomp and the ceremony. Tired of being the national brand, since she was to be the next queen.

She wondered if her title and her future role were all worth giving up for her privacy. The public scrutiny of the media into every detail of her life to live like a royal among Europe’s elite families was overwhelming for sure.

Charlotta had long planned to experience becoming a normal person. She diligently prepared in advance to obtain a false US Passport and a new identity. She also stored aside the cash needed for the trip without anyone in her family or the staff finding out, even her personal assistant did not know what she had in the works.

Charlotta boarded her plane to Chicago as Cindy Mason. Charlotta’s departure was perfectly planned, as both of her parents were in Switzerland on business. No one should notice she was missing until it was too late. Charlotta pondered about the new change in her life. She needed to think of herself solely as Cindy Mason in America. She would explain her Swedish accent by claiming to be from Minnesota as it claims a large Scandinavian immigrant population from the early 19th century.

Cindy was excited to have the freedom she planned for. She felt that her parents viewed her as state property and not as a person. She knew her parents loved her, but they seemed to pattern their relationship with her based on proper royal traditions and other protocols mandated by their constitution. She never really felt close to her family.

She grew up being sent off to the best boarding schools her whole life, and then to the finest private prep school and university in Europe. Everything was always so formal and cold. Cindy wanted to be free to live life. She also hated the tabloid media that plastered her all over the news whenever she partied with her friends. Cindy didn't want the responsibility. She only wanted fun. Simply put, no accountability, unrestrained fun, and most of all freedom. But she realized that if she lived the crazy party life with any of her friends, her secret would be out soon enough, and her family would find her. Cindy accepted the fact that she was a troublemaker for her family. She felt that she never fit in with any of her family. She needed to be left alone, and away from them so she could live the life she so desired. But how can she achieve her goal without someone from the Swedish government finding her?

Little did Cindy know at the time, that such a party lifestyle is an unreachable dream unless you're a movie star or pop diva. Cindy would soon learn that a young single girl in America without a job or a source of income would soon find herself homeless.

Cindy arrived in Chicago and quickly went to the Amtrak station and took the first train to California. She exited the train in Rockville California, a suburb of Sacramento, to rest for a few days in a local hotel and plan where to go next. Cindy turned on the TV to see if there were any news accounts of her missing. Then she inventoried her cash and assets to plan her life. She realized that she might need to look for a job here. She planned to lay low for a while and save money before moving on to Los Angeles. Cindy didn't want to arrive at the party capital of the world broke. There was nothing on the news about her yet, so she turned in for the night.

Chapter 2

Jack completed boot camp at Parris Island and was assigned to a new Marine unit known as a Marine Raider Battalion, later known as Carlson's Raiders. In the spring of 1942, Jack went to fight at Guadalcanal. Jack proved himself among his fellow brother Marines. He never told them about his family background in order to fit in with the group. They quickly called him "Man" short for Manchester. Jack fought with distinction during the war and earned a silver star.

After leaving the Marines, Jack found it difficult to support his family since his father had used every business and political contact he knew to prevent Jack from succeeding. Jack was blacklisted from elite society. He needed to escape his father's powerful influence preventing his success. Jack decided to move to California and changed his name to Jack "Mann" (adopting his nickname from the Marines) in order to become invisible in the world and disappear from his family.

After moving to California, Jack married a nurse he met earlier during the war, they had a son, whom they named Reginald after Jack's younger brother.

Reginald grew up as a normal and happy kid in Northern California completely oblivious to his father's family background of extreme wealth and privileges. He graduated from college and became a police officer for the Rockville Police Department. Reginald was also very active and served his community with honor. He was awarded the Medal of Valor for single-handedly saving a classroom of children from an active shooter at an elementary school. Reginald also valued the same honorable attributes as his father; honor, duty, discipline, integrity, and most importantly sacrifice. Reginald was taught by his father, Jack, that family meant everything. Family was worth sacrificing everything for, after all, Hence the quote, "We're all of us there are". This was kind of a mantra, so to speak, that Jack always said when he felt alone or downtrodden. Somehow, he felt comforted with the few close family members he had left, even though they were few in number they were a sanctuary to him.

Jack never told his son Reginald about his family (the Manchester's) and how they disowned him in life. Jack always said he was alone, orphaned, and then found a true family in the Marines.

He realized now with a wife and a child of his own that his family is everything, and they need to stick together no matter how hard life hits you with difficulty. Jack wanted to make a universal change for himself and his descendants. The Mann's would leave a legacy of loyalty and honor, not money and power.

Jack's son, Reginald married Samantha Clark and they had a son whom they named Scott. Reginald and Samantha met each other while in college. Samantha grew up in a foster care group home and didn't have any family or relatives that she knew of. She vowed that she would protect her kids from the loneliness she knew growing up in the system. She struggled hard and put herself through college and then went on and earned a master's degree. She did everything she could to elevate herself from the world that she grew up in. Samantha was so grateful for her marriage and family, and the opportunity to be there for her kids, that she doted heavily on them their whole lives.

Reginald diligently taught his son Scott the same values and character traits that Jack had instilled into him when he was a child. The Mann's also had twin daughters about twelve years after Scott was born, Annabelle and Maryanne. Samantha became pregnant again four years later. Reginald remembered his father's mantra about family, "We're all of us there are". He laughed after thinking of his growing family that God has blessed him with, and yet now, another one on the way. But he continued to teach his children and tell them about the short "Mann" family line that they knew of, and of course the mantra, "We're all of us there are".

Cindy sat in her hotel room and watched the breaking news story on cable news. Her face was once again plastered on the media. She was reported as the missing Crown Princess and possibly kidnapped. Cindy laughed at some of the conspiracy theories about her disappearance, not realizing how terrified her parents (the ruling Monarchs of Sweden) must be.

With the current media coverage, Cindy knew she needed to disguise herself and had to stay out of the public eye. The wig she wore on her flight from Sweden wouldn't do. Cindy donned a pair of plastic-rimmed, plain, prescription style, eyeglasses and decided to grow her blond hair out longer and wear a baseball cap. Baggie jeans and t-shirts or sweatshirts were what most young people seemed to favor wearing these days. That would work for her.

She would wear popular middle-class style clothes avoiding the expensive designer dresses and elite name brand outfits she was famous for wearing in public. She would blend into Northern California society simply as a normal person. Cindy laughed thinking to herself how eyeglasses and a change of clothes worked perfectly as a disguise for Superman and Clark Kent. Sometimes a lifestyle and a personality change are a better disguise than a complete makeover. Excluding the British Royal family, Americans don't really keep up with the royal families of Europe, especially Scandinavian royalty. Cindy just wasn't well known in America, let alone small-town Northern California. So, she wouldn't have any problem at all to blend in and disappear here for a while.

After working on her disguise, Cindy meditated on her choices and in a split second of doubt wondered if all of this was worth it. She is alone at this moment, running away from home, and being in a strange country. Now after all the travel expenses, she is running low on money and started feeling especially vulnerable and there is no-one to turn to. There is no safety net for her in case if something goes wrong. Cindy realized that even her personal safety could be at risk.

She regained her resolve by meditating on one of the reasons she left home in the first place. Cindy grew up in a cold and formal environment. She felt family love was void in her life. She never bonded with her mother and got to dream about girly things. Cindy blamed her mother for being sent off to boarding schools her whole life. Cindy felt that being the oldest child in this family monarchy was nothing but a business proposition. She wanted a life where she could drop the formal facade, relax and live a little. Most importantly, Cindy believed she just needed to have fun with other people. Sometimes freedom can come with a risk, and she was willing to go forward, at least for now.

Chapter 3

For I know the plans I have for you," declares the Lord, "plans to prosper you and not to harm you, plans to give you hope and a future...

Jeremiah 29:11 (NIV)

The world seemed to suddenly come apart for 18-year old Scott Mann. He was in his college math class when a Rockville Police Officer and a Police Chaplain entered his classroom. They escorted Jack to the counselor's office and informed him that his dad, Reginald, was just killed in the line of duty. "Scott", Chaplain Ken said with a soft but blunt tone, "I need to tell you that your father was shot during a traffic stop, and he did not survive."

"Are you sure it's my dad", Scott replied? Scott felt like someone just kicked him in the stomach hard enough to make him dizzy. He was still trying to process the information and didn't quite manifest the deep emotional sadness yet at this point.

Scott hoped it was a mistake, but he knew they would not be here with him unless it was true. Scott cried briefly, then fought back the tears to talk.

Chaplain Ken continued, "This is devastating, but we will be here with you through this whole process. Your mother is at the hospital right now."

"How is my mom doing? She is ok, right? Are people with her right now?"

Scott then started to feel a deep dread thinking about how sad his mother must be.

He looked around and could see everyone through the windows in the office as he looked out into the student services building. Many students and staff were gathering and were staring at them through the windows. Scott realized that it must have already broke on the local news about a Rockville officer killed on a traffic stop. His lip started to quiver, and his breath shortened taking in quick breaths. He started a muffled sob, but then he bit down hard and fought the tears as best he could, as he was afraid to make a scene while walking off the campus.

The chaplain drove Scott to the hospital where his father was taken, he told Scott how Reginald was shot without warning during a routine traffic stop. Scott saw dozens of marked police cars from every nearby law enforcement agency parked in the parking lot of the hospital with more arriving every minute. They walked into the lobby and saw dozens of police officers consoling each other. Some of them were crying. More police personnel continued to pour into the lobby to comfort each other and the family. Several other police officers were with his mother Samantha. He recognized Sgt John Weathers, who was his dad's best friend. Sgt Weathers wasn't helping console Samantha as much as he was crying himself and mourning with her over his best friend. Scott then noticed that each of the officers near his mother was also crying. Scott immediately went to his mom, hugged her and cried together with her. Scott then realized at the moment how important the police family is. Each of the officers near Scott's mother was grieving as if losing their own brother. It was somewhat comforting to share the loss of his father with so many police officers.

That night, someone from the police department brought a home-cooked meal over to the Mann home. Scott realized it was the first meal he had since breakfast. Samantha set the table and served everyone their dinner. Scott felt so awful himself but knew his little sisters and his mother needed comfort. He tried to encourage everyone there as they sat crying together with their first meal without Dad.

"Mom, I love you", Scott said softly. "I know it's so bad, but I'm going to be here for you mom. I won't leave you stranded. I will do anything we need to get through this as a family. We're all of us there are."

Scott looked so caring at his mother and was so grateful for her. He thought to himself that this nightmare is unbelievable, but at least mom is here to be with us. Scott pondered at how much she was always there for each and every one of her kids.

She was a beacon of strength for them right now. He definitely felt better, comforted in just being with her. However, he noticed that she didn't touch the food.

She didn't eat the next morning either. Over the course of the next week, several of the officers and their wives brought meals every night. If it wasn't for them, his family would not have eaten. But Scott seriously started worrying for his mom because with being pregnant she should have been eating more. Scott realized that the sadness he felt over his dad's death had completely taken over any appetite he had for food. He knew it was probably the same with his mom.

Scott grieved very much for his father, but he also hurt deeply for his mother. She cried every day all day. It wasn't right for a son to see his mom hurting so much. Scott worried for his mom as she often sobbed that the pain was so deep that it was unbearable. His mother cried so much during the day that her eyes were constantly swollen and red. Scott also noticed that his mom started dropping weight after his dad died. He wasn't sure if it was the stress and lack of appetite, or loss of water weight from crying so much. Besides, he noticed how tired he was as well at the end of the day. The grieving was extremely tiresome and physically exhausting.

Scott sat with his mother and sisters during the memorial service. There must have been thousands of police officers in the auditorium. The Rockville police chief sat next to his mother along with the Mayor and the Governor of California. Nothing could take the place of losing his father, but the family felt comforted by the outpouring of love and support from the community, more importantly, they did not feel alone.

Scott marveled with his mom and little sisters about the size of the procession of police cars. He tried to capture a video of the event on his cell phone as the procession continued farther back than he could see from his vantage point. It seemed to go on for miles. Even his mom seemed momentarily comforted to see so many police cars from every city and state imaginable file in behind them. Scott took the opportunity to try to encourage his mom and plan ahead.

“Mom I want you to know that I want to drop out of my college classes to get a job and help with our family finances. I just want you to know I'm here for us. I'm not going to do anything drastic in my near future. I'm staying right here at home to help in any way that I can. I'm going to be there for the girls too. I'll even keep up on the yard work and things around the house. I'll do everything that dad did.”

“You'll do nothing of the sort Scott”, she answered gently. We're going to do fine, I promise. I think you need to still focus on school. College is everything. It is hard to think of where we are going to be in the future. I never thought I would live without Reginald. Not when we were so young at least. I feel lost and without a vision of what to do. I feel without a purpose. Everything in my life was about us as a married couple. Scott, all of our plans, our dreams of retirement plans that we made together, and now he's gone.”

Samantha felt like less of a person without her husband. She felt diminished. She then felt a little insecure that she might be sharing too much of her feelings to her son or if he could even understand her unique grief. She worried about how close she could or would lean on her son during this time of incredible emotional crisis. Now that her husband is gone, she would need to find a new best friend, maybe a woman from church. Someone that she could open up too and talk with about all of her feelings, sadness, and grief.

She turned back to Scott, “Son, I’m so proud of you and so glad you’re here to be with all of us and help with the family. I’m sure we’re all going to be very close as a family, each of us is going to need to lean on the other for emotional support and love. But most importantly, you’re still my little boy. You are always going to be my little boy no matter how big you get. I’m not going to leave you either. I’m always going to be there to comfort you and just be your mom.”

“I love you so much, Mom.”

“I love you too Scott.”

Scott still worried about his family and their future. He noticed his mother, Samantha, was not doing well with the loss of Reginald. He could still hear her crying very hard through the walls into her bedroom. Several times just the sadness of his mother evoked strong tears from him as well. Scott pondered that his mother was much more affected in losing a spouse, as he was in losing his father. She grieved far more than he did, and he sometimes felt guilty that he wasn’t as sad as she was all the time.

Scott still felt a dread though, a feeling of despair that never seemed to cease. That dread started to get worse when he noticed his mother’s health seemed to decline each day. She started experiencing serious complications with the pregnancy. Samantha would not tell her son exactly what the health problems were, but he could see she was getting worse. She felt it was not appropriate to tell her son due to the circumstances and the nature of her illness.

Samantha was very dignified and discreet and felt there were some things a mother should not tell her son. Scott asked her if there was anything he could do to help. "No son, I'll be alright," she said.

Samantha pondered in her mind the next few days about all the things happening to her and their family. Her health problems were not getting any better. Samantha decided that she needed to plan for every outcome and try to see to the survival of her babies if things got even worse. She waited for Scott to come home and spoke with him alone while the twins were still at preschool.

"Scott, I need you to sit down, we need to have a serious talk that may decide the future and survival of our very family. I need you to know there are some serious health risks for me to have this baby".

"Ok, mom, but don't talk like that, you're going to be fine".

"No Scott, things may not be fine. If something were to happen to me during the delivery. I need you to promise that you will take care of your sisters. You can't allow them to grow up in foster care or group homes like I did."

"Mom!"

"Scott no. We have to make decisions now. Your two sisters are five years old. It will be hard enough for anyone to want to adopt a five-year-old, let alone two of them. The odds are not good, they will most assuredly split them up into different families. This will destroy your sisters, do you understand? How can they face losing a father, and a mother, and then being split up? You can't let this happen. I know as an 18-year old kid, it will be hard enough to convince CPS that you are capable and will be a good guardian for the children. As you know; 'We're all of us there are'".

"I promise mom, but I think you're just freaking out."

~~~~~~~~

Cindy was unable to find any kind of employment. She really didn't have any experience in job hunting anyway. But Cindy also found that every place she applied to, would not hire her because she did not have a social security card. Cindy realized that her finances were becoming dire now. She couldn't afford to continue staying in her hotel much longer.

She began to panic thinking how she would take care of herself if she ran out of money. The weather didn't help her feelings, it was a cloudy day with slight drizzles that added to the feeling of despair. She walked to the bus stop to go back to the hotel and thought that she may end up calling home for help after all. She stood under the clear plastic awning of the bus stop shielding herself from the mild wind and drizzles. It seems her whole adventure was about to fail.

Then she noticed two Hispanic women standing near the bus stop on the other side of the bench. She overheard them speaking together about wiring money to their families in Monterrey Mexico. Cindy knew that she was trying to survive under similar circumstances. How do they make it here if they have the same struggles as she? They are also in a strange country and yet have successfully navigated through all the cultural and legal barriers of life to live here and support their families.

Cindy asked the women in Spanish, "Excuse me, can you help me, please? I'm not from here, I'm not an American, and I need to find a job." The two young women stared at the young blond-haired, blue-eyed, girl speaking to them in perfectly pronounced European Spanish. She looked like a typical California girl wearing a pink baseball cap, faded blue jeans, and a sweatshirt with a gym logo on the front, yet she was speaking Spanish as if it was her first language.

Usually, if an American speaks Spanish, it's with an accent and sometimes imperfect grammar.
~~~~~~~~

"How do you know Spanish so well and so very formal", they asked?

"I'm from France but grew up in Spain", Cindy answered.

She couldn't tell them that she was the missing Crown Princess of Sweden. But in reality, she was related to the Royal family of Spain. Cindy actually went to boarding school in Spain, and practically grew up with her cousins in the Spanish palace. As with most European royal families, they are related either by marriage or blood with the other royal families in many of the countries in Europe.

Cindy went on to explain to the women that she was stranded and needed to make some extra money in order to get herself back home to France. They explained to Cindy it was best if she could work under the table for cash, doing personal work for an individual, and not a company. They recommended that she try the bulletin board at the local library, post office, or even at the nearby community college. People usually post small job opportunities for college students to make some quick cash.

One of the women went on to explain to Cindy, "I know you're not a Mexican citizen, but we have a Consulate in Sacramento, and I believe another one in San Francisco that may have pamphlets or other information in the lobby to help you with special programs or guidelines to help set up bank accounts or other things you will need while staying here."

Cindy thanked the women, then went to the local library and found the bulletin board. There were several flyers for an upcoming concert, postings for missing pets, firewood for sale, handyman needed for small carpentry projects, and one posting for a babysitter.

Chapter 4

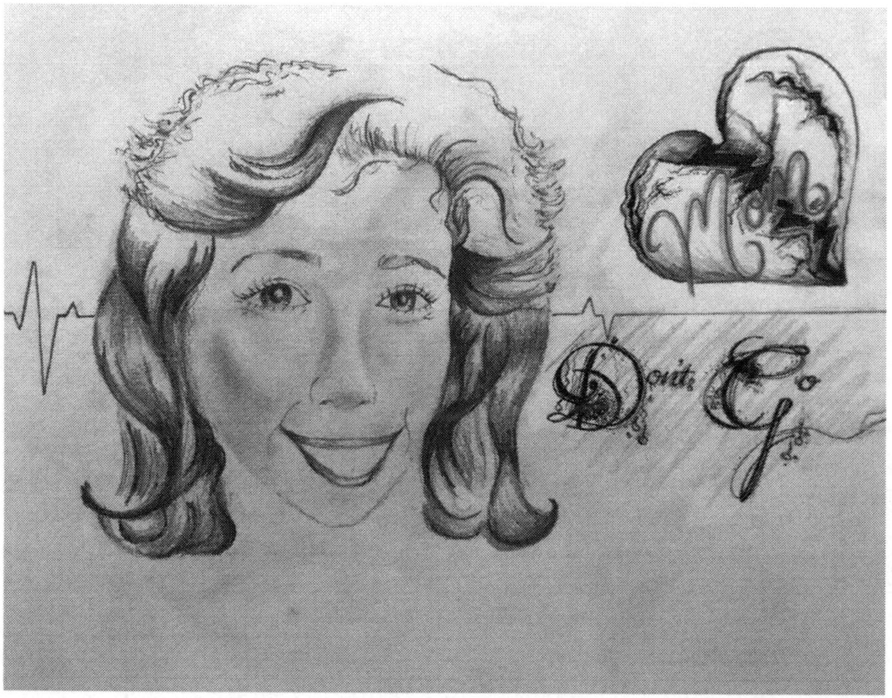

Samantha went into labor in the middle of the night. Scott called Sgt. John Weathers, his fathers' best friend, from the Rockville Police Department to come to pick up the kids to watch the twins while he drove his mother to the hospital. John Weathers had been best friends with Scott's dad, Reginald, ever since they went to the police academy 21-years earlier. John had promised Samantha that his family would never leave them stranded or alone after Reginald was killed.

Scott waited in the waiting room for hours while his mother was in labor, and finally two doctors, and another person, who did not appear to be a medical professional, entered the waiting room to talk with Scott. The doctor told Scott in a blunt but gentle manner that Samantha died just after the delivery. The baby girl survived.

Scott felt the same dizzying kick in the stomach as he felt when he was notified of his father's death back in the counselor's office at his college. Time seemed to stop in an instant for Scott. He couldn't understand what was happening. How could this mean his mom is gone now too?

The woman with the two doctors identified herself to Scott as Amanda Peters, from social services. She could tell Scott had a glazed look over his eyes as if he wasn't able to grasp this new bit of crushing information. Amanda spoke with Scott about helping with any immediate needs for himself and his other two sisters. She offered to have a hospital chaplain come to assist if needed, but Scot declined. Scott told her that the twins, Annabelle and Maryanne, were with a family friend and would be fine staying with him the rest of the night.

Again, Scott needed to process…

What does he do now? Who does he call? Who can help him? Scott panicked as he thought of his sisters and how this is going to just destroy their little hearts.

Scott asked to be left alone for a few minutes, he walked outside and cried.

He called Julie, his girlfriend since 9th grade. Julie, Julie, (as he cried) My mom died! "Oh my gosh", she answered. I'm coming over to meet you right now. No please, don't. I have to talk to the social workers about my sisters, and also the baby. She survived. What are you going to do? I don't know. I don't know what to do. Everything is so wrong, "Why me, why us, I feel so punished in life. This is way too much. How am I going to make it? I don't know what to do. I'm lost, Julie."

Julie feeling uncomfortable simply said, "It's ok Scottie, you always do the right thing."

"Ok thanks, Julie, I gotta go. I'll call you in the morning. I need you, honey, more than anything right now because I feel that everything is against me."

Scott thought about the loss of his mom and dad, all in just a few months. He felt the world on his shoulders, and that there was not much more pain any human could take. “I'm at the end of my rope”, he uttered to God in a short prayer under his breath.

Then he remembered the new baby girl. Scott went back to the lobby and found Amanda. He asked to see his baby sister. Amanda escorted him to the pediatric ward and presented him to “baby girl Mann”. Amanda said she was 100% healthy and would be ok. Scott saw how beautiful she was and how she resembled her mother. He also thought she had her father's ears.

Amanda asked, “Would you like to hold her Scott?”

“Yes”, he answered. The nurse lifted her carefully out of the nursery crib and handed her to him.

Scott cried thinking that his mom would never get to hold her. He was also sad thinking that this baby would never know how wonderful her mother was. He adored her as he stared long at her while he held her into his arms. Scott determined that she would get all of the love she could get, all that he could give. He admired her perfect features as he looked at this beautiful little girl. He could hear her precious breathing and it just melted his heart. He decided that he would do anything to keep her. Not only her but both of his other sisters as well no matter what.

Amanda Peters cried as she watched Scott. She realized how devastating this is, and she thought to herself how this job never really prepares you to help people in this type of crisis.

Scott stared into the face of his perfect baby sister and admired her for another short moment. Then a stinging fear came across him... What if he couldn't keep any of his sisters, what about his family right now?

"Mrs. Peters, what about our family, what's going to happen to her? And what about my other sisters. We're a family, and, 'We're all of us there are'."

Amanda answered, "Please Scott, please call me Amanda. I don't know how things are going to proceed from here. We need to see how we can help you, and the other kids, what will be best for everyone. I need to meet with my peers at CPS and start working out a plan for this family. We will need to meet with our supervisors after this and plan out the best possible outcome for all of you."

Scott replied, "I understand. But, you need to know, I promised my mom I would keep us all together with no matter what. We are the Manns' and we will stay the Mann family. This is the only option for us. This needs to be the whole goal of your discussions on how to make us work and thrive as our own family. I don't want to be separated from my sisters, and worst yet, I don't want my sisters separated from each other. Amanda, I also want to name my sister, I need too. I'm her oldest relative, and I have a right to name my own family. She has a right to be named by her own blood relative".

"Yes, you do honey!" Amanda stated in agreement. "But there is also a lot to do, and much to think about right now in regard to all of your family's needs".

Amanda assured him that she was on his side and was there to help him, not to hurt him. Amanda also said this was now a time for him and the girls to grieve for your mother. Then she told Scott, "I promise you, we will take care of you and the girls." Amanda thinking to herself for a moment just to make sure she didn't forget anything, then smiled and asked, "Scott what would you like to name her?"

He thought about it as he looked down at how perfect she looked. He realized how sad he is with his mother not here to see her beautiful daughter. He also remembered how much his dad had wanted their small family to grow.

He was also afraid that CPS would take his sister's away from him, separate them, and send them out to different foster families.

Sadness, grief, and fear seemed to dominate his thoughts and feelings at the moment. But he wanted to make a statement that by naming his sister, he was claiming her.

Scott thought of the Bible story of Ruth and Naomi, and how Naomi was specifically mentioned in the Bible as so very sad and bitter at losing all of her loved ones close to her. Yet Naomi later received a blessing of a new family after all of her first family died.

Naomi grew very close to the people that were still around her, and then God blessed her with a new family through Ruth and grandchildren she could call her own. He wanted her middle name to be Pearl because she was perfect. She was a beautiful pearl found in a sea of sadness around her.

Scott said, "Her name will be Naomi Pearl Mann. Mom and Dad would have loved that name for her."

Amanda and the nurse both fought back tears as they listened to Scott. "Ok Scott", Amanda said, "I will inform the hospital administration to put your sister's full correct name on Naomi's birth certificate. We should go to meet with Sgt. Weathers, and your sisters Annabelle and Maryanne.

We need to talk to them about your mom. Scott, I know this is tremendously hard for you. I want you to know that I can tell you're an exceptional young man and I am on your side. I will do everything to help you, but you are not going to have much time to grieve in between taking care of kids. You will need to prove to me that you are able and capable to provide for all of these young ones. This is very, very rare for a young sibling to take custody of three children including an infant. But not impossible, I do recall a story of a young, 18-year old, woman adopting her three siblings in Southern California".

Amanda continued as they walked to the parking lot, "I don't want to overwhelm you because I can see that your family has been through so much sadness. Your sisters are going to need you right now Scott, tonight, more than ever. So, I am going to approve you keeping them for tonight. But I can't promise anything to you after this. Let's take it one day at a time. Tonight, we're going to keep the baby in the hospital. We'll talk more on her status later".

Chapter 5

Cindy wrote the number down for the babysitting advertisement that she read at the library. She fluctuated in fear of whether or not to call. Cindy had never worked for anyone, ever. Then she debated with herself if the money was really worth it.

She was running low on cash, another first for her to experience. Cindy hated counting dollars and looking for bargains on the food she purchased at the grocery store. Cindy called the number thinking she could always decline the job if she felt uncomfortable, besides the person she was calling wouldn't know her and probably would never see her again.

The woman who answered the phone said she was going shopping all day with her mother this Thursday on a long-planned outing. She needed someone to stay with her 13-year old, and 10-year old sons. The woman felt the kids were old enough to be home alone, but she was just too uncomfortable to leave them home alone together. She worried that they might get into trouble with no supervision.

Cindy took the bus to the woman's Granite Beach neighborhood and walked the rest of the way to her house. Cindy looked at each of the homes as she passed by noticing that this seemed like an upper-middle-class neighborhood. Some of the houses had expensive cars in the driveway, and she could see some houses with boats or travel trailers parked in back yards behind fences.

Cindy found her address and knocked on the door. The homeowner answered and said, "Hi I'm Linda Maxwell". Linda wanted to speak with Cindy first about her qualifications, although she was not too picky since her two sons were older and could take care of themselves. Linda seemed a little condescending toward Cindy when she realized she took the bus.

Linda also noticed her plain clothing style. Cindy explained she was a college student from Minnesota (little did Linda know that Cindy already graduated from Cambridge University in England with a degree in economics and could speak five languages). Linda, of course, took the opportunity to encourage Cindy to continue with her education and boasted of her own position as a marketing executive for a medical insurance firm. The day went easy enough for Cindy. The boys were polite and played video games all day. Cindy marveled how some American boys could spend so much time in front of a TV playing video games.

Linda was exhausted when she returned at the end of the day, but grateful for Cindy's help. She gave her $100.00 for the six hours. Cindy thanked her and prepared to leave. Linda stopped Cindy on her way out and asked her if she could call on her again in the future if she needed help. Linda also told Cindy she could use her as a reference if she needs one.

Cindy thanked Linda and left. Cindy realized the $100.00 would pay for only one night in her hotel and food for the day. Not bad, but Cindy needed more easy jobs like this one. Cindy found it refreshing to meet new people and find out about their lives without anyone trying to impress her. She decided the working middle class was not so bad after all.

~~~~~~~
~~~~~~~

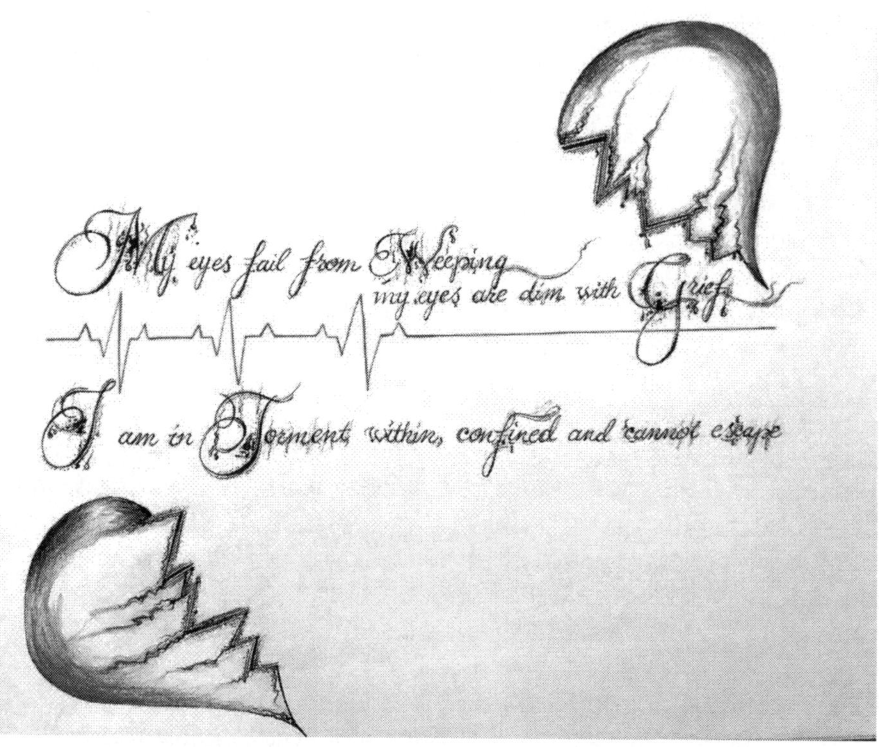

Scott and Amanda arrived at the Weathers' house in separate vehicles. He cried so much after leaving the hospital that he almost had to pull over. This was especially hard since he was driving in his mother's car.

All of her things were still in the vehicle bringing back fresh memories of his mom. The car smelled like her perfume it just seemed like she should be in the passenger seat with him. Her overnight bag was in the passenger side floor, he could see her change of clothes she packed for herself to come home in as well as a small cooler with some bottled water and fruit that she packed for her stay in the hospital. He couldn't believe that she was gone. It was just hours earlier they were in the car together on the way to the hospital to have a baby, and now this is just so painfully unacceptable.

Scott waited for Amanda before walking to the front door of the Weather's home so they would be together. Scott started crying again before they rang the doorbell thinking that he had such horrible news to tell everyone.

Sgt. Weathers and his wife both knew something horrible was wrong for him to arrive with someone from CPS. They could see Scott's red watery eyes and knew he had been crying.

They sat everyone down in the living room and explained to the girls what happened with their mom and comforted the girls in their grieving as best as they could. Scott sat with the girls and held them, he reassured the girls that he would not leave them alone and would keep their family together including Naomi. Amanda took notice of how important it was for Scott to comfort his sisters. She also noticed how they clung to him during this whole process.

Mrs. Weathers' stayed with the girls in the living room, holding them and crying with them, while Scott, Amanda, and John went into the kitchen to talk. Amanda informed them about her concern of Scott only being 18-years old.

The question is could he provide food, shelter, and clothing consistently, as well as the emotional needs for all three "very small" children? John Weathers vouched for Scott's character and also added that Scott would inherit the house which was nearly paid off as well as his mother's economy car and his father's lifted 4WD extended cab truck.

Scott was also going to receive the lump-sum payout of his father's retirement which would pay off the remainder of the mortgage and anything left on the vehicle payments. He told Amanda that the police department would also hold a community fundraiser for the family. There is no doubt that they would have the financial means to survive for some time before he had to go back to work. Scott could take this necessary time in between jobs to bring the baby home to adjust to life with her. Scott said he would drop his classes at school for the time being too. Amanda stressed that as soon as Scott settled down with the kids it would be mandatory for him to get a job in order to have custody of any of the children. Scott agreed.

John promised that he would check on Scott on a weekly basis as well to make sure the family thrives. Amanda said she would take all these points into consideration and speak with her supervisors. Amanda also determined that the girls needed Scott now during this family crisis and should not be taken from him at this time.

Amanda met with Dr. Joan Spencer, the director of Gold Country CPS, the following morning. She explained Scott's passion to keep the family together and about the promise he made to his mother before she died.

"Dr. Spencer, Scott is a young man of fine character. He has a home, transportation, and food in the house. Scott has a desire to care for all of his sisters and to do whatever it takes to keep them. How can we make this work? We need to come alongside this family and help them, not dissolve it."

"I understand you Amanda, but he is only 18. Does he have the maturity to take care of a newborn infant including two small children, what about income for their future needs? There are a lot of questions here that need to be answered. I'm not sure we can take on the liability if we leave those children in his care. What if something disastrous happens that we could have prevented?"

"Ok", Amanda answered, "What if we send Scott to newborn parenting classes this week before he takes the baby home? Besides, he already has two young sisters, he is not completely unaware of what it takes to care for a baby."

"Scott has a home, and sizeable savings left over from his father's life insurance and retirement. There will also be a memorial fund given to the family that the police department is raising. He can sell one of the family cars if needed. The money will not be an issue for the near future as long as he is coached on how to budget and care for those funds responsibly".

"Ok, Amanda, you will be their caseworker. I want weekly home visits, as well as random welfare checks on the children. I also need to see him get a job, this is a requirement. He has to agree to this, or he cannot have the kids.

I like the idea of Sgt. Weathers meeting with Scott once a week for a positive male influence in his life. Let's make this part of the guardianship agreement."

Chapter 6

The following morning, Scott waited at home with his two sisters to meet with Amanda to find out what is going to happen with his family. He closed the door to his parent's bedroom and kept it shut. It was too painful for any of them to look inside.

He called Julie again for comfort. "Hi Julie, it's me. I'm just waiting for the social worker to come by to find out what they are going to do with my family. 'We're all of us there are'".

Julie answered, "What do you want from them, Scott? You're only 18 and have your whole life ahead of you."

"I know, but I don't want to lose my sisters. None of them. Annabelle and Maryanne need me more than anything in the world right now. They have to feel more alone than ever. Can you imagine how afraid they are after losing their mother?"

"I'm sure Scott, I know they need you. I'm here for you. But, do you think you are going to be able to take care of two five-year-old girls?"

"Yes, I am going to have to figure it out and do what it takes to give them a caring home where they feel safe. I'm going to protect them and give them love. Including Naomi. They all need a family identity."

"Ok Scott, I'm here for you. Just let me know what I can do to help."

"Julie please just don't leave me alone, I need someone too, or I am not going to make it".

Scott tried to make the girls breakfast but couldn't find any of the proper cooking utensils or dishes after looking through several cupboards. Scott was ashamed that he rarely helped his mother in the kitchen, although she was very protective of her kitchen. Scott's mother had certain rules about how things were to go in the kitchen. She never allowed anyone to use her pots and pans or even wash the dishes. Scott knew that only a few dishes went into the dishwasher, but mostly everything was hand washed. He remembered certain pots required plastic scrubbies, some pots were washed with a sponge scrubbie with the scouring pad on one side, some were washed with only a washcloth.

Nevertheless, Scott panicked thinking about the simple task of making breakfast and cleaning up. His mother took care of almost everything in their lives. What about taking care of little girls? Scott being a young man didn't know anything about their unique needs and how to take care of them. Scott felt like crying again after looking through the cupboards one last time, realizing that his mother was the glue that kept their family together. She managed all of their lives, he realized this more than ever now and wished so bad he could tell her one last time how much she meant to all of them. Scott had a searing sadness as he realized he was so lost without her. He then noticed the two dried wash clothes that had been wrung out and placed on the kitchen window sill. The wash clothes had been squeezed into a ball and had become hardened as they dried. Obviously, one was for wiping down the countertops, and the other was for dishes. Scott realized that the last person to use the wash clothes was his mother.

She wrung them out with her own hands before going into labor. Scott stared at the dried washcloths and started crying very loud and uncontrollably. Annabelle and Maryanne ran into the kitchen and hugged Scott, holding on to his legs, crying with him for a few moments. He then told them they needed to get dressed in nice clothes while he made breakfast. They needed to get ready for Amanda Peters first visit at their home.

Scott knew he needed to be strong for the girls. He needed to reassure them that they were safe and would be loved and cared for in a warm home. But, how could he face his sadness and not outwardly grieve while being in this house? Every room reminded him of memories of his parents, and just a few months ago they were a family of five, laughing and bustling, dreaming about the future with so many bright hopes and joys. At any moment he could see any random object in the house that would evoke a painful memory and then tears of sadness and loss. Sometimes this house seemed like a dark place of pain, fear, and unrecoverable loss, along with the feeling of punishment looming over him. How could he overcome this tremendous sadness and provide a loving, stable, and warm home for the girls?

Scott decided that he would make every effort not to cry in front of the girls. If he had too, he will wait until he gets to bed at night to cry. Whenever he gets sad during the day, he will try to be loving to the girls at the same moment. Besides, if he is sad they are sad too. When he feels like crying, he will smile at them, and tell them how wonderful they are. Yes, he will even try to make them laugh.

Amanda arrived at Scott's home soon after he finished cleaning up after breakfast. She noticed Scott's eyes were bloodshot red and could tell he had been crying just before she arrived. Amanda sat down with the family and asked them how they were doing. Maryanne started crying. Then Annabelle stated, "This is our first morning without mommy. Please let us stay living here with Scott". They both held onto him as they talked to Amanda. Annabelle started crying also.

Amanda reached over and hugged each girl and cried herself. She answered, "I know both of you baby girls are so afraid". Amanda caringly looked intently at the twins. "We're not going to take you away from your brother little girls!"

Scott interrupted, "What?" and stood up as he looked straight at Amanda.

"Yes, Amanda answered with a huge smile on her face, you will keep both girls here for now. It's obvious to all of us, that you three need to stay together, actually you four".

Scott started shaking and crying, it seemed the stress all at once had just lifted off of him. He shook as he asked, "You mean I get to bring Naomi home too?"

"Yes Scott, but there are a lot of things that the county will need from you first before Naomi comes home. There is a two-day infant care course for parents of newborns held at the children's center. After these two days, you can bring Naomi home."

“Then there are several more things you will need after this. Next, you will need to attend the 10-week fathers and men caregivers for infants and children classes held every Tuesday night at the Gold County family counseling offices. You will need to find suitable and approved child care so that you can attend the classes.”

“You will be required to meet with me on a monthly basis for follow-up counseling and there will be unannounced periodic general welfare checks on the children and the condition of your home.”

“Finally, you will also need to meet with Sgt. Weathers once a week for mentoring.”

“Eventually, in due time you are required to find a job as well. This will all be in the county’s contract with you”.

“Scott, this is not going to be easy for you. You will basically be a father to these three children. You will be the only parent Naomi’ will know. These little ones will depend on you for all of their needs, love, and support. Honestly, you will feel like you are losing your life in a sea of laundry, cooking, diapers, and house cleaning.”

“There will be sacrifices, I know you were going to go to college this year on a scholarship. You will need to look for a job right away. I’m sorry, but you will have to put all your life plans on hold for now. Including your friends. You know you’re not going to be a regular 18-year old guy anymore. You are the sole mother and father to three children. Your friendships are all going to change. You may lose some friends, I’m just being honest…”

She continued, “But you will find out who your real friends are, and you will make new friends, the kind of people you would never think of befriending before.”

Amanda completed some paperwork with Scott then she checked the kitchen to ensure there was plenty of food in the fridge and the pantry. She also checked the rest of the house for any safety issues that might pose a risk for a newborn. Amanda assured Scott that she was his biggest supporter and fan. "Scott, I want you to make this work. Here is my business card with my work cell phone number, please call me anytime day or night."

Julie came by shortly after Amanda left. Julie hugged Scott when he opened the door. "Hi Scott, I had to come by and check on you." Scott couldn't help it and started crying immediately as soon as he saw Julie. Julie didn't know what to say and felt uncomfortable. How do you comfort someone who just lost his mother and father?

She held him and cried together with him for a short time as they stood in the doorway. Julie seemed overwhelmed by his emotional needs, and it scared her as she thought about the enormous sadness this family is saddled with right now. She felt that she wasn't up to being able to meet his needs. Julie felt nervous and wanted to just run away.

They went inside and sat down on the couch to talk. Julie asked Scott, "So what are your plans for the near future? I just want to help you, Scott."

"The girls are my responsibility. I need to care for them and provide a warm home. I need to preserve our family and keep us all together. I'm starting newborn parenting classes tonight and will pick up baby Naomi from the Hospital tomorrow night".

"Scott, are you for sure this is what you really want to do?"

"Absolutely, these are my sisters. There is nothing more important to me and to the girls than to keep us all together. They are depending on me. Besides I promised my mom. It was the last thing we talked about before she died."

Julie realized that this whole scenario is way more than she was looking for in a boyfriend. She liked Scott, but maybe she was just afraid of the changes. Or maybe she was afraid of what things would like with her in the picture. “Scott, I can’t stay for long because my mom needed me to help her in her shop today.” Julie then thought maybe she would just wait a few days to think things through and perhaps she would feel better about the kids.

Chapter 7

Gold County Family Services
Case Name: Scott Mann
Case File: #4237
Case Worker: Amanda Peters
Date: May 2019

Scott agreed to the terms of the family contract to keep Annabelle, Maryanne, and Naomi. There seems to be a deep family bond between the two sisters and with Scott. Scott is determined to keep the whole family together. It appears the bond of unity in this family is helping each of them to heal and to cope with the trauma of losing both parents in such a short time. Scott is determined to become the primary caretaker for all three children. The home is clean and in order. There is plenty of food in the pantry and in the refrigerator. There are no safety issues in the house that would present a danger to an infant.

Scott called Julie later that afternoon. "Hi Julie, I am going to my parenting classes tonight at the Children's Center. I was wondering if you wanted to come with me to visit Naomi in the hospital and then come with me to the classes."

"No Scott, I can't. To be honest, I am a little uncomfortable about going to the class with you. People might think I am a pregnant teenager. I'm a little afraid of how it might look."

"That's ok honey, I get it, I understand. This is a lot for anyone to digest right now."

"Thanks, Scott, bye…"

Scott dropped the twins off at the Weathers' home and went to the hospital maternity ward to see Naomi. One of the nurses from the nursing station led Scott to an empty room nearby for privacy and brought Naomi to him. Scott held her gently, rocking her back and forth, and felt an overwhelming bond with his baby sister. Looking into her precious little eyes as she awkwardly flailed her little arms about, he realized how deeply he missed his mom right now. He meditated about many good memories with his mother at that moment while he held Naomi. Then he cried quietly so he did not alert the nurses. Scott began to pace in the room holding Naomi.

"Dear sweet little baby Naomi, hey you little cutie, I am your brother Scott. He cried softly as he spoke gently and lovingly to her. I want you to know I love you so much. I think you are perfect. You were born into a loving family little baby. I promise you that you will always be loved and protected. I promised mom, that I would take care of our family. I am going to be there for you always and forever. Soon, I'm going to bring you home and you'll get to meet your two sisters Annabelle and Maryanne. I need to tell you about mom and dad. Dad was a cop, he was so brave. He was the best dad ever, he was always there for me. He loved mom so much, and he would have loved you too so very much. I'm going to do my best that as you grow up, you will get to know all about him. Mom was the coolest mom ever. We were so lucky to have the best parents. Mom loved her kids. She loved us all so much. She was pretty and she was so refined, she is the true example of what a woman should be. Mom always wanted the best for us. I am going to try to be everything they both were, for you. I don't know if I could ever live up to their character though, but I'm going to try. I'm never going to forget them, and I will keep our family together. Because their heritage needs to be remembered in this family."

Scott didn't know the small group of hospital staff that gathered at his door. Some of them were crying as they heard him. One of them had a cell phone and captured the whole moment on video. The video of Scott and Naomi was anonymously posted onto an internet video sharing site shortly after Scott left the hospital.

Scott finished his visit with Naomi and went to the new parent class. He immediately noticed he was out of place. He walked into a room with several people seated at desks. Some of the desks had rubber baby mannequins for instructional purposes. The room was full of new moms and moms to be. Most of the women had their husbands with them.

The host of the class stopped Scott and asked, "Excuse me, are you lost?" Scott was only 18, but he looked even younger than his appearance.

"No, I'm enrolled in this class."

Some of the moms wondered why a teenage boy would take this class alone. Other than a few odd looks he received, everyone else left Scott alone. That night they learned all about caring for and handling a newborn baby ranging from carefully bathing them, health issues, and even all the popular baby products sold in supermarkets.

Scott picked up the girls from the Weathers' and went home to prepare the house for Naomi's arrival. He moved the crib into his own bedroom so he could be with Naomi. Scott moved all the baby shower gifts his mother received into their proper places. He also installed the infant car seat into the family truck.

He decided to keep dad's larger 4-wheel drive truck. In his mind, it was an additional safety measure. Scott didn't want to take any chances with his family. He wanted to make sure they were traveling in the largest vehicle with the most metal surrounding it. He decided to sell mom's smaller economy car and add that money into his savings for the time being.

That night just before bedtime, Scott had a family meeting with Annabelle and Maryanne.

“I wanted to let you guys know that tomorrow evening we will be a whole family. Naomi’s coming home! There will definitely be more noise in our home. But, I will need both of your help to make us work as a family. Amanda will be checking in on us to make sure we're ok so we all need to be on our best behavior at all times and we have the house looking its best.”

Both girls were so excited and agreed to work together as a Mann family team. They prayed as a family that night and asked God to bless the next day.

The following morning Scott got up to finish preparations for bringing Naomi home. He decided to go to the store to pick up last minute baby items that he already didn’t have. He noticed that there was a large plate of homemade cookies covered in plastic wrap and a card left on his front porch from a neighbor.

“Scott we are so proud of you for keeping your family together. Please ask us if you need anything. Love, The Thompsons.”

He wondered, why the spontaneous gift was left on the porch. Scott and the two girls got in the truck and went to the local supermarket.

The three walked inside the store and noticed they received numerous stares and smiles from other shoppers. Annabelle overheard a woman gasp as they walked by, “Oh my god, he’s so young”. They finished their shopping and entered the checkout line.

“That will be $87.92 sir”, the clerk stated as she finished scanning the groceries. At that moment, another store employee approached Scott’s check-out clerk.

“Excuse me, Sandy, his groceries have been paid for by an anonymous customer.”

“That will be it for you,” Sandy told Scott. “Someone else picked up your grocery bill.”

Scott looked around and saw several customers holding shopping carts standing in the other checkout lines looking at him. Some of the women had tears in their eyes, but no-one said anything.

Scott took the girls out for ice cream after leaving the store and noticed once again that they received the same looks from everyone nearby. They went home and prepared for the afternoon.

Scott took the girls over to the Weather's home when it was time for his last class. Hi, Mrs. Weathers, it's just us. "Oh my" she cried. She hugged Scott and kissed him on the forehead when he entered the house.

John entered the room, "Scott can you come with me to the kitchen?"

"Sure, what's up?"

"Well did you know someone posted a video of you and Naomi online last night? I guess it went viral pretty quick, there are already two million views and growing."

"What", Scott answered. "I didn't see anyone taking a video of me yesterday".

"Yes, it was taken of you in the hospital room when you were holding Naomi. It seems you have captured the hearts of America son. I have to admit, I am proud of your determination to keep your family together."

"Thanks, well I have to be honest, I am just winging it. I am doing everything I can to keep myself together. I feel like breaking down every moment of every day. On top of that Julie quit talking to me. I think she is freaking out about the kids."

"Scott, keep in mind, she just graduated from high school. She has plans and dreams of her new adult life and new freedom. That's what every kid looks forward too about growing up. For her to be saddled with this huge responsibility of two kids, and, especially the addition of a newborn baby might be too much for her. I think it's hard for an 18-year old girl to take on this idea of three kids instant motherhood."

"I know, I just feel like I need my girlfriend right now. She seems so distant from me after everything that's happened with my mom. I feel like Julie is being taken from me too."

~~~~~~~

Cindy sat at the picnic table near the lake in Hansen park when her cell phone rang. "Hi Cindy, this is Beth Klingson. Linda Maxwell gave me your number. She said you were a great help for her yesterday. I was wondering if you could help me this evening..."

Cindy arrived at Beth Klingson's house at the arranged time. Beth was extremely grateful for her help in such short notice. She didn't seem to have a superior attitude at all toward Cindy as Linda did. Cindy enjoyed watching all three of her children that evening. They were all very well behaved and were no problem for her. Cindy was fascinated by being in another American middle-class home. This was a huge culture shock for her in every manner when she first arrived.

It wasn't just the cultural and language differences but the social class differences for her as well. Cindy had never been exposed to this lifestyle. She walked through the house and looked at the family pictures that were hung on the wall. There were wedding pictures and family portraits. But it was the little league pictures of one of the boys, the Girl Scouts pictures all framed and hung with care and importance that intrigued her.
~~~~~~~

It seemed the family wanted to show their guest's how important the children's activities were as if they were on the same par as special family events. She felt there was a certain warmth to this American middle class.

Cindy watched both Linda and Beth's kids a few more times that month but realized she either needed to make more money or lower her overhead. Cindy wondered if she could find a cheaper place to live than the hotel she was staying in, but she did not want to live in a bad part of town. Cindy enjoyed her freedom for the time being. She was staying in a nice hotel in a wonderful rustic small-town setting. She wondered how long she could keep the best of both worlds.

The money she earned was not enough to support her living out of this hotel and the expense of her food budget. It's obvious that she would be forced out on the street soon enough unless she didn't increase her income.

Cindy went back to the Rockville post office and checked the bulletin board again. She saw a piece of paper underneath a flyer for a rap concert at the fairgrounds. The request said, "Small family looking for live-in childcare. References required".

This is something she is looking for, maybe an answer to her dilemma. Cindy read the flyer with excitement. If she could find a job with room and board, this would certainly solve her financial worries.

Chapter 8

Gold County Family Services
Case Name: Scott Mann
Case File: #4237
Case Worker: Amanda Peters
Date: June 2019

Scott shows continued interest in providing a loving environment for each of the children. Someone took a video of Scott at the hospital and posted it to the internet, which seems to have made him a momentary internet sensation. Scott does not appear to let the new attention affect his focus on caring for the children. Scott completed his required parenting class and brought Naomi home. He placed the crib in his own bedroom and has the adequate formula, diapers, changing station, and all other infant care needs are in place in the home. Scott seems a little depressed as his girlfriend Julie has stopped calling or seeing him anymore. It appears she feels to be too young to become involved with someone with three children. However, he is still focused on taking care of each of the children.

Scott entered the classroom for the last night of the parenting class. Everyone's eyes were on him.

One of the ladies near him asked, "I saw the video of you and your little baby sister... Can I give you a hug?" The instructor also walked over to Scott and hugged him. No-one today seemed to wonder about his age but were amazed at his attention to the class material and his desire to learn how to be a dad. One of the dads to be approached Scott shook his hand and told him how inspired he was about the video he saw online.

After the class, Scott couldn't wait even though it was tempting to stay and talk to people. He was so excited and immediately drove over to the hospital to pick up Naomi. Scott was directed to bring his truck around to the loading area by the front double sliding glass doors. Some of the nurses assisted him out to his truck and helped to load her into the car and to ensure the infant seat was installed in the proper manner.

Others carried the diaper bag and several other free bags of sample baby products. Scott felt they doted on him too much and loaded him down with extra free stuff. Little did he know a newborn goes through diapers like a maniac.

Scott arrived at the Weather's home and brought Naomi inside. Everyone came to the front door. Mrs. Weathers cried when she saw Naomi and repeated, "She is so beautiful Scott. She looks just like Samantha. Scott, I am so proud of you for bringing your sister home. If you have any baby questions, just call me anytime Scott."

Scott turned to the girls, "Annabelle, what do you think of your sister? She is part of our family now. Isn't she pretty?"

Annabelle kissed Naomi on her forehead and said, "She so perfect. Smell her Maryanne, she smells like the baby smell."

Maryanne drew near to Naomi smelled her too, and said, "She does, but look how tiny her hands and fingers are."

Maryanne then started crying thinking how much she wanted her mom to be here to see Naomi. Mrs. Weathers comforted her and said, "Maryanne honey, your mommy is looking down right now at your precious family with so much love. She is also right here right now in all of your hearts. She is in Scott's heart giving him so much love for each of you to be there for each one of you."

Annabelle asked, "Do you really think, mommy, knows Naomi and can see her?" "Yes, honey she knows each of her babies. Her love for each of you will never ever go away."

John took Scott aside, "Scott before you leave, I wanted to say, my wife, Sandy volunteered to come by your house each Saturday for a few hours to watch the kids. This will give us time to get together and talk. We need to get you out of the house once a week for some 'guy time' we can hang out and talk about things".

“Ok, that’s a great idea, John, I can’t thank you enough for everything.”

“Cool, I’ll be by this Saturday morning at 9:30. Oh and Scott, you’re doing great bud, I’m proud of you. Your father would be too”.

Scott loaded the girls into his truck and headed home. Once they arrived at the house Scott sat everyone down in the living room.

“Ok Girls, before we get ready for bed. Let’s have some family time. First, we need to pray together as a family. This is the first time Naomi is coming home. We need to ask God to bless us and keep us safe. I want to ask God to bless little Naomi to grow up and be safe and strong, and to commit her to Him. I want to have all of us stand before Him tonight, and declare that we are still His people and that this family in this house will live for Him. After that, I want you two to pick out your favorite book, and I am going to read it to you. From now on we’re gonna have family time every night. Sometimes we will read books together, sometimes we will play board games or make puzzles, and sometimes will have arts and crafts. Sometimes we will just talk...”

Scott prayed with the girls and read to them a story from a book Annabelle picked out. It was a beautiful story of a kingdom with a beautiful princess who had adventurous travels who finally met her prince in another kingdom far away.

Scott awoke Sunday morning and decided it was important to gather the girls up and go to church. He thought it would be healthy to get everyone out of the house and socializing with others as soon as possible. Girls wake up, I have a surprise for all of you this morning. Annabelle asked, “What are we going to do?”

"Well honey after breakfast we're going on a walk through the park (there was a community park at the end of the street in the neighborhood) and then go to church. You know that big church at the other end of the park. Then after church, we're going to get ice cream and play in the park."

"Yeah!" Maryanne yelled in excitement.

After breakfast, Scott cleaned up the dishes while the girls watched cartoons on TV. Naomi peacefully slept in a wind-up baby swing in the living room with the girls.

Scott then loaded Naomi into a baby stroller and the four of them left the house to walk through the park to the other end of their housing development. They walked past the baseball field, then a playground, and nearby, a wooden bridge crossing over a year-round running creek. Scott and the girls rounded the corner after the bridge there was a large meadow which was a well-manicured grassy area with some trees and brush as a form of a perimeter for the grassy area at the edges. The park path wound its way through the trees into a clearing which opened up into a large parking lot for Rockville Victory Church. The main sanctuary was massive as it seated several thousand. Scott's family had been to this church a few times in the past but his dad felt it was too big. He called it an impersonal mega-church and felt they got lost inside the service. Scott wanted to get lost. He wanted to be unnoticed.

He knew this church had a large children's ministry that would provide a time for the girls to be with plenty of other kids with healthy activities this summer in a good environment.

Scott entered the church into the foyer and was greeted by a couple passing out church bulletins for the service. "Hi, good morning welcome to Victory. Here is a handout."

"Thanks", Scott said. "Where are the kindergarten class and the nursery?"

"The Kindergarten class is through those doors and down the hall to the right. The nursery is three doors down from there. Your parents will need to sign in the children though."

"I am the parents", Scott answered and walked through the doors past the foyer.

Pastor Jim, the assistant pastor, was standing nearby and saw the greeters meeting with Scott. "Hey, Sandy what did that young man say?"

"Hi pastor Jim, He asked for the kindergarten class and said he was the parents, but he looked no older than sixteen" (although Scott was 18).

"Sandy, I think that was Scott Mann with his sisters. You know the kid on that internet video." Pastor Jim turned and hurriedly ran down the hall toward the church office.

Scott walked down the hall and found the kindergarten room. He signed the girls up and listed himself as the parent on the sign-up roster. The teenage girl handling the roster didn't even notice anything unusual and didn't bother to ask any questions.

After dropping off the girls, Scott entered the nursery. There was no-one else in the room so he took Naomi out of her stroller and held her. Scott looked around the room and the first thing he saw was a large TV on the wall with a live video feed from the sanctuary.

He noticed the worship group was still setting up their instruments getting ready for church. There were changing tables with assorted diapers, baby toys, a playpen, and several rocking chairs for nursing mothers. Scott felt totally out of place. The nursery was designated for nursing moms to take care of their babies during the service.

Two women carrying babies entered the room with Scott. One of the women whispered, "Why is that kid in here with that newborn baby, where is her mother?" Neither of them said anything to Scott. Two more women also entered the nursery soon after. Occasionally one of them looked at Scott then whispered to the others. Scott felt so out of place, he wanted to run away. He was so uncomfortable he didn't know what to do.

Senior pastor Frank Billings was in his office for the last-minute preparations for today's message when his assistant pastor, Jim Henley, entered. "Hey Frank, you won't believe it. Remember that video we all watched last week of that kid who became the guardian of his little sisters. I am almost positive he's here now, he just walked in and checked them into the children's ministry. I believe he is in the nursery with the baby girl."

"Are you sure?", pastor Frank asked.

"Yes, he told the greeters that he 'was the parents' after they told him only the parents could check the kids into children's ministry. Besides, it looks just like him. I'm sure of it."

Pastor Frank immediately stood up, "Thanks, Jim. Hey, I need to find him and go talk to this kid if I am a little late cover for me during the church announcements ok".

"Ok Frank, no problem". Pastor Frank ran down the hall to the nursery.

Frank knocked on the door to the nursery and entered. He saw four women with babies and a young teenager with a newborn infant girl. "Excuse me, son, hi, I'm pastor Frank Billings, are you Scott?"

"Yes sir, I'm Scott Mann".

"Scott, thank you for visiting our church this morning. I want you to feel welcome here. But, I think we as a church have a responsibility to come alongside you and lift you up, even if it's just for this one day. Will you and your sisters be willing to come with me into the sanctuary during the service, up onto the stage so we as a church can pray for you. We normally do baby dedications for families with new babies. We pray for that child to dedicate it to the Lord all the days of her life. That God would bless the parents and provide for that family. Also that He would protect and keep the baby all her days. Usually, we make these appointments in advance so we can schedule it in within the church service and have the baby dedication certificate ready for the family. But I think in this circumstance we should pray today for you and your precious little one including your other sisters".

"I don't want to be an inconvenience", Scott answered.

"You won't be I promise, this is our responsibility to greet you properly when you walked under our roof this morning. I will take care of what to do, I promise it will be ok, you don't have to worry about the crowd".

"I'm not nervous in front of people pastor. I've already had enough fear and sadness in the last few months since my dad passed. I'm just worried that my sisters will be afraid in front of the large group in the sanctuary".

"Don't worry, little kids don't have the same stage fright we grown-ups have. I can soothe them up on the stage, I do it all the time. It will be just fine, trust me. (Pastor Frank smiled to assure Scott) Let's go get your sisters ok."

Scott carried Naomi and walked with Pastor Frank. They gathered Annabelle and Maryanne from the children's ministry and walked to a small but cozy room located just behind the stage. There was nothing in the room except two large couches and a few chairs. There was also a video monitor in the room like the one in the nursery with the cameras fixed on the stage. There were a few other people sitting inside the room, each awaiting their turn to walk out onto the stage to present their message or announcement to the church body. Scott noticed some of them were silently praying.

Pastor Frank explained to the girls what they were going to do. He asked them for their names and ages and wrote each child's name and age down including Scott's on a separate note pad and gave it to a woman standing nearby. She immediately left and went to the church office. Pastor Frank explained that he would first go out and give some announcements and then ask for them to walk out to join him on the stage.

Pastor Frank walked out of the room. Scott watched the monitor as Pastor Frank walked out onto the stage and greeted the church. Then Pastor Frank began his introduction, "Good morning everyone. I need to say that you never know when God is going to present you with a tremendous opportunity. This morning we have a visit from an angel so to speak. Our church family has an opportunity and the responsibility to provide the proper hospitality, as you never know when an angel will come through your doors. Hospitality to a special family, who just walked in to visit our church this morning. I'd like to invite Scott Mann and his sisters Annabelle, Maryanne, and Naomi to come out onto the stage. We are going to lift this young family up in prayer."

Just then another person wearing an earpiece walked over to Scott and whispered it's time for you and the girls to walk out onto the stage.

Scott walked out carrying Naomi. Annabelle followed, holding on to his rear belt loop with Maryanne holding her hand. Several people in the crowd gasped loud enough for others to hear.

“Now some of you might have seen Scott and Naomi on a recent viral video. Scott is the legal guardian and caretaker of his three sisters. They happen to live literally right here in our own backyard.”

Scott, tell us a little about your family (as he held the microphone near Scott).

“This is Naomi Pearl. She was born just a few weeks ago. God called her home, so Mom went to be with the Lord when Naomi was born. Dad was a police officer with Rockville PD and was killed in the line of duty a few months ago. Here are my two wonderful little sisters Annabelle Rachael and Maryanne Elizabeth. They’re five and will be starting Kindergarten in the fall. I promised mom that I would take care of our family because we're all of us there are. These little girls need to grow up and know the heritage of our parents and grandparents and not be adopted out to other families. I will fight with all that I am to make sure that we stay together as a family. Several people in the crowd could be heard weeping while Scott spoke.”

“Scott tell us, who named Naomi”, pastor Frank asked.

“I did. I wanted to let social services know that this was my family. I needed to exercise my authority as the leader of this family right away, to send a message that we are a family and no-one can separate us.”

“I’m sure not many brothers get to name their baby sisters Scott. Why ‘Naomi Pearl’?”

"Because I was sad and bitter. So very bitter at losing both of my parents in such an abrupt manner. I remember in the book of Ruth, of the story of Ruth and Naomi, how Naomi was so bitter at losing everyone close to her. Everyone that she loved. Naomi and her family were so reduced. It was just her and two surviving daughters' in-laws, and then only Ruth stayed with Naomi. I felt reduced like Naomi was. Because my family was reduced. But when I saw this little baby girl for the first time when she was born, she was so perfect so beautiful she was a treasure from God. So I knew her middle name was to be Pearl, Naomi Pearl."

"Scott, I need to tell you something. Naomi in the bible held what was left of her family together with all the strength that she had. It was her faith. Naomi's faith was the bond between her and Ruth. God must have been so pleased with Naomi's desperate effort because he blessed her descendants to come from royalty. Many kings were in her family line after that, ultimately the King of all kings and the Lord of all the lords were in her family line. God has something special for you too Scott, you need to know that."

"And who are you, young lady" (as Pastor Frank held the mic toward Annabelle)?

"I'm Annabelle and this is Maryanne."

"Wow, you guys are the prettiest twins I have ever seen."

"Are you proud of your big brother?"

Maryanne answered, "Yes he takes care of us and reads to us every night and prays for us. He cooks and does all the work in our home like mom used too". Annabelle interrupted and said, "And he does puzzles with us too and takes us to the park".

The crowd laughed loudly bringing a sense of comfort to those on the stage.

“Wow, it sounds like your big brother Scott is taking great care of you?”

“Yes, he is”, both girls answered in unison.

“Scott let me hold little Naomi Pearl, so I can lift her before the Lord in prayer...”

After the prayer, Pastor Frank leaned over and whispered in Scott’s ear, “Please wait to see me before you leave church today, it’s important”.

Scott and the girls exited the stage. Scott escorted the girls back to the kindergarten Sunday school class. Then he went back to the nursery with Naomi.

Scott entered the nursery and noticed each of the moms were crying. The women immediately came over and wanted to see Naomi. During the rest of the service, each of the ladies in the nursery gave Scott advice on their favorite diapers and infant care products. They gave him advice on everything from bathing infants, waking up at night to feed them, and the best way to keep your sanity when you’re always attached to a baby. Several of the moms hugged him when the service ended.

After Scott left the stage and returned to the nursery, pastor Frank addressed the church and asked the ushers to come forward with the offering plates.

Pastor Frank continued, “I don’t think we should send this young man away empty handed. I want to hold a special offering besides our regular offerings, something just to help with the financial needs of the Mann family. We will send him home with a check this very morning. Pastor Frank then walked over to the nearest usher and opened his wallet and placed all the cash he had on him into the offering plate.

One of the men in the congregation sitting with his wife said, “Wow, what a young man of character. What an example Scott is for all of us.”

Scott's girlfriend, Julie, who was sitting next to the couple also commented, "He sure is". However, she thought to herself that Scott is a fine catch for any young woman. But also knew she was not ready to be a mother for two little girls and a baby. She realized that she needed to break off her relationship with him as soon as possible.

After the offering was received, the assistant pastor Jim went to the office with the ushers to count the offering. They met the church secretary who just finished typing the baby dedication certificate for Naomi Pearl. She gave it to pastor Jim and said it was for Scott. The total offering for Scott was a little under $5,000.

Pastor Frank met with Scott at the nursery after the service. He gave Scott two envelopes. One large manila envelope containing the baby dedication certificate, and the other envelope contained a check for $5,000.

"Pastor Frank, thank you so much for your hospitality. Your church is just on the other side of the park from our home. Perfect for a Sunday walk for my family. I think we will make this a regular thing. I want Annabelle and Maryanne to have some activity outside of our home for them to be with other kids and do things in a positive environment. It would be helpful for them to heal. Can we make this our home church?"

"Yes, Scott you are so welcome to become part of our church family".

Scott walked out into the foyer with the girls and several people approached him to hug him and the girls. Several people gave Scott warm words of encouragement.

One person waited until she could speak with him alone. "Hi Scott, I am Janet Stilwell, the principal of Hope Classical Christian Academy. This is a very exclusive private school in Granite Beach. I want to offer you a scholarship for Annabelle and Maryanne for this fall. We would be proud to open our school up for your girls. They are starting kindergarten correct?"

“Yes, they are, wow. I knew I needed to start the enrollment process for school soon. It was the next thing on my ‘to worry about list’. This is so wonderful thank you.”

“Scott please come by my office on Monday, and we will give you the enrollment packages for your daughters. I would also like to introduce you to several of my staff and give you a personal tour of the campus.”

“Thank you so much I will be there.”

Scott and the girls then left the church and walked through the park. They stopped at an ice cream vendor along the way and went over to the playground. Annabelle and Maryanne played in the playground while Scott sat at a park bench nearby pushing and rocking Naomi in her stroller.

Scott sat and reminisced how nice everyone at church was to him today when he received a text from Julie.

“***Where R U can we meet***?”

“***At the playground in the park by the church***”

“***Be there in 5***”

“***Great, I can’t wait to see you***”

Scott excitedly watched as Julie walked up to sit with him on the bench. He hoped she would just be his girlfriend like she was before and that she was here to tell him the good news.

“Hi Scott, I saw you in the church today. You and the girls were adorable. I am so proud of you for your decision, you did do the right thing for you and your family, I know that now. But I need to tell you I think our lives are simply taking different paths. I don’t want you to hate me, but I have my own path to follow and it’s not with children and a new family right now. I felt it was the right thing to meet you in person and be honest with you about my feelings.”

"Julie", Scott answered, "I thought I was your guy, I mean we were a couple, way back since we started high school. Just because I am taking care of my sisters, all of a sudden, I'm not in your path for life? I can't afford to lose someone else in my life that I care about. Look I will miss you. I will miss your friendship. I miss the company of people my own age. I like you, Julie. I don't want to break up. But I get it, I also know it's not fair to saddle you with my family's issues."

Julie interrupted, "Scott, I need to go."

"Whatever…" Scott answered as he angrily turned his head away from her. Julie turned to leave, her eyes teared up as she walked off. Julie wondered if she should turn back to him, but resisted the temptation and continued walking away, never to return.

Scott thought to himself that it really wasn't fair to Julie, for him to be so demanding. She didn't do anything wrong. Sometimes God only intends a person's trials solely for that person who is afflicted. He intends for them to go through that darkness alone for them to endure and grow from it. This trial was his alone to bear. Scott realized It was Julie's choice to make for the vision she had for her own future, and she should follow it in peace.

Chapter 9

Gold Country Family Services
Case Name: Scott Mann
Case File: #4237
Case Worker: Amanda Peters
Date: July 2019

Scott and the family have adjusted to a new routine. The girls seem to be adapting well to the new stability. Scott and the family have joined a new church to provide and encourage much needed healthy social activity for each of them. There seems to be positive a support system developing from within the church for this new family. Scott has received a scholarship from Hope Classical Christian Academy for Annabelle and Maryanne for Kindergarten beginning in the fall. Scott also has begun the process of looking for employment and possibly taking on one college class in the fall or winter semester. The changes will require full-time childcare. I inspected the home on this month's welfare visit. The house was immaculate and well organized. There was plenty of food in the pantry and the refrigerator.

Cindy called the number from the flyer she saw posted at the post office bulletin board. The position had been filled. Cindy knew her situation was now at a dire crossroad. She only had enough money for a couple more nights in the hotel. Cindy scraped up some change to buy a granola bar out of the vending machine in the hotel lobby. This would have to suffice for her dinner. She knew she was almost broke and unable to go any further, but somehow, she felt that something was telling her to stay here.

After she got up the following morning, Cindy made coffee for herself in her room from the free packet of condiments left in her room along with the shampoo and hand soaps. The coffee was nasty, and it only reminded her of her dilemma.

Cindy took a long walk from her hotel room and somehow ended up at Rockville Victory Church. Cindy's royal family belonged to the Church of Sweden, which is Lutheran. But she decided that the peace one felt from any Christian church might help to calm her spirit while she tried to think of what to do. The front doors were open but no one was inside, so she walked past the foyer and into the sanctuary.

Cindy was comforted that no one was around so she sat in the front row and decided to meditate on her problems. Cindy felt scared and alone and began to cry.

Pastor Frank walked past the sanctuary on his way to the church office and overheard the muffled crying.

"Hi, I'm pastor Frank Billings. Usually, we don't see anyone here on weekday mornings. Is there anything I can get for you?"

"Oh, I'm sorry, am I not allowed to be in here?"

"You're fine, what's your name, and how can I help? If you just want privacy I can leave."

"Oh, I'm Cindy Mason, that's ok. I have a big problem right now and I don't know what I need to do. I have made a big mistake. I left home, my family, everything I knew, all for very selfish reasons. I traveled pretty far to get here and now I'm stuck."

"I'm not sure I understand your whole situation. But you're an adult and you have the choice to go back home if you want right, why not just go home?"

"Yes, I'm 21 almost 22, but I'm not sure where to go or how to go actually. My story is very complicated. It's something I'm sure you have never dealt with, and so unusual it would be hard to explain."

"OK well, can't you just get a job until you decide what to do? What about asking your family for help?"

“No, I can’t. You see I planned and saved for so long to come to California. It took everything I had worked to get to this point, but I still haven’t been able to enjoy what I wanted to do. Now I’m broke, and If I called my family it would be an embarrassment. You don’t understand, this is bigger than you think.”

“Cindy let me ask, are you in legal trouble, or is your safety a concern?”

“Yes, I am in trouble, more than you realize, but not legal trouble. I’m perfectly safe too. It’s just politics and…”

“Cindy, why do I get the feeling that you’re not telling me everything?”

“Do you keep matters in confidence like confession is to a priest?”

“Cindy yes, I have a spiritual responsibility to keep things in confidence. But every clergy member in California has a legal responsibility under state legal codes for clergy confidentiality. We have the same privilege as lawyers and medical doctors to keep people’s information confidential.”

Cindy hesitated, then she looked around and stared at the wall for a moment. She turned back and looked back at pastor Frank, “I am invoking this clergy confidentiality.”

“OK, go ahead Cindy.”

“Actually, I am Princess Charlotta, the crown princess of Sweden.”

Pastor Frank stared at her and held back a smile seemingly in disbelief.

“Pastor Frank, unless you need me to go back to my hotel room to get my passport I could, but just search my name and images on the internet on your phone for right now.

Cindy removed her glasses and held her hair up on top of her head in a sort of informal pose. Pastor Frank noted her strong European accent and looked at his phone then back at Cindy/Charlotta.

He quickly stood up, "Oooh my, Princess! The whole world is looking for you".

"Just call me Cindy for now. That's what I am calling myself here in California. Please sit with me."

He sat down and she continued, "I left the palace thinking I could escape the paparazzi and the whole stress of all the public scrutiny. My family seemed cold, and too formal my whole life. Being the eldest child, I feel like I have been groomed since childhood for the throne but nothing else. The crown and the whole public image is all that matters. I missed the hugs of a father and mother as I grew up. I missed the attention parents give their children. I just wanted normalcy. So, I rebelled. Planned my escape and decided to go to LA. I was going to party it up incognito so to speak. I never thought of anything past that. I also never realized life is so hard without money. I know I'm never going to make it to LA. However. It would be a huge public embarrassment for the monarchy, which is already unpopular in Sweden, for me to call my family completely destitute and on the streets.

But there is something else. I also feel something pulling me to stay. I can't say how or why, but something in my heart, it's telling me to stay for now. What do I do? Should I call my family or try to stay?"

"Cindy, first and most important, you need to find a way to let your family know you are ok. There's no doubt that your mother and father are so worried."

He showed her an article on his cell phone. The article was about the royal couple who were publicly appealing for the whereabouts and safety of their daughter (not even mentioning her title of the crown princess). It's obvious this was the picture of an emotionally wrecked husband and wife. They did not hide the emotion on their faces in reporting the loss of their child. Cindy cried when she read the article on pastor Frank's phone.

"I know, I can't call or email them, they can trace where I am. I agree with you though and I promise that I will figure out how and try to get a message to them."

"Cindy, I can't give you an answer to your dilemma. But I can give you advice. Sometimes God uses emotions and events in our lives to lead us to places where He wants us to be. Then, He often allows us to reach rock bottom in our trials for several reasons: First to empty us of our selfish desires and thoughts so we can hear His voice. Secondly, He wants to empty us of pride so we are dependent on Him to guide us to where we need to be. Thirdly, He wants to build character and patience in us to prepare us for the new calling He is leading us into."

Pastor Frank continued, "I can't answer for God in your circumstances. But you can seek Him. I encourage you to fast and pray just for today for what God is leading you to do.

But I do not want you to wait for long. After a day or so, if nothing happens you need to call your family to come to pick you up. It's dangerous to be alone in a strange land with no money. Here is my card with a number you can reach me directly if you are in an emergency situation. I sincerely ask that if God shows you something, that you let me know if you are safe and ok, just so I don't worry too."

"I promise. Thanks, pastor Frank."

They prayed together and then Cindy got up to leave. She walked into the foyer towards the exit and saw a flashing glimpse of light on the wall. It flashed several more times with each step she took. Cindy walked over to the bulletin board to see what had captured her attention. Then she saw this note thumbtacked into the cork board. The paper was covered in glitter that reflected the lights from the room with each step that she took. It said, "Live-in child care needed for small loving family".

The name was covered up with glue and glitter but the phone number was readable. Cindy took the note off the wall and placed it inside her pocket. She walked outside through the parking lot and into the park and then called the number on the glittery note.

A teenage male voice answered, "Hi its Scott…"

~~~~~~~

The first thing Monday morning Scott got the girls up and dressed them in their best dresses and took them to the new school to meet principal, Janet. Scott was given the enrollment papers for kindergarten. He met with several of the office staff members but was advised that the teachers were still out for Summer vacation.

Scott and the girls also met with the school nurse who stated she needed copies of Annabelle and Maryanne's vaccination records. They were given a tour of the school and left the campus. The girls were so excited to see the playground and the classrooms.

Scott and the children then went to their pediatrician's office on the way home from school to get a copy of their medical files. The receptionist looked up their family on the computer to access the needed records. She printed out the records and then advised Scott that their medical insurance was going to expire next month as they were all on his parent's insurance plan. Scott realized the seriousness of the situation.
~~~~~~~

He had enough money in the bank to live on for a while but would not have medical insurance, which was mandatory as part of the contract he signed with CPS. Amanda had offered Scott state-funded medical insurance earlier. But Scott decided he wanted to keep the same doctors and medical plan if possible. He didn't want too much change, besides they all liked their doctors. Scott knew he needed to find a job as soon as possible.

Scott stopped at the grocery store for diapers on the way home from the doctor's office. He put Naomi (while still secured into the infant car seat) into the child seat portion of the shopping cart. The car seat fit right into that portion of the shopping cart. The girls followed him into the store. A woman approached him when he neared the check-out line.

"What are you doing young man?"

"I'm just shopping for diapers. We're running out at home. It's surprising how fast a baby goes through a pack of diapers."

She stared at Scott threateningly, "What is a teenager like you doing with all these babies alone? You can't responsibly take care of an infant out in public and watch two little ones at the same time. Where is your mother? I bet she is drunk and passed out on the couch. Somebody needs to report this to the authorities."

Scott didn't know what to say as the situation appeared to escalate. Annabelle started crying which only caused the stranger to become even more irate. He wanted to leave, then she stepped in front of his cart blocking his path.

At that moment, an African American woman intervened, and angrily said to the other woman, "Huh-uh, I know you're not talking to my kids like that! These are my babies! All of them! So what do you have to say!"

The other person seemed exceedingly shocked and embarrassed, she quickly abandoned her cart in the line and walked out of the store.

"Scott, are you ok honey?"

"I'm fine, how do you know me?"

"I'm Paige Wilson, you were in my church last Sunday."

Annabelle still crying hugged Paige and buried her face into Paige's thigh. Annabelle cried deep and hard.

"It's OK little baby, Paige answered. I know your scared honey, and you two little ones have carried more pain on your shoulders and in your hearts that no one your age should have to do. It isn't right. But I tell you that you're not alone. More people are loving your family more than you could ever know. One day God is going to look down from heaven and see all the tears you cried, and His righteous vengeance is going pour out of heaven with flames and shaking. Kingdoms are going to rattle. Kings and queens are going to shake when God moves on your behalf because God is going to change your lives and bless you with so much happiness and wonder that you won't be able to contain all the joy."

Paige held Annabelle patiently for several minutes until she stopped crying.

Scott thanked Paige, and apologized, he also struggled unsuccessfully holding back his own tears as he watched his younger sister unload her grief. Scott noticed sometimes grief in their family was contagious. Once one sibling seems to get sad, then the others begin to suffer. It starts with thinking about how unfair it is for your little sister to mourn so hard, then somehow it invokes your own grief.

"I'm sorry I think Annabelle just misses mom. I feel inadequate because she needs the special kind of love that a kid can only get from a mom."

Paige gave Scott her phone number and promised she could help him babysit on some occasions with Annabelle and Maryanne, but she just couldn't watch the baby. Scott felt completely overwhelmed at this moment.

Paige's kindness unlocked this dread that had engulfed him. Sometimes, even when talking to a complete stranger the grief and fear start coming out, nothing can stop it. It doesn't matter where you're at. Scott noticed this feeling of dark sadness has been with him constantly since his dad died. It doubled down with his mother's death. His mom was everything to him. How could she be gone? He started sobbing as he spoke with Paige.

"I don't know how to do it all he said as he cried. On top of this constant sadness, It hurts so bad. Now I also worry about how to take care of the girls. How do I shop for them with School coming up? The pediatrician also told me there are things I need to do for them too. But I'm just a boy, I don't know how to be a mom."

Paige hugged Scott and promised to help him with any girl stuff, shopping, anything that he needed advice for. To just call anytime. She also comforted him with the knowledge the whole church is behind him. That more people are with him than he realizes.

Scott thanked Paige again, wiped the tears from his face, and went into the checkout line. The clerk scanned the three packs of diapers. Then told Scott as she fought back her own tears, "That will be all". One of our other customers took care of your groceries for today. Scott looked around at the other check-out lines to say thanks, but no-one looked back at him.

The family left the store and went home. They decided to watch a movie for the rest of the day instead of going outside.

Chapter 10

Gold Country Family Services
Case Name: Scott Mann
Case File: #4237
Case Worker: Amanda Peters
Date: August 1, 2019

The family is adjusting very well to their new lifestyles. Scott recognized the need for a job in order to obtain medical insurance since the family insurance plan runs out next month. He has an appointment for a job interview with the city of Rockville next week. He also applied to the local community college and will take one class next semester. Scott is exhibiting financial and emotional maturity in recognizing the need for a job and pursuing that need without outside prodding. Scott confided in me during our last home visit that he still struggles with depression. He feels alone during the greatest emotional crisis he could endure. Scott decided to take the college class in order to "push himself out" publicly, to make friends and place himself in a new environment outside of home and babies.

That night after the kids were put to bed Scott went online looking for Jobs. He filled out several applications, one of them for a position with the City of Rockville in the Public Works Department as a landscaper. It was easy enough work, but it had medical benefits, and a tuition assistance program for employees to go back to college.

While filling out the job applications Scott realized his own birthday was coming up in two days. He had simply forgotten with everything going on. He hoped someone would notice it was his birthday. He just wanted to feel appreciated and loved. The fear of no-one to celebrate his birthday with accentuated the loss he already felt.

Scott also filled out a college application online for the local community college. He took a math class the last time he was enrolled here. Scott had already completed five college courses when he was a high school student assigned on the academic enrichment program.

Earlier, Scott had earned a partial athletic scholarship for the Taekwondo team for North State Bay Area University. Scott had always dreamed of going to the Olympics on the US Taekwondo team. He had trained for years in martial arts with his father since he was a small boy. There was also a world-famous kickboxing gym nearby where Scott had trained religiously before his father died. He has not trained since.

Scott's life was not always all perfect. He was academically advanced, and an athlete, but he was sort of a snob toward other kids his own age. He often refused to go to school functions or hang out with any of the kids from the church simply because they were “Nerds”.

Now Scott would give anything for friends his own age.

Scott’s Birthday came and went. Not one person recognized his special day. No one sent a birthday card or even texted happy birthday to him.

Scott laid in bed crying, and told the Lord, “I feel like You are punishing me. I feel so alone, no one cares for me at all. Everyone even CPS seems to care for the welfare of the kids, but no-one cares for me. My dad and mom are gone. The pain is still there Lord but no one is helping me through this. Will you help me?” Scott cried quietly until he fell asleep.

Scott awoke the next morning and turned on the news while making his coffee. He briefly listened and overheard a commercial, “*...to receive your* ***gift***...

Scott finished getting ready for his job interview with the city of Rockville, as this was the big day. Sandy Weathers arrived to babysit for Scott.

“Scott here is your newspaper, I picked it up in the driveway on my way in.”

“Oh, that’s the Thompson’s paper, they live next door. Sometimes it ends up in our driveway by mistake.”

Scott took the paper and noticed a crumpled flyer inside the rubber band on the paper. "…***Gift*** for **S**..**tt**…" He uncrumpled the flyer and it read the whole add, "Door Prizes and ***Gift*** giveaways at the grand opening of **S**unset Park Tra**tt**oria".

Scott left for the interview and couldn't help noticing the giant ad on the side of the City Bus, "*Special* ***Gifts*** at Mom's Boutique".

He turned on the radio and "The Great ***Gift***", the latest popular pop song, was playing on Hot Hits 102.3 FM.

Scott finished the Job interview at City Hall for a position on the public works department and was given a background packet to complete. It looked like he would get the job after the City of Rockville finished checking all of his background credentials.

Scott continued to hear the word "Gift" being pronounced in every medium possible throughout the day.

He gathered the girls together that evening for family time. He decided to read a passage from a daily devotional about giving and serving others in need that ended with a verse from **2 Corinthians 9:15, "*Thanks be to God for His indescribable gift.*"**

Scott smiled and felt that maybe the Lord was telling him that a gift from God, for his birthday, is coming soon. Scott realized that he is not alone even if he feels alone. Maybe something good is about to happen to change the current course of darkness, and the sunshine of joy will shine on his family once again.

John and Sandy Weathers arrived at Scott's house on Saturday morning. Sandy took the kids while John and Scott went into the den to talk.

John looked around the den, it was a sort of man cave with bookcases filled with books, a desk and a computer, and a gun safe.

“Scott, I see your dad’s gun safe is still here, did you have the combination?”

“Ya, I found it in a file folder in the garage that contained the owner’s manual. Don’t worry, I put the owner’s manual somewhere else more secure.”

“What goodies do you have inside? I’m just being a guy right?”

“Here, I’ll show you. Some are my grandpa’s guns and some are dad’s. I’ll pass all of these on to my kids too in time.”

Scott removed a handgun from the safe. “This 1911 .45 pistol is my favorite.” Scott then pointed to a rifle inside, “This is an M1 Garand, the .45 and the M1 were grandpas. They were his, from the war. There’s also this old pump action .22 rifle that was grandpas too.”

“Wow, Scott, that .22 rifle is also a collector’s item for sure.”

“Dad has a few handguns in there, a pump action 12-gauge shotgun, and a bolt action hunting rifle as well.”

Scott removed each gun from the safe to show to Mr. Weathers. He cleared each gun to ensure it was ‘safe’ before handing it to him to look at. Scott also wiped down each gun with an oiled gun cloth after they handled them before placing them back into the safe.

“Mom keeps her jewelry in there too. Scott’s eyes teared up, but he continued. Here is my mom’s wedding ring. She took it off before going to the hospital, I guess people don’t wear jewelry in hospitals.”

John looked at the ring but didn’t touch it. It was a single diamond in a raised setting over a solid thick yellow gold band. The diamond looked like at least two carats.

The wedding band itself contained seven ¼ carat diamonds lining the circumference of the band.

"Wow Scott, that is awesome. What are you going to do with all this jewelry?"

"I'm keeping the wedding ring for sure. I will give that to my future wife. Hey, it was my Grandmother's ring, then my mom's. I want to keep it in the family. I will probably split up the rest of the jewelry for the three girls when they get older."

Scott changed the subject, "John, you know I wanted to ask you. This is embarrassing ok. But, I find myself crying at night, a lot, almost every night when I go to bed. Is this normal to still be so sad?"

"Yes, Scott it is very normal, it's going to take a long time for you to get over the grieving process. The girls won't take as long since they are so much younger.

But also, you need to understand something. You are taking on the whole world of responsibility right now, and it has to be so scary for you. Besides, you are now a mom and a dad to two children and an infant, as well as managing a whole house. Honestly, my wife cries at night sometimes too. I think a lot of mom's do. The workday becomes overwhelming and it's a natural way for coping, for unloading of all of the day's stress. Scott, you have sadness and fear on top of a huge workload. Sometimes we endure critical stress. There are healthy ways and unfortunately unhealthy ways people try to overcome this type of critical stress.

Avoid alcohol and drugs or locking yourself up alone in the house to mope. I encourage you to manage your stress in a healthy manner. Eat healthy foods with a lot of fruits and vegetables and drink plenty of water during the day, keep hydrated.

Avoid junk foods and sugary drinks. I also encourage you to exercise daily. I know you liked martial arts so when you can, go into the garage and work the heavy bags. I know you and your dad had a good routine for your martial arts training. Hitting the bag will help you sweat and get in some good cardio, it will release some of that tension. Lastly, spend intimate time with God. Also, continue to find and get involved in new family projects. Build a new set of family traditions with you and the girls. When you can, I do encourage you to get that job and to eventually start taking college classes again. Getting outside and doing positive productive activities will help release that stress. Believe me, in time life, will get better, and you will find happiness and laughter once again in your life and in this home."

Scott decided he wanted to sign up for college class soon after meeting with his Mr. Weathers. Scott changed schools so he could be closer to home and enrolled at the community college in town. Scott was able to get into the class easy enough even though he registered so late. After all, it was just an "English A" class. He was only trying to take care of most of his general education units while attending the more affordable community college. Scott gave up his athletic scholarship during the summer after his parents died. He was actually glad to attend the nearby community college. The only problem was child care.

Scott thought He would try one of the mom's he met from church until he could arrange more permanent child care on the nights of his classes.

Tuesday was the first night for his English class and no-one was available to help on such short notice. Scott didn't think he would get a class this soon after applying and didn't make childcare plans in advance. Scott remembered Paige Wilson from the grocery store and had seen her a few times in passing at church. He found her number and gave her a call.

"Hi, Mrs. Wilson this is Scott Mann from the church."

"Hi Scott it's so nice to hear from you, how are you?"

"I am fine thanks. I am trying to jump start my life and add more activity. I want our lives and get back into a new normal. I'm getting a new job and I also signed up for a college English class. My first day of class is Tuesday."

"That's fantastic. I am so glad to see you moving forward Scott. That's healthy."

"I'm almost embarrassed to ask, but I wasn't planning on getting into the class this semester since I enrolled late, kind of spur of the moment type of thing. I didn't make plans in advance for a babysitter."

"Scott honey, you can bring the girls over no problem. However, I am not able to watch the baby. My home is simply not childproof enough for a baby."

"That's fine. I will take her with me to class in the stroller, it's big enough, and maybe she will sleep through class."

Scott dropped off his two sisters at Paige's house and went straight to the campus. He parked his truck in the back lot and unloaded the baby stroller. It was the big old-fashioned type of strollers on four wheels. Scott gently placed Naomi in the stroller, but she seemed fussier than normal tonight. He hoped she would fall asleep while being pushed through the campus on the way to class.

Scott ignored the other people staring at him as he pushed a baby stroller through the campus. Scott arrived at his classroom and waited outside, pushing the large stroller back and forth as some of the other students went inside. Scott went inside a minute before the class started.

He heard a light whisper from one of the students, "That's Scott Mann". Scott sat in the rear of the class still pushing the stroller back and forth, but Naomi did not seem to want to cooperate with the plan and started fussing again.

The professor walked into the room and stared at Scott showing slight displeasure that he brought a baby into the classroom. He thought, "Why would this teenager bring his baby to class couldn't his 'baby mama' take care of their illegitimate child? Why do we all have to suffer because of their lifestyle problems?"

He took roll call and then, passed out the syllabus, and introduced the class goals for this semester. During his speech, Naomi seemed to get even more impatient and fussy. Scott removed her from the stroller and stood in the back of the room holding and rocking her to keep her quiet.

The professor grew increasingly agitated about the disturbance in the classroom and decided to embarrass this selfish student who lacked sensitivity to anyone else wanting to learn.

"Young man", he said. "Why don't you come up here and write the four major types of essays on the board."

Everyone turned and stared at Scott and Naomi to see what he would do. At that moment, an African American young man who was sitting in the back of the class got up and walked over to Scott. He reached over and said, "I'll take her for a minute man." Scott hesitated, then handed Naomi over and walked to the board in the front of the class. Scott wrote, 'Persuasive, Narrative, Expository, Descriptive'.

Scott turned around and saw the guy in the back of the class smiling, holding Naomi as he whispered to her and rocked her gently.

The professor seemed humbled and said, "Well done Scott, you can return to your desk." Scott walked to the back of the class and said to the young man holding her, "Thanks so much, I can take her".

The other student said, "Take a break, I'll keep her for a while". Scott sat down at his desk, and during the course of the class, several students, male and female, each got up and walked to the back of the class and took turns holding and rocking Naomi allowing Scott to sit at his desk for the entire class.

After the class, several students gathered around Scott to meet him and talk with him about his family. Some of the students showed the professor the videos on the internet about Scott Mann and Naomi.

Scott realized that people have been generously kind toward him, but he could not take advantage of everyone's willingness to help. He must find full-time help with childcare in order to work and go to school.

Chapter 11

Gold Country Family Services
Case Name: Scott Mann
Case File: #4237
Case Worker: Amanda Peters
Date: August 15, 2019

Scott started college by taking one class this semester at the local community college. He also got a job with the city of Rockville in the department of public works. Annabelle and Maryanne started school at Hope Classical Christian Academy, a prestigious private school in the neighboring community of Granite Beach. Scott hired Cindy Mason as a live-in childcare helper. Cindy had several local references but is very quiet about her past and where she is from. Cindy seems to be very refined in her posture and demeanor. She communicates with a very formal speech and vocabulary hinting that she comes from a very refined family background. Cindy will be a good influence in the home for the girls. Scott is determined to keep a professional atmosphere in his relationship to Cindy and to be above reproach since she is an employee. However, I do believe they are both attracted to each other. I believe the family is on the path to healing and a positive future.

It was Monday, the first day of school, Annabelle and Maryanne were starting Kindergarten. After the girls got dressed Scott stopped for a moment thinking with a sadness in his heart that the first school day was that proud and fearful moment that a mom and dad shares with their child as they start to grow up. Scott felt a deep sense of loss and missed his mom tremendously thinking she should be here taking them to school. He determined to himself that he would not show any grieving or sadness as he loaded everyone into the truck.

They arrived in the parking lot at the school which was located in an exclusive neighborhood in Granite Beach. Most of the moms were arriving in their compact luxury cars or expensive SUV's. Scott felt a little out place arriving in a lifted 4X4 truck, but he didn't care what they thought, he knew they were safe while they drove.

Some of the moms and older kids watched as Scott unloaded Naomi and the other two girls. He put Naomi in a smaller, folding stroller, and held on too Annabelle's hand. Maryanne walked on his other side. Scott walked through the hallways and located their Kindergarten class and walked inside. Mrs. Judith Bell introduced herself to the moms and new kids in the class.

"Hi, I'm Mrs. Bell I will be your child's Kindergarten teacher. Please take this additional information packet about school materials you will need to purchase for your child this year, as well as information about our school lunches. Please fill out the forms if your child has any food allergies that we need to know about. We encourage the parents to get involved with several class projects during the year including a school Christmas play. There is a sign-up sheet in the information packet in how you can get involved in the activities."

Some of the moms looked suspiciously at Scott, others knew who he was. Mrs. Bell finished her introductions and used this time to meet any parents that wanted to talk with her.

"Hi Mrs. Bell, I'm Scott Mann. You get two of mine. This is Annabelle and Maryanne."

"Hello, you are the two most beautiful twin girls I have ever seen. You will have so much fun in our class."

"Hi, Mrs. Bell," both girls said simultaneously. Annabelle continued, "Can we go over to the play area?", pointing to a large matted area in the center of the class with some toys.

"Yes, girls you may."

Mrs. Bell turned to Scott and said, "Ohhhh is this little Naomi, she is so beautiful". Her eyes teared up, as she continued. "Scott I am so proud of you for taking in all of your sisters and caring for them as your own children. They are so lucky to have you. I am so lucky to be their teacher this year. I will never forget this opportunity in my whole career."

“Thank you. I’m still learning what to do. Please forgive me for the mistakes that I know I will be making, but I am trying my best to be a good parent. I’m sure I will have a ton of questions as the year progresses. If I get too bothersome just let me know.”

“You already are hon, a good parent that is. The fact that you worry and want to learn to be better means your conscientious. One thing you do need to understand though is that you are their parent now. You’re not a brother anymore to them. You will find that parental role you have with them will continue to change that way more and more, and in time, each of these little ones of yours will start to look at you as their father. Naomi already does.”

“About asking questions, please anytime, I will never be too bothered to help. I also wanted to tell you that our entire school staff is aware that your children are enrolled in our school. We are all so excited to have your girls here. Some of the other parents may be suspicious of you at first, others may be kind of snobbish too. But overall most of our families are good people. The others will all come around in time.”

Scott said goodbye and left with Naomi.

That night Scott and the girls were having family time after dinner. Scott said, “I have an arts and craft project for us, girls. We’re going to make a few flyers to post up for childcare. We need a babysitter so I can work and go to school. I would like you guys to help me design and decorate them. Tell me who do you guys want, what kind of person do you want to live with us.”

Annabelle said, “We want someone like a mommy.”

“Maryanne said, “But someone your age Scott, it would be weird having an old lady in here. She needs to be young and pretty.”

“Well, that’s a tall order girls. If you decorate the flyers appropriately maybe we will find that right person huh?”

Scott filled out the information on several flyers that he would place on bulletin boards at the post office, churches, and some college campuses. Maryanne spilled glue on the last flyer, smudging some of the information but sprinkled glitter on it anyway.

The next morning Scott took the flyers and dropped the girls off at school. He placed the flyers at the various planned locations and went back to pick up the girls after school.

Annabelle and Maryanne were both crying in the principal's office when Scott arrived to pick them up. Mrs. Bell explained to Scott that some of the other girls teased them on the playground today. "One girl, in particular, told them that they were orphans and didn't have a parent. She told your girls that orphans don't belong in our school."

Scott comforted his sisters in the office. "Hey, girls you guys DO have parents. Your mother and father were honorable and good people. Your dad was a hero. They are still your parents looking down from heaven with such great love and concern for you both. But you need to know that I am here for you now. I might be your brother, but I am as a parent for you both now."

Annabelle asked, "Can I call you dad"? Maryanne yelled out, "No you can't he's not our dad".

"He is too Maryanne. He makes our food every day and takes care of us. He takes care of Naomi and changes her diapers. He takes us to the park and plays with us on the playground."

Maryanne feeling guilty for ignoring what Scott has been to her started crying and turned to Scott and hugged him and said, "Thanks for being our dad." Annabelle joined in hugging Scott.

Scott looked up and saw Mrs. Bell and Janet Stillwell, watching from the hallway, both crying. After Scott left, Janet turned to Mrs. Bell. "This is so hardcore isn't it?"

“I have never seen anything like this Janet. That poor family, Scott is doing a great job though. They are going to be ok.”

Scott took the girls home, and they all got their bikes from the garage and went to the park for a bike ride.

Scott's cell phone rang when they were near the playground. He dug his phone out of his backpack as quick as he could and answered, “Hi this is Scott.”

“Hello, my name is Cindy Mason I am answering your advertisement from the church for live-in child care.”

Scott noticed Cindy spoke with a strong accent, but she had a beautiful voice. She seemed young.

“Yes, hi Cindy thanks for calling. I would like to meet you in a neutral place first before I introduce you to the family if that is ok. I have a college class late this afternoon. Can I meet you at the coffee shop on the corner of College Avenue and Rockville Road at 4:00?”

“Yes, that would be great Scott. Will I meet your parents then?”

Scott didn’t feel it was appropriate nor was he comfortable in talking about their family situation over the phone until they could at least meet in person. “I need to meet with you first just to get your references so we can check them out before a more formal meeting with our family. I can give you more information about our family when we meet, I’m sure you want to check up on us too. If everything works out, if we're still comfortable with each other, we can schedule the next day for you to meet the rest of us. We are a family of four and live in Rockville.”

“Ok Scott, I’ll meet you tomorrow. I have blond hair and I’ll wear a pink baseball cap.”

Scott couldn’t stop thinking about meeting Cindy. He knew this was a job interview, but he thought she had the most beautiful voice he had ever heard in his life.

Scott walked into the coffee shop and saw Cindy sitting down and the corner table. He knew it was her because she was wearing the pink baseball hat. Scott immediately got butterflies in his stomach. She was so beautiful and she sat with such perfect posture. Somehow, she gave off this vibe of being super classy but he couldn't put his finger on it. Scott had a hard time focusing on the fact that he needed to interview her. Scott walked over and nervously asked, "Cindy"?

"Yes, it's me, Scott?"

"Yes, it's me too", he answered.

Scott noticed she had the bluest, sapphire blue, eyes behind dark-rimmed plastic eyeglasses. She had the most appealing thin beautiful lips. The face of a model with perfect features. But no make-up. Why no make-up he wondered?

As they spoke, her accent and the sound of her voice was even more attractive than he could stand. Scott noticed Cindy spoke with a very formal vocabulary and her posture was so perfect she must have been trained to maintain such a perfect bearing.

When Scott walked into the coffee shop and started speaking to her, Cindy noticed he looked young. She guessed about 16 at first, but he was very tall. He was about 6'1" and walked standing straight up with his shoulders back. He had big muscular arms for a kid and noticed the athletic definition to his shoulders and trapezius muscles through his t-shirt. He was very attractive nevertheless. Maybe he was a couple of years older than her estimation but he still had a baby face.

He had the brownest eyes and light brown hair. Cindy felt guilty for being attracted to the son of her possible new employers.

"Cindy, please tell me about yourself," Scott asked.

She handed over a small list of names and phone numbers of her references. Including Linda Maxwell and Beth Klingson, whom she had still been providing occasional babysitting. “I’m 21 years old, and I’m from Minnesota. I recently moved here to California to start a new life. My family is wealthy but very cold and distant to me. I do not feel close to them at all. I really haven’t got out into the world to do much, so I don’t have much to tell. Please tell me about yourself and your family Scott.”

“I just turned 19 and started taking a college class. My goal is to finish as much of my general education units as possible at the community college and then transfer to a 4-year university after that. I can save a lot of money on tuition this way. I also start working next Monday for the City of Rockville. I love martial arts and usually work out regularly. I have three sisters, whom I would love to introduce to you when you meet the rest of our family.”

“Can you meet us tomorrow afternoon after the girls are out of school? Let’s say 2:00 ok? Everyone will be home by then for you to meet.”

“Yes Scott, I’ll be there. I would like to meet your family.”

Cindy thought it was odd Scott told her he had three sisters, and yet earlier on the phone, he said they were a family of four. Maybe he was only counting the children in the family and not their parents.

After their informal interview, Scott went home and called the names on Cindy’s list. Linda and Beth gave excellent recommendations for Cindy, but they each only knew her for a short time.

Scott worried about Cindy because she was very guarded about telling him about her background. There wasn’t much information for him to discern if she was going to be ok fit with the children. Scott conducted an internet search to try to find out more information, but Cindy did not have any social media accounts. Her name came up blank on the search.

That night after dinner, Amanda Peters arrived for an unannounced home visit. They sat at the table as Scott told her about all the new changes and especially about Cindy. Amanda was also a little concerned but praised Scott for checking into her. He told her how she seemed very refined, about her rich vocabulary and perfect posture.

She obviously came from a refined background and did not appear to be a bad person. Amanda agreed but asked Scott to get one more reference, someone not involved with childcare.

The following day Cindy took the bus and walked the rest of the way to Scott's house to the address provided. The neighborhood was a middle-class subdivision of well-manicured landscaped houses built from the same set of architectural plans. Cindy saw Scott's truck in the driveway when she arrived at his address (The same truck she saw him driving when he met her at the coffee shop). There were no other vehicles parked in the driveway or parked in front of the house.

She assumed the parent's cars were in the garage. Cindy rang the doorbell, and Scott answered the door with the most beautiful blond-haired little girl peeking around his backside to look at her. He invited her inside and introduced Annabelle. "And this is Maryanne." Standing on the other side of Scott was the identical picture of Annabelle.

"I am pleased to meet you both. Hi, I'm Cindy Mason."

Scott interrupted, and said, let me get the rest of the family. He walked upstairs to his bedroom to awake Naomi from her crib. Cindy scanned the room and saw a bible on the end table by the couch. She noticed a church bulletin for Rockville Victory Church near the bible. The bulletin gave her a sense of comfort knowing that he attended a church where she felt safe. She guessed the family can't be too scary.

Cindy sat on the couch with the two girls sitting next to her as Scott went upstairs.

Annabelle whispered to Maryanne, “She is so pretty”. Maryanne agreed.

Cindy said, “Well you two are the prettiest little girls I have ever seen. How old are you two?”

Annabelle answered, “Were five” as she held up five fingers.

“Maryanne please tell me what fun things do you like to do?”

“Scott takes us to the park and ride bikes with us. He makes puzzles with us and reads to us every day.”

Cindy seemed puzzled and thought he is so very involved for a brother, where are the parents? As she pondered that thought, Cindy heard footsteps coming down the stairs. She stood up to meet the rest of the family.

Scott came down the stairs alone holding an infant. He walked over to Cindy, and said, “This is little Naomi Pearl. We’re all of us there are”.

Cindy said, “I don’t understand, where are your parents?” Scott turned to the girls, “Why don’t you two go outside out back to play.” After the girls left to the back yard, Scott continued, “My parents died not long ago, they both passed away”.

Cindy trembled stared in surprise at Scott and gasped holding her hand over her mouth, “Oooohhh”. She thought to herself, “How could this be?”

Scott continued, "My dad was a police officer and was killed in the line of duty a few months ago. My mom died in childbirth when Naomi was born. I didn't want my family to be separated and the girls taken away from me. I fought hard to keep them. This is my family, we are one, we need each other, and we will stay together no matter what. I'm lucky, CPS worked with me, and helped me with what I needed to keep us together. So, I am the legal guardian, the only real parent for my sisters. We still have a lot of sadness and grief in our home that we're dealing with, each of us, and the most important thing is that we have each other. We cling together for comfort when we need it, and push forward, looking to the day we develop our new family identity."

Cindy stared at Scott open-mouthed for a second. She had never ever been exposed to this kind of struggle, and yet this young man was fighting for the life of his family.

"Cindy, I'm not sure if this is the type of work you were thinking of. But there are a few things. I will still need one more reference from you. I will need a reference of someone else outside of babysitting that can vouch for your character."

Cindy nodded still not saying anything.

"Now if everything is ok with you, I mean if your final reference checks out, and you still want the job, You can have the master bedroom downstairs with your own private bathroom. Our bedrooms are all upstairs. We can work out your pay later, I'm sure it will be ok with you. We'll all have meals together as a family so you won't need to worry about anything, except just being part of our family and help to watch the kids so I can work and go to school two nights a week."

Cindy thought about it for a minute and said, "I need to make a phone call in private. I will have another reference in a minute". Cindy stepped into the kitchen and called Pastor Frank Billings on the personal number he gave her.

"Hi, this is Frank."

“Hi pastor Frank, this is Cindy Mason, you know, Princess Charlotta”, she said whispering into the phone.

“Yes, your highness, how can I help you?”

“I found a flyer posted on your bulletin board as I was leaving your church the other day after we spoke. Something caught my eye about it and drew me to it. It turns out it was a posting for help needed for live-in childcare. It’s for Scott Mann and his family. Do you know them? I’m only asking because I saw your church bulletin at his house. I am with him now at his house.”

He excitedly answered, “Yes, I know them. Scott is a wonderful young man. This is a very special family Cindy, I believe the hand of God is with them in a powerful way. Scott is a man of fine character. Cindy if you’re thinking of helping them, this may very well be why God called you all the way here in the first place. Honestly, maybe this family is meant to help you and minister to your needs to my dear. Do me a favor before you make a final decision about working for him. Look him up on the internet, there are a couple of viral videos that were posted. You should take a look at them as soon as you can.”

“Ok I will, Oh, and can I list you as a reference for me. I know you only just met me, but I need someone for another reference. You know my real family background and where I came from. Please don’t tell him anything about me. I also think you should only refer to me as Cindy Mason for now. Yes, I agree, Cindy. I will be honored to be your reference.”

Cindy hung up and then found the videos about Scott and the children. His love for his sisters is so evident, one of the most emotionally powerful things she ever saw. Cindy quietly cried while watching the videos. As soon as she gathered her composure, she walked back into the living room.

Chapter 12

Gold Country Family Services
Case Name: Scott Mann
Case File: #4237
Case Worker: Amanda Peters
Date: September 1, 2019

Scott started his new job and is enjoying the freedom to go to school. Scott hired Cindy Mason as a live-in childcare helper. Annabelle and Maryanne are adjusting quite well to their new school and are getting involved in school activities. The family is beginning to develop a new identity and moving forward with a positive outlook. Cindy Mason's involvement with the family seems to have a very positive impact on all in the family. I believe that each one is forming quite a bond with her. It's possible that Cindy may have a larger role to play in the family in the near future. Cindy claims to be from Minnesota, but not much is known about her background. She should open up more about herself which would allow a deeper trust to develop between them all. I do notice quite an attraction developing between Scott and Cindy. Scott has assured me that he will continue to be above reproach in every manner. He understands he is her employer, and anything beyond that would be unacceptable.

Cindy agreed to work for the family and move in with them. Scott gave Cindy a tour of the house. He showed her the master bedroom but did not walk in the bedroom with her.

"Cindy, this is my mom and dad's room. It's now yours. There should be enough room in the dressers and closet for you as my mom got rid of most of my dad's clothes after he passed. My mom's clothes are still in her dresser. You can take what you want or need and pack up the rest of the clothing. I will take it to the donation center later. It would be very hard for me to go through my mom's clothes and things without falling apart. This would be a great help if you could do that for me."

Cindy wondered how Scott could give away his mom's clothes so easy. But she is sure he has grieved and healed a lot in his own way. She has heard it said that there is no uniform or right way for people healing from grief. Each person heals uniquely.

They walked through the kitchen and into the garage. The garage was typical for any American garage. There were boxes stored in the rafters, a workbench with tools, Two small child bicycles and an adult bike with an infant trailer attachment. Cindy noticed three heavy punching bags of assorted sizes hanging from the rafters and two free-standing kicking bags. This must be where Scott works-out she thought to herself.

Scott showed her the den which was more of a personal office with a desk, recliner chair, bookcase, and a gun safe. Scott advised Cindy there were guns in the safe, but it is kept locked at all times. It was part of the signed family agreement with CPS. Scott said the computer in the den is free for her to use anytime and there is nothing he keeps secret in the house.

Scott assured her that he is extremely cautious about not having any appearance of wrongdoing on his part so he does not endanger his status with CPS.

The upstairs consisted of the two bedrooms and a bathroom. Cindy thought the house was very quaint and comfortable.

The backyard had some toys, a swing set, a barbeque, and some outdoor furniture on the patio. There was also a small landscape pond near the side of the house with a running water feature with water cascading from some rocks into the pond. It added greatly to the peacefulness of the backyard.

When they finished the tour of the house, Cindy told Scott that she needed to go back to the hotel to gather her things in order to move in. Scott excitedly said, "You're not going alone since it's getting dark. We will all go together. I'll give you a drive!"

“Girls let's get ready to go, we're going to take Cindy to get her things. Then we're going out for dinner to celebrate. Cindy is moving in with us”. “YAY!” the girls yelled out.

Annabelle said, “Our home is getting bigger”. Both girls danced in the hallway as they were putting on their shoes. Cindy looked at this picture for a moment. This young man holding a baby in a bassinet, with his two young sisters dancing in the hallway. The biggest smiles imaginable were seen on their faces. This is so amazing she thought to herself. She never saw this kind of enthusiastic celebration in her home growing up.

They walked out to the driveway and Scott put each of the girls into the truck. Scott walked over to her door and opened it for her. Cindy had never climbed into the cab of a lifted truck before. Scott said, “Here grab the handle on the inside of the roof there and step up on the step side”.

“Why do you drive such a large truck Scott?”, Cindy asked.

“This was my dad's truck, I had a choice between my mom's economy car or this truck. I felt it was safer to put the girls in the largest vehicle possible. I don't want to lose any more of us, ever. I just feel safest in this big truck. I know it's a pain to drive, but you get used to it. Besides if you back into all the parking stalls instead of driving straight in you can get into almost any parking spot.”

Cindy thought, “Wow he puts careful thought into the welfare of his family into every decision he makes.”

They picked up Cindy's things, much to Scott's surprise she only had one small bag of clothing. She was more than welcome to take some of his mom's things if they fit her.

Scott stopped at a local diner just around the corner from his neighborhood. “Let's eat guy's, dinners on me.” “Yay!” The girls said in unison. Scott assisted each one of the girls out of the truck including Cindy.

Cindy couldn't help but wonder how involved she was going to get with this family. She didn't plan on helping to take care of two small children and an infant. Especially with a 19-year old boy whom Cindy worried that he wouldn't know how to care for these children on his own.

They entered the diner and were seated at a table in the middle of the room. Cindy noticed a few of the patrons looking at them as they ate. Cindy realized she had lived this life before. It's Scott they are looking at, not her! Scott is a public figure and he is oblivious to the attention.

Moments later, an older couple in their 70's got up to leave. They walked near his table, and the lady stopped near Scott. She said, "Excuse me, young man, God Bless you", and then she kissed him on the forehead and left the restaurant.

Cindy also noticed a large group of Bikers in the back of the room sharing several booths and tables. The men were wearing patched jackets, it's obvious they were part of a motorcycle club or gang. They continued looking at Scott's table during their meal. Cindy tried not to look back at them or stare because she didn't want to capture any more attention they were giving them. Cindy saw they had tattoos everywhere, some of them even had tattoos on their faces. Scott was oblivious to anyone around him. He simply made funny faces at Annabelle and Maryanne and just kept eating.

The waitress came over to their table and advised them that their meal including the tip was paid for by a customer. Soon after, another waitress brought two plates, each with a piece of cake and scoop of ice cream for Annabelle and Maryanne.

The waitress said the goodies were also from the same special admirers. Scott and Cindy guessed the meal and the desert was a gift from the older couple.

The bikers all finished their meal, and as a large group stood together to exit. Cindy was impressed as they stood up together, and in such a disciplined ordered fashion as they started walking out. They went out of their way walking straight toward Scott and Cindy's table before going to the exit. Some of the men patted Scott on back walking past him, one of the men said "Respect", and some walked by stating "good job kid" or "were with you". Finally, one of the last men in line patted Scott on back and said, "Good job son, we're proud of you. Dinner and dessert were on us."

Scott graciously thanked him and said his little sisters loved the cake and ice cream. Annabelle excitedly spoke out, "Yes it was yummy thanks". Maryanne exited her chair and hugged him. He seemed to get choked up and turned to leave with the rest of his group each of the men had large smiles on their faces.

Cindy turned to Scott. "You are a very interesting young man". She then thought to herself thanking God for bringing her here.

Scott answered, "It's not me, I was really pretty selfish before all of this happened. It's moments like these that help with the overwhelming sadness that we still wear on our hearts. Running into the kindness of strangers is like meeting real-life angels. Sometimes the hurt.... it's still so heavy (Scott teared up as he spoke), but this very unexpected kindness helps us all recover."

Cindy couldn't remember when the last time she had an honest discussion with someone so open about sharing their emotional hurt and pain.

"You're so honest with your feelings Scott. I wish I could tell you more about me. One day I will tell you about my family. It's just not the time now for me to talk about them. I can say that I am not used to such expressions of joy openly displayed in your home and the honesty you have about how you feel. I enjoy talking to you".

Scott answered, “Cindy I really enjoyed getting to meet you and I can tell so do the girls”. I really look forward to having you with us.

After dinner, they arrived home and Cindy started to move into her new bedroom. Cindy walked over to the sliding glass door that opened to the patio, there was a statuette that she didn’t notice before next to the rocky water feature in the landscaping that provided the trickling sound of water into her bedroom. This room was quite peaceful.

Cindy walked over to the dresser to put some of her things away. Most of the drawers were empty, but there were still some women’s clothing left in some of them. Cindy saw a photograph of a handsome couple on the top of the dresser along with with some antique figurines, and a blue and white 1800’s antique porcelain self-winding clock. Cindy wound the clock and set the time. The ticking of the clock was beautiful. She hoped the chime was not too loud.

Cindy took a moment and stared at the photograph. This must be the parents. They were wearing formal clothes as if they were dressed for an anniversary night out. The woman in the picture seemed very refined and dignified. She was beautiful. Cindy noticed the wedding ring on her finger. It was classy, beautiful, it seemed more expensive than what a middle-class couple could afford.

Cindy looked closer at the couple in the photograph. The husband was looking so lovingly at his wife, there was no doubt he completely adored her. Her facial expression reflected the confidence that she knew she was the most loved and adored woman in the world.

Cindy opened the closet door and saw a few modest but classy dresses hanging on the right side of the closet, there were also a few blouses, slacks and women’s dress pants.

She noticed the only thing hanging on the left side of the closet was a formal police dress uniform. There were several ribbons and badges on the uniform, it was apparent the husband had a very full and diverse career in law enforcement.

The top closet shelf was empty except for a large velvet box. Cindy opened the box and saw a law enforcement Gold Medal of Valor.

There was a folded newspaper clipping underneath the box: *"Off-duty police officer stops a school shooter. Reginald Mann was jogging on the school track when he heard a single gunshot. Mann ran toward the sound of the shot turning the corner into the first corridor, surprising the gunman. Mann tackled him before a second shot could be fired. There were several full classrooms nearby. Officer Mann is credited with saving the lives of dozens of children. Mann was unarmed during this incident".*

"Wow Scott's dad is a hero", Cindy thought to herself. This is an amazing family! It's no wonder Scott so willingly stood up to keep them together as a family." The sound of children's laughter interrupted Cindy from her thoughts.

She walked back out into the living room. Scott was sitting on the couch reading a children's book. Annabelle and Maryanne were sitting on the couch scrunched up next to him on both sides so they could see the pictures in the book. The girls looked so cute as they sat with their heads resting on his arms.

Baby Naomi was sleeping in the wind-up rocker nearby. Cindy couldn't resist watching. Her own father never bothered to read a bedtime story to her that she could ever remember.

Shortly later, Maryanne noticed Cindy and excitedly motioned with her little hand for her to come and sit next to her on the couch. Cindy sat down and thoroughly enjoyed the peaceful sound of Scott's voice as he read the entire book. She couldn't remember feeling so much love and peace as she felt that first night in the Mann's home.

Scott quickly got everyone off to bed after reading to his sisters, and then went to bed himself. Cindy turned in and went to bed listening to the sound of the mantle clock on the dresser and the sound of the water feature outside. Moments later, she heard the sound of muffled crying upstairs through a vent in the roof of her bedroom. She snuck out quietly and tip-toed up the carpeted stairs to the sound of the crying. It came from Scott's room. Scott cried for a long while. It's obvious he was crying himself to sleep.

The amazing thing was that none of the children were awakened by the sound as if they were used to hearing it at night. Even Naomi slept through the sound of Scott's tears. Cindy marveled that Scott could love so much even when he is hurt so much. His broken heart was still able to give out unmeasurable love to his three sisters.

Cindy snuck back to her own bedroom and meditated on the day's events. She was so humbled by this family. Cindy felt ashamed for her own selfishness and immaturity. Scott is a public figure yet he doesn't care for or feel bothered by the attention. His sole focus is taking care of his family.

The people of this community adore him, not out of vanity, or because he is wealthy, famous, or simply because he was born into a certain elite class. They adore him for his personal character and sacrifice. They adore him because he loves his family. They adore him because he never gave up on his own.

Cindy realized that each person needs to know that they matter to someone else, so much that, that person will do anything for them, simply because they love them. Cindy knew now that God brought her here. She was sent to serve this family, to learn true love and service. She felt unworthy to be here with them. There was no doubt in her mind that this family is heavenly royalty. Character trumps bloodline.

Chapter 13

Gold Country Family Services
Case Name: Scott Mann
Case File: #4237
Case Worker: Amanda Peters
Date: September 15, 2019

Scott and the children continue to grow an attachment to Cindy. Cindy is very refined and seems to come from a prominent family background. She is helping each in the family to grow past their hurt and move forward with life. However, each family member is starting to view Cindy as more than a child care provider. Scott has relied on each his church, his mentor, Sergeant John weathers, and myself as positive support systems and as accountability partners. Scott started his new job and is able to begin a new life path with school and work. Annabelle and Maryanne\are fitting in well in their new school and taking part in school projects. I recommend this case to be closed.

Scott and the family awoke to start the new school day. Cindy stayed home watching Naomi, while Scott took the older girls to school. Cindy decided to still work on her bedroom and empty out some of the dresser drawers. Cindy emptied undergarments and socks into a large plastic bag which was to be discreetly discarded per Scott's request.

Cindy understood that these were their mother's clothes and it might be hard for the family to see mom's stuff.

She bent over to pick up her bag of things and noticed something underneath the bed. Cindy pulled a long flat plastic tub out from underneath the bed. It contained photo albums.

She opened the oldest most worn album first. It contained many black and white photographs and some color pictures dating from the 1950s and 1960s. She saw a black and white picture of a young man in a military uniform. She guessed it was from World War II. Cindy wondered if this was a picture of Scott's grandfather.

There were many other pictures of this same man and his family, a beautiful curly dark-haired woman and a small boy. This must be Scott's grandparents and his dad. His grandfather was pictured as very affectionate with his wife. He seemed so in love with his wife.

He usually looked so lovingly at her in each of the pictures instead of posing or smiling at the camera. There was also a portrait photograph of Scott's grandmother. Cindy noticed the ring she wore was identical to the one Scott's mother wore in the picture she saw on the dresser. Maybe it was the same ring that was passed down.

Cindy scanned several of the other albums, in each album. She noticed the pictures were all family pictures with people in them, rather than pictures of homes, cars or material possessions. There were not many pictures of landmarks or nature scenes either. The focus of the photographer seemed to be more intent on capturing the family members rather than stuff around them at the time.

She decided to show the albums to Scott when he returned home.

Scott returned shortly later and asked Cindy if she would join him and Naomi on a walk in the park. Scott placed Naomi in the big stroller and they walked out into their neighborhood toward the park. Scott stopped briefly to say hello to Mr. Thompson, his next-door neighbor, as he washed his car in the driveway. Scott introduced Cindy to him. Mr. Thompson was so polite and glad to meet her. He told Scott that if he needed anything to let him know. Cindy noticed that some of the other neighbors also waved at Scott as he walked by.

Cindy walked alongside Scott as they walked past a row of houses to the park entrance. She studied the houses, the landscaping, and even the vehicles parked in the driveways. This neighborhood was not as wealthy looking as Linda Maxwell's in Granite Beach, but it was a comfortable middle class or working-class neighborhood. It had a more intimate feeling for sure.

Cindy surmised that perhaps the wealthier one became, the less one was involved with their neighbors. Cindy had never been exposed to the concept of having a relationship with your neighbors or what it was like to participate in living in an intimate community because she had grown up in a palace sort of shielded from those around her.

"This is such a friendly and welcoming neighborhood Scott."

"Ya Cindy it is, we have lived here since before I was born. I grew up knowing everyone on our block. It's comforting to know that we all look out for each other.

Scott showed Cindy a park at the end of the block, "This park is part of our neighborhood. If you walk through the entire park and come out on the other side, that is where our church is".

"Oh", Cindy replied. "Have you gone to church there very long?"

"No, my parents always considered it one of those user-friendly mega-churches. I guess we wrongly judged them. You see, I went there just after Naomi was born just because it was so close. I really thought that if it was so big that I could just disappear inside, and no-one would bother me. But that wasn't the case. Once I got there, they embraced my family. The pastor reached out to us in a big way and I fell in love with the place. It's not the size or all the special stuff that they have. It's just very personal to me. I really like Pastor Frank. I feel like he is someone I can come to no matter what and he would be there for me."

Cindy thought about his answer and agreed.

They walked to a wooden bridge with a small creek running underneath. There were plenty of shade trees and a bench just past the bridge. There was also a playground nearby. They stopped talking for a moment to listen to the sound of rushing water and playing children.

“Cindy, this is my favorite place in the whole park. I like to sit here when I need to be alone and meditate. I love being near the trees and listen to the sound of the water, it’s so peaceful.”

Cindy just soaked in the peacefulness of the scene. This is the first time she felt secure and safe while being in America.

Scott interrupting her thoughts…

“So, I talked to Pastor Frank Billings, since you listed him as your last reference. He thought very highly of you Cindy. He said you come from a very prominent family with a refined background and are a woman of great character. He said you would be fantastic for the kids. Interestingly, I asked him where you were from and about your family (Cindy cringed as he continued), but Pastor Frank refused to say. He said that was going to be up to you to tell me when you are ready. You know, Pastor Frank is a man of integrity and a great pastor. His word is more than good enough for me. I am so glad you are here with us. Cindy, I’m glad you’re here with me now in the park.”

“I am glad to be here Scott. I really want to be with you and your family.”

Cindy continued, “However, Scott, yes, I am from a ‘well to do’ family. I felt abandoned by my mom and dad my whole life. They sent me off to boarding school. When I came home for holidays they were too busy with the family business to spend any time with me. To make matters worse, I was even sent off to stay with other relatives on my summer vacations.”

"I can't remember my mother or father reading a bedtime story to me as you do with your sisters, let alone holding me and telling me they loved me. Cindy started to cry as she talked. I wish I grew up a love-filled home like yours Scott. I graduated a semester early from college and left home right after that. My mom and dad haven't seen me since."

"So, you already finished college? What did you major in?"

"Yes, I'm almost 22. I majored in economics."

"I'm taking college classes and do have a semester of units under my belt. I will graduate, in time. My major is going to be in History. I am fascinated by the past and where we came from."

Cindy stared at Scott making and holding eye contact with him while they spoke.

Scott continued, "But now I have three kids. Life threw me a hard blow, Cindy. I know I will recover. I grew up in a very loving and supportive home. My mom was always at home, she was always there for us. My dad was involved in everything I did. Our family was so close. I am going to keep it that way just like they were with me, even more. My sisters are going to know how much love was always in our home."

"Cindy, I do believe every parent loves their kids, deep down God put that love there. I believe it's possible that your parents just got sidetracked. You need to get in touch with them somehow to tell them you are ok and safe. Tell them you love them, talk to them, tell them what you need from them. I am sure they are worried sick about you. I wish I had the chance to tell my mom and dad just once more how much I love them but they are gone."

Cindy meditated on what Scott said. Pastor Frank also told her she needed to contact her mom and dad. They sat in silence for a while. Scott was intimidated by Cindy's beauty and didn't know what else to say or talk about.

Regardless time seemed to fly as they visited with each other. Scott was sad they needed to leave as the girls would be out of school soon.

He thought it was a great idea to invite Cindy to come with him. “Cindy, would you like to come with me to pick up the girls. You should probably come so I can introduce you to the school staff in case if you ever have to pick the girls up from school.”

“Sure Scott, I’d love to see your girl’s school. Scott smiled at her, showing his delight that she wanted to come.”

Cindy climbed up into the truck and thought to herself, “I like being with him.”

When they arrived at the school in Granite Beach, Cindy also noticed they seemed out of place. Scott’s truck was the only vehicle that was not a luxury car. Cindy knew the neighborhood, as the school wasn’t that far from Linda Maxwell’s house. Her first impression was that people here seemed to feel more entitled. They tried hard to express their affluence.

They walked into the office to complete the paperwork authorizing Cindy to pick up Annabelle and Maryanne from school. Cindy saw a blonde woman wearing designer sweatpants and a t-shirt blouse walk over to the counter next to her. The woman rudely interrupted the receptionist in the office and arrogantly demanded to see the principal.

“Excuse me, I’m Cheryl Adams. I’m here to see Mrs. Stilwell. She’s got my kids in her office”.

The receptionist turned to Cheryl, and said, “One moment. I’ll let her know you're here”. Cheryl turned toward Scott and Cindy. She stared rudely at both of them without saying anything.

A few moments later, Cindy spied Beth Klingson (whom Cindy babysat for earlier) in the hallway walking past the office. Beth stopped, looked at Cindy, but didn't seem to want to acknowledge her. Cheryl turned and also saw Beth in the hallway.

"Hi, Beth honey how are you today?"

"I'm fine, Cheryl. What are you doing in the office?"

"They said my kid was picking on other kids again today. If you ask me, it's the teacher's fault for not watching them, after all, kids will be kids."

Beth walked into the office as she talked to Cheryl. She looked over at Cindy and Scott. "Hi Cindy, what are you doing here?"

Cheryl interrupted, "How do you know her" pointing at Cindy.

Beth answered, "She helped babysit my kids a few times. She's ok".

Cheryl looked back at Cindy and stared at her and simply exclaimed, "Ewh"

Cindy said, "I'm here with Scott Mann getting the authorization so I can start picking up his sisters from school".

Cheryl said, "Ya you mean those 'Scholarship kids'".

Scott and Cindy finished the form and left it on the counter with the receptionist. They quickly left to go get the girls. But couldn't avoid overhearing Cheryl saying to Beth, "You let one needy kid in on some 'feel good premise', and soon there's a bunch of those kinds of people who need handouts at our school."

Scott wondered if it was Cheryl's kids that were the ones that bullied his sisters on the first day of school.

They picked up the girls and returned home. Scott then told Cindy he was going to his class tonight and asked her if she could watch the kids.

Cindy decided to do her laundry after Scott left. It's a nice change for her since she came to America, she had to use coin laundries while staying at the hotel. When her money ran low, she ended up hand washing her clothes in the bathroom sink using the hotel shampoos and hand soap as a clothing detergent.

Cindy found a pair of women's sweatpants and a colorful t-shirt in the dresser in her room and put those on so she could wash all of her clothes.

Maryanne walked by the laundry room while Cindy was loading up the machine. Cindy's back was toward the hallway while she sorted her laundry. Maryanne saw Cindy in her mother's house clothes, and screamed, "Mom, mom", and ran into Cindy grabbing her legs tightly and cried very hard as she buried her face into Cindy's side.

Maryanne wouldn't let go of Cindy's legs as she continued crying very hard. Cindy literally picked up Maryanne and carried her into the living room and sat on the couch with her holding her. Maryanne buried her face into Cindy's side and continued crying. Annabelle entered the living room and also sat on the couch next to Cindy leaning against her as she held Maryanne.

Maryanne cried very hard for a long time, then the crying changed, it was now obvious to Cindy, Maryanne was fake crying now at this point, but she continued with the crying noises, just so she could still hold on to Cindy. The laundry buzzer on the dryer went off, but Cindy sat on the couch with the twins, in silence at this time, the three of them still holding each other. Moments later, both girls got up and decided to go outside in the backyard to play. The girls didn't say anything as they got up, it's almost as if they just needed to be held for while in a way that their brother Scott was not able to provide.

Cindy just experienced more emotional contact with another human being that she has ever had in her whole life.

Cindy went to bed that night and thought about this family. She decided that she didn't want anything to change in her life right now. She thought about Scott and realized she was becoming more attracted to him every day. This wasn't just a physical attraction. She felt good around him and the girls. There were peace and comfort in this house. She also realized that she needed to contact her parents somehow. Scott and Pastor Frank were right. They needed to know she was safe, and that she loved them. But how to tell them without anyone finding out where she was or who she was?

Chapter 14

Scott held Cindy's hand as they walked in the park toward the wooden bridge. She felt so loved by him and cherished every moment. She tried to freeze the moment and stop time. Cindy listened to the birds in the nearby trees, and the sound of the water running in the creek near the footpath. She felt his warm hand in hers and oooooh, he smelled so good, as she leaned into his shoulder and pressed herself against him. Scott put his arm around her and continued walking. Cindy knew that he was her forever protector and that he loved her with a love that is unmatched by anything she has ever known. Scott has constantly demonstrated his ability to be faithful, caring, and loving even at his own expense. She knew she would never leave his side. They stopped at the bridge. Scott drew her near to him and he kissed her gently on the lips. His lips felt so soft in this first kiss, she would never forget this moment in time. He caressed her face with his hands and continued that soft sweet gentle kiss. Cindy could smell his breath with their faces so close together.

The wind started blowing through the trees, Cindy caught a scent of pine adding to this magic moment. The wind blew harder and harder until Cindy awoke, hearing the curtain shades banging gently against her bedroom wall bringing her back to reality. She could also hear the mantle clock ticking on the dresser. She opened her eyes and could see her nightstand as it was illuminated by the small nightlight she left on in her new bedroom. Cindy got up out of bed, shut the window, and got a drink of water before going back to sleep.

Cindy was standing in the Stockholm Cathedral wearing the most beautiful wedding dress ever made. She was wearing the same ring she saw in the photographs of Scott's mother and grandmother. Moments later, both women from the photographs walked into the church and went directly to Cindy.

Scott's grandmother said, "Look Samantha (Scott's mother), our princess is so beautiful. No one could deserve our Scott more than her."

"Princess Charlotta", Samantha said, "Thank you for taking care of all of our babies including Scott. He is still our baby. We're so happy you are going to be part of our family forever. We know you will be loved and cherished by him until the end of time".

At that moment, Cindy was then somehow instantly standing at the altar with Scott. He was so handsome. She was so proud to declare to all Europe and to the world that Scott Mann is her prince charming. Cindy looked out into the crowd of guests to rejoice in her moment. She saw on the bride's side of the church her parents, The King and Queen looked so regal as they sat in the front row. Her younger siblings, and cousins, aunts and uncles, all European royalty, was also sitting in the first few rows.

Nobles, politicians, and other famous people filled the ranks of the other rows behind them until that side of the church was full.

Her family seemed to be genuinely happy for her, but many others were there for politics or because they just needed to be there for the proper political protocol.

Cindy looked at the Groom's side of the church. She saw Annabelle, Maryanne, and Naomi sitting alone in a bare field of pews. Annabelle looked at Cindy and said, "We're all of us there are. But we love you so much."

At that moment, Cindy suddenly saw people sitting behind the girls. The pews weren't empty after all. Jack Mann and his wife, Reginald and Samantha Mann, each of them smiling so adoringly at her. Cindy then noticed there were many others sitting with them. John and Sandy Weathers, Amanda Peters, and Pastor Frank Billings. Cindy even saw Linda Maxwell, Cheryl Adams and Beth Klingson who seemed so happy for her.

There were so many others. Suddenly the back door of the Cathedral opened and a very old man entered. He stood in the hallway looking at Cindy and at Scott up at the altar. The gentleman seemed exceedingly wealthy beyond anyone she knew. He turned and motioned for many others outside. “I found him, my brother, Jack’s grandson. Come inside!” About three dozen people entered the church adults and children, all of them so happy and smiling. They entered the church and walked up to the altar weeping and embracing Scott into their midst.

Cindy awoke in the morning with the sun shining through her windows and the sound of the water feature on the back porch and the chiming mantle clock on the dresser. She wondered about the dreams she had during the night. She was amazed, however, because she dreamt in English. Everyone in her dreams spoke in English. Cindy had only ever dreamt in Swedish her native tongue her entire life. Cindy noticed she felt strangely exceeding warm and happy as if she had been hugged all night long.

That night after dinner, Cindy showed the photo albums that she found underneath her bed to Scott.

Scott decided that during the family time after dinner Scott would show the albums to the girls and tell them about their grandparents and more about their parents. He did not want the girls to forget where they came from.

He started with the oldest album and stated, “This is my grampa, Jack Mann.” Cindy immediately remembered her dream. No-one told her “Jack” was Scott’s grandfather’s name. Maybe it was from the newspaper clipping that she remembered his name.

Then she asked Scott, “Were your parents Reginald and Samantha Mann?”

Scott stared at her in amazement and stuttered, “How, how did you know their names, I don’t think we spoke about them before?”

Cindy exclaimed that she read it off something she found in the bedroom. However, Cindy knew it was something else that even she couldn't explain. Somehow that information came to her in those strange dreams last night. Those dreams were not just emotions in the subconscious. Or something else originating with her own mind. Cindy realized that somehow, she is meant to be here.

Cindy listened as Scott so affectionately explained to the girls all about their parents and grandparents. He told several stories and relived memories about each of them and made sure they knew they were loved very much by their parents.

She watched in awe as the girls were mesmerized as they listened to their older brother. Cindy knew she was falling for him.

Amanda Peters stopped by shortly after dinner during family time. She came to tell Scott in person that CPS is going to close their case with him. The last concern CPS had was for Scott to find a job. CPS does not need to monitor his family anymore because he found employment with the City of Rockville.

"Scott you have done such an amazing job with your new family. I am so proud of you. However, I want to still be here for you, son. I feel connected to you and to your kids. If it's ok with you, I wouldn't mind stopping by from time to time."

"Amanda I am so grateful to you. You helped me make it through the worst moments in my life. You were with me on that first awful day my mom died. You fought for our family in front of your superiors at CPS, scheduled classes for me, counseled me in our frequent meetings, you were like another mom for me."

Scott teared up as he continued, "I can't imagine not having your help anymore. I don't have all the answers there still are things I don't know how to do."

Amanda also cried as she answered, “I am touched Scott, your family will always have a place in my heart. I’ve watched you all these months and I know there is no problem that you won’t figure out. You are going to be fine honey. But I need to go, I can’t stay long tonight. I have an early day tomorrow I am going to San Francisco for some errands.”

Cindy interrupted, “Excuse me, Amanda, I also had a very important errand that I’ve needed to run in San Francisco for some time now. I don’t think I’m needed here tomorrow since Scott does not have class on Friday. If it’s ok with him, is it possible if I can hitch a ride with you?”

Amanda thought this would be a great opportunity to get to know the secretive Cindy Mason. Maybe she could get her to open up more about herself if she could get Cindy alone in her car. “Sure Cindy, I will be here at 6:30 since we need an early start or we will be fighting rush hour traffic. That should easily get us there by 9:00.”

Scott was glad Cindy got to spend some time with Amanda. Amanda seemed more cautious about her than anyone else. Scott hoped Amanda could see how cool Cindy was now.

That night after dinner Scott, Cindy and the girls started a new puzzle in the living room. It was a colorful puzzle of a candy shop. They all laughed and had so much fun sitting together, laughing, and talking while they tried piecing together all of the border pieces before bedtime.

What touched Cindy the most, was how excited both girls were that she participated with them. They both insisted on putting their chairs next to her so they could sit next to her. Cindy was very moved after realizing how much the girls craved her attention. She realized she wasn’t just falling for him. She was falling for all of them.

Chapter 15

Amanda and Cindy arrived in downtown San Francisco just when most businesses were opening on Friday morning. Cindy remembered meeting a woman at the bus stop that recommended Cindy should go the Mexican Consulate for various pamphlets and information for immigrants.

Cindy didn't need information, but she wanted to contact the Consul General of Mexico in order for him to send a confidential diplomatic message from Princess Charlotta to the Swedish government. Cindy decided the best way for her to contact her family to tell them she was safe, was to do it this way. Cindy believed if she called or e-mailed, they would easily trace her directly back to Scott's house. However, if she sent a message from San Francisco, she could still remain anonymous, the closest anyone would be able to track her would be to the Mexican Consulate in a city over 2-hours away.

"Amanda, can you take me to the Mexican Consulate. I need to pick up some paperwork for a close friend."

"Ok, Amanda answered, this is a strange request."

They arrived at the Consulate and entered the main lobby. The lobby looked like a DMV office with almost a hundred chairs where people waited after taking a number at the front row of windows.

Cindy turned to Amanda, "Just have a seat, I promise this won't be very long. I think they will take me right away."

Cindy walked up to the window and took off her glasses. She placed her hair into a ponytail and then handed the clerk behind the counter her passport, her real Swedish passport.

Cindy spoke in perfect Spanish. "I am Princess Charlotta Dorothea Katarina Maria Bergfalk of Sweden, the missing princess. I know this is unannounced, but I would like to see the Counsel General for diplomatic assistance."

The clerk nervously opened the passport and looked at the information inside and stared at Cindy.

Cindy hoped she could get a message to her parents without causing too much commotion.

Amanda watched from her vantage point in the lobby as a commotion began behind the counter.

Several people gathered to look at Cindy's passport. Immediately, a very loud alarm sounded inside the consulate stunning everyone sitting inside the lobby. A few armed men in uniform quickly entered the lobby.

More guards closed the consulate doors and stood to watch. Two others stood next to Cindy and bowed their heads to her speaking something, moments later, a refined gentleman entered the lobby from the office area. Amanda watched in awe and confusion at the ensuing incident. The gentleman bowed his head to her as he began to speak with Cindy and handed her back her passport. He then motioned for them to enter an office. Amanda could have sworn she overheard them all speaking Spanish together. She was confused, among other things, that Cindy could speak Spanish.

Cindy waited at the window as soon as she handed the clerk her passport. The clerk stared at the passport for a moment then she handed it to a man standing behind her desk, she motioned at some nearby office workers one of whom sounded an alarm inside the consulate, a moment later some guards came out into the lobby to close it off to the public. Some other guards stood next to Cindy They bowed their heads to her and politely asked her if she was ok and if she needed immediate assistance.

Cindy simply stated, "I need to speak with the Counselor General please".

The Counselor General entered the lobby and also very politely gave the Princess back her passport. He asked, "Are you safe Princess, are you ok? How can we help?"

The Princess answered, "Please may we go into your office, this is very complicated?"

The Counselor General escorted Princess Charlotta into his office and closed the door.

"How may I help you, your highness?"

"Thank you for your gracious hospitality. I would like to ask the government of Mexico to assist me to send a diplomatic message to the government of Sweden. Sir, do you have a daughter?"

"Yes, I do your highness."

"Please understand my simple request in the light of a loving parent. That this is the most personal issue between the King and his daughter, a sensitive family situation that I have selfishly created. I would be most indebted to you if you could help."

"Of course, how can I be of assistance?"

"I simply need to send this message to the King of Sweden in your next diplomatic pouch to the Swedish Ambassador."

She handed him a handwritten note:

Dear Father,

I have acted selfishly and am ashamed of the original behavior that led me to leave you and mother unannounced. For that, I am truly sorrowful and humbly ask for forgiveness. However, God has brought me here regardless of my human intentions. I know that I am meant to be on this spiritual quest. I am fully convinced it to be an honorable and worthwhile endeavor that will make a father proud of his daughter. I cannot tell you my location at this time, or what I am involved with, for fear of disrupting God's plan for me and the future of the Monarchy. I am not abdicating my position, nor deserting the Kingdom. I promise I will return to you in the proper time. Please understand that I deeply love you and mother more than you can know.

Your loving daughter Charlotta

"I assure you, sir, Mr. Counsel General, that my mysterious disappearance will come to an end soon and I will return to my country. This is a very noble cause that I am involved with for now, and in time I will return. My country will be deeply indebted to the government of Mexico and you for your kindness and assistance to their Crown Princess in her time of need."

"Yes, your highness. I will deliver this message at once to the Swedish ambassador."

Cindy was escorted back out to the lobby where she met Amanda. Amanda stared in awe at Cindy. Cindy sensed she needed to give a quick answer for the strange commotion. She simply said there was a weird mix up with paperwork.

She assured Amanda it was all straightened out. Cindy exited the Mexican consulate with Amanda Peters. During the drive home, Amanda wasn't sure what to say of the matter so she kept things to herself and hoped Cindy would tell her about this mysterious visit.

The following morning Amanda awoke and made her coffee she turned on the TV to see "Breaking News, Missing Princess Found" on every news channel. The King of Sweden, the Swedish Prime Minister, and the Mexican Ambassador to Sweden were giving a news conference from Stockholm Sweden.

The King of Sweden spoke to cameras with his wife standing beside him. The Queen stood behind him as he spoke, she quietly cried without hiding her emotion. The Prime minister and Mexican Ambassador stood on each side of the King.

"Last Friday morning the Mexican government had contact with the Crown Princess Charlotta. The Princess is safe and there was no foul play involved with her disappearance. The Princess voluntarily left our country on a spiritual quest and will return soon to Sweden. She is not abdicating her position nor deserting Sweden. The Princesses activities will be made public in the proper time. She assures all of us that Sweden and the Monarchy will be proud. We cannot disclose her location or any other information about her at this time. I must say that the Kingdom of Sweden is deeply indebted to the government of Mexico for their help and sensitivity in this matter. They have been most helpful."

Several reporters shouted out questions, "Is she currently in Mexico?", "Is she working for the church?" and other related questions about her location and safety.

The Swedish Prime Minister interrupted, "We will not be taking any other questions at this time. The important thing to report is that the Princess is found, and safe, and she will return soon. Thank you."

Amanda Peters stared at the TV in disbelief. She conducted an internet search on Princess Charlotta and looked at various images of her. "Ohhh my gosh, oh my gosh, oh my gosh, oh my gosh, no way! Scott Mann is falling in love with a real Princess." Amanda decided to speak with her supervisor first thing Monday morning before doing or saying anything else on this matter.

Meanwhile, Cindy woke up to the peaceful sound of the water feature in the backyard trickling down into a rock pool which she could faintly hear through her open bedroom window. She loved sleeping with her window open on the warm California evenings. Cindy sat up on her bed and cherished the peace for a second before getting up to get her coffee.

Cindy went into the kitchen and found the coffee and filters in a counter just above the coffee pot. This was much better than hotel coffee, and excitedly made herself a pot of coffee. Suddenly Scott walked in startling her.

“I’m sorry Cindy, I didn’t mean to scare you. I heard you moving about downstairs and thought I would get up and get ready to make breakfast for the kids.” He lowered his voice, and continued, “We need to be quiet because Naomi is still sleeping.”

Cindy smiled and poured Scott a cup of coffee. They sat at the table together to enjoy a moment alone before everyone got up. Scott realized that he didn’t know what to say.

He mildly feared that he would seem boring to Cindy if he didn’t start talking and bring up something interesting. He was always so nervous when alone with her. He doesn’t usually have this problem of shyness, but they always had something to do with the kids and all. They were fine thinking of things to say with the distraction of chores, with life happening, but now he is alone with her. He couldn’t get over how beautiful her she was as he looked into her deep blue eyes, but he didn’t want to seem weird just by staring at her.

“What do you usually do on Saturday’s Cindy, I mean what are your hobbies? What do you like to do for fun?”

"I like to visit my friends and family. I also liked going to the park near my last home with my family." Although she didn't tell him about the elaborate palace gardens. She continued, "I play piano, so I guess that's a hobby. But I've been in college for a while so I buried myself in my studies. I didn't have much of a social life because of my studies, you know homework and assignments. I took a packed schedule so I could graduate early. What about you Scott. What did you like to do, what are your favorite activities?"

"As you know, I practiced martial arts and trained. I went to school too, but I quit and dropped my scholarship when my parents died. It is nice to take this class now. I feel like I'm with kids my own age again in an environment that I'm used to."

"Didn't you have any friends to help you when things started happening with your family?"

"Well I had a couple of friends in school but we weren't close. Not close enough that they would want to help me with babies. I also had some friends in the martial arts school but that was only centered on our training. I never knew how much of a loner I really was until this happened. I also had a girlfriend (Cindy stared up at him in elevated interest as soon as he brought this new information into the conversation)".

Scott sensing Cindy's enhanced interest followed up with, "I mean we weren't super serious or anything. We hung out, I met her in school. She was someone fun to talk too. But then when I took over the responsibility of being the guardian for my sisters. She walked away very fast and made it clear she was moving on with life without me."

"I'm sorry Scott."

"No that's ok, I get it, I'm not mad at her. Were both only 18, and how can I ask her to date a guy suddenly with three kids? She has a future right?"

“Ya Scott, but she still should have had the character to help and not leave you alone. You were her friend. One thing for sure Scott, I know we're just getting to know each other, but I hope you know that I won’t stop being your friend just because of life hardships.”

Scott felt a bit uncomfortable and changed the subject quickly back to Cindy, “Did you have a boyfriend?”

“No Scott, I never had a boyfriend. I was focused on finishing school so I could help my family out with their business and other responsibilities.

“What kind of business is your family involved with Cindy?”

Cindy quickly searched for an answer but decided not to lie. “Scott I’m still dealing with some issues with my family. I’m sorry there are some things I’m trying to work out in my heart. I do promise you it's not bad. I’m not in trouble, and no-one did anything wrong. I will work these things out eventually. I just can’t talk about them right now. It’s important to me just to try to sort everything out for myself. This is why I came here to California Scott. I promise you though one day I will tell you everything.”

Scott sensing Cindy’s discomfort wanted to assure her that he wasn’t judging her. “Cindy it's ok. You a good person. There is no one I would rather have here with my family than you. I really like having you here with us actually. So, I’m not judging.”

Cindy smiled and thanked Scott. She was so comforted in the fact that Scott seems to prioritize keeping a relaxed environment here and in her relationship with him. She totally felt at ease with him.

Chapter 16

Special Agent Sandra Boyd poured herself a cup of coffee as she started off her Monday morning. Sandra enjoyed working at the FBI office in Washington DC. She has had a very decorated career with several successful investigations against corrupt politicians, lobbyists, and judges. Agent Sandra Boyd has earned a reputation for doing the extreme “Secret Squirrel” work, in other words having the ability to do the sensitive and confidential investigations that need to be kept secret until the case is closed. Her last case was against a sitting congressman. There was a report he was taking bribes of sexual favors for his votes.

Agent Boyd infiltrated a secret and exclusive swingers sex club in order to get close to the congressman. No-one in her office knew about her work until the case completed with the arrest of the congressman. Her reputation of managing a secret investigation to the completion has led to many assignments for her as the lead case agent for several sensitive cases involving national interest.

Sandra sat back with extreme satisfaction as she enjoyed her morning coffee and meditated on the events of her most recent arrest. She was on the fast track for a stellar career with the FBI. Sandra majored in government and finished top of her class at Smith College. Sandra then went on to complete her Master's program for American Studies at Brown University. Sandra was raised by her mother in a single parent home and considered herself a reasonable feminist.

Sandra sat at her dining room table reading the news on her laptop computer when she received a call from her office. Boyd’s SAC (Special Agent in Charge) told her she was to report to the US State Department offices immediately. Sandra wondered what this was about since her SAC did not know why she was being summoned to the State Department.

She reported to the lobby at the Harry Truman building in Washington and informed the receptionist she was there for an appointment, “Hi I’m Agent Sandra Boyd with the FBI, I have an appointment, but I don’t know who I am meeting with”.

The receptionist made a phone call, and moments later, an official entered the lobby.

“Agent Boyd, please come with me.”

She asked him as they entered the elevator, “Do you know why I am reporting here this morning?”

“No Ma’am. I do not. I am to escort you to the Deputy Secretary of State’s office.”

Agent Boyd wondered, wow, this must be huge.

Agent Boyd was escorted into Deputy Secretary of State Liam Jackson’s office.

“Agent Boyd, thank you for coming this morning on such short notice. You will be assigned to work for this office for a special circumstance of an international nature. This investigation is ordered directly from the President. You were recommended to lead this case from the director of the FBI himself. This case is highly confidential and no-one except those you handpick to work directly for you will know about this case. I am the only person you will contact and report directly to. No-one else in the FBI knows about this case. I cannot stress the sensitivity of this investigation do you understand?”

“I understand sir, how can I help?”

"As you know, the United States is currently enduring an unpleasant demeanor with several European countries due to economic and political differences with our new administration. There has now arisen a circumstance that has the potential to significantly further damage our relationship with some of those nations. However, there is the remote possibility that we may be able to heal those wounds if things can work out for the good. Agent Boyd, you have a unique opportunity to help positively affect and shape the US and European relations for the near future."

"Here is a file folder on the Crown Princess of Sweden. As you know, she disappeared several months ago. She showed up at the Mexican consulate in San Francisco last week. She is believed to be somewhere in Northern California. Now, the Swedish government has reached out to the US state department for assistance. We have been requested to locate her and to find out what kind of activity she is involved in. They do not want you to interfere or interrupt her in any way until the Swedish government decides if her activities are an embarrassment to Sweden and the Swedish Royal Family."

Agent Boyd thought to herself, "You gotta be kidding me, I am being assigned to babysit a royal spoiled brat".

"You must understand the dynamics of this investigation Agent Boyd. Imagine losing your child completely for months, not knowing anything. This is a family matter Boyd. We must be sensitive at the most basic level, that of a parent and a daughter in order for you to have the proper perspective for what you are doing. This is a first for us, to work together with the Swedish Royal Family. Perhaps our assistance can improve our relationship with Sweden. We hope, this case will not only soothe the Swedish governmental view of our administration but maybe other European countries as well. Many of the Royal families of Europe are related in one way or another anyway. Most Europeans seem to follow these families as celebrities. They do in a way have an understanding about the royal families of their neighboring countries as well. We can hit a PR home run with all of Europe if you can be of help."

"Listen, I also want you to focus on somehow providing executive protection, security for the Princess without her knowing it. God forbid anything to happen to her while she is on our soil, especially if we knew where she was. You will also find, in your file, the surveillance video footage of the Princess's visit to the Mexican consulate. There is additional footage of her getting into a vehicle with another female. You should be able to capture the license plate information to begin your search. Remember, at all costs do not allow her to find out what you are doing. This is a completely confidential operation. As trivial as it seems, a case like this could ruin a career if it goes south, your career is no exception."

Agent Boyd was disturbed but understood the seriousness of this investigation. She wished someone else could have been assigned to do this. But she also pondered that even a basic police officer on patrol knows that the simplest and seemingly stupid calls for service may unfold to make or break a career.

Agent Boyd stared in awe at the TV monitors in the airport lobby while waiting for her flight to California. She caught herself not believing celebrities could be like normal people in that they could have normal fears and concerns for their own children. The breaking news of the press conference in Stockholm was being shown on every airport TV. She noted the emotion clearly visible on the faces of the king and the queen.

Boyd could sense they truly missed and worried for their daughter. Boyd decided she had to push aside any prior bias or slanted view she had of the rich and famous in order for her to move forward with her assignment.

The following morning, Agent Boyd met with the SAC of the Northern California FBI office. The SAC had already been notified from Washington of Boyd's arrival and asked how he could assist her with anything she requested. He wondered what the case was about since he had not been briefed about the nature of her investigation. Boyd was issued her own private office and a vehicle. She then informed the SAC that she would handpick some agents to assist her in a surveillance detail later.

Once she got set up in her office and signed on to her computer, Boyd ran the license plate of the vehicle the princess was seen getting into after leaving the consulate. She immediately left the FBI office and went to the Gold Country Family Services office. To meet with Dr. Joan Spencer.

"Good Morning Dr. Spencer. I am Special Agent Sandra Boyd from the FBI in Washington DC. I am working on a case that may involve one of your social workers, an Amanda Peters.

Boyd was able to get the license number of the vehicle provided from the video footage from the Mexican consulate. Dr. Spencer, this is not a criminal investigation nor is your caseworker involved in anything wrong."

At that moment, Amanda Peters barged into Dr. Spencer's office, "Joan, you wouldn't believe it! She's a princess!" Amanda turned and noticed Agent Boyd. "Oh, I'm sorry, I barged in. I was so excited to tell you the news."

"Amanda this is Special Agent Boyd with the FBI. She came from Washington to meet with us."

Agent Boyd showed Amanda Peters a still photo from the video footage from inside the Mexican Consulate. "Who is this woman?"

"That's Cindy Mason", Peters' answered. "She asked to come with me to San Francisco to run an errand for a friend. I was with her in the consulate". Amanda didn't think she needed to keep any secrets since it was obvious the FBI knew who Cindy was. Amanda explained to Agent Boyd and her boss everything about her knowledge of Cindy Mason and how she learned, after watching the news, of the true identity of Cindy.

Amanda started to worry that the government was more worried about politics and international affairs than Cindy or Scott. It's obvious that Cindy wanted to be alone and she wanted to be with the Mann family.

Agent Boyd briefed both women about the circumstances of her case and admonished them to keep this entire case confidential. She also warned them of federal obstruction charges if they interfered in any way or told anyone about Cindy's true identity. She then demanded copies of Amanda's entire case files on the Scott Mann family.

Agent Boyd's demeanor continued to worry Amanda. Scott, the children, and even Cindy were all very vulnerable right now. They were kind of huddled together after each of them faced fearsome trials. It seems Cindy needed to be with the Mann's as much as they needed her. They were all drawing tremendous strength and encouragement from each other.

Agent Boyd arrogantly thought both women were shaking in their boots after giving them the "Official I'm in charge thing".

Again, Amanda sensed that Agent Boyd was a threat to the miracle happening in that home. The healing and love and the comfort they are all finding in each other cannot be interfered with.

Immediately, Amanda Peters confronted Agent Boyd. "Listen, I don't care what you do to me. I am the one that's warning you! You will not hurt this family. If you hurt Scott, Cindy or anyone in this family I will go public and out you personally. Your reputation will be crap."

Dr. Spencer stood up and also agreed with Amanda Peters, but in a calming tone to de-escalate the situation. "Listen, this family is precious, and so is Cindy. They have done nothing wrong, but each of them is very vulnerable right now. I implore you to read the case files before you embark any further into this investigation. This is very complicated no doubt. Let's work together ok?"

Amanda offered to re-open the case if that would help in keeping Agent Boyd from getting too close to the princess and upsetting anything with the Mann's at this time. "Agent Boyd, they know me. I will keep up my family visits and document everything."

They agreed to their discussion points. Amanda would continue to be close to the family in order to document how Cindy is doing. Agent Boyd would keep her distance to avoid upsetting any of the family dynamics at this time.

After Agent Boyd left, Dr. Spencer told Amanda, "listen, I think our plan is the best one. You need to be in that home to look out for Scott and the girls above all else".

Amanda replied, "I agree, but I don't think Cindy, or the Princess if you will, poses a threat. I think she innocently came to help Scott. However, there is no doubt that they are falling for each other now. I can't believe it, Scott and a Princess! Dr. Spencer, I looked her up. I mean a full search of everything about her I could find on the internet. She speaks five languages, and recently graduated from Cambridge University with a degree in Economics."

Dr. Spencer added, "I know it's exciting, Scott deserves a Princess no doubt. But, we just need to be there for Scott, just in case. This is the last thing he needs now is another heartbreak."

Agent Boyd drove to a nearby park after leaving the CPS office. She read through the CPS reports as promised. Boyd realized this is definitely not what she thought she would find the Crown Princess of Sweden doing. She imagined finding The Princess shacked up with a rock star and hitting the night time party scenes, not changing diapers and babysitting five-year-old twins.

Agent Boyd decided to contact Pastor Frank Billings as he was also mentioned as a person close to both parties. Boyd felt she needed to get more background information. Sometimes pastors have a different perspective than a social worker because people confess their secrets to their minister.

She drove away from the park and went straight to the church parking lot. Boyd was impressed by the size of the parking lot, she felt like she was entering the parking area to a large shopping mall. The building itself was massive

.

Boyd wondered how Cindy could be involved in a church this large without anyone finding out who she was. Boyd walked into the Foyer and followed a sign on the wall with an arrow pointing toward the church administrative offices. There were other signs pointing the way to the church bookstore, and yet others directing people to the children's ministries. This was indeed a true megachurch.

Agent Boyd entered the offices and was greeted by a receptionist. Boyd identified herself and asked if Pastor Billings was in the office and if she could meet with him.

"Pastor Billings, I'm Special Agent Sandra Boyd from the FBI. I am working on a case involving Scott Mann and Cindy Mason. I need to tell you this is not a criminal investigation but it is of extreme national interest."

Pastor Frank just stared at her thinking to himself and wondering why she was interested in Scott and Cindy. He worried that the FBI would disrupt what was happening between Scott and Cindy. He also worried for Scott as he had just overcome the death of both of his parents and had overcome so many other obstacles. He didn't want anything to happen to Cindy or to have yet another person pried out of Scott's life. Pastor Frank guessed that the FBI wouldn't be here asking about Cindy unless they knew who she was.

Agent Boyd continued in her line of questioning about Cindy. Then Pastor Frank started to get irritated as he realized Agent Boyd tried to pressure him for information about Cindy or Scott.

"Listen, Agent Boyd, with all respect, I do not care about how much the federal government wants to know about these people. I know who Cindy really is, but confidentiality was invoked. I won't be helping you with any information. Furthermore, I want you to understand one thing. I know there are kings and leaders of nations involved with your investigation. But the King of all the kings and the Lord of all the lords are also involved, more so than anyone in this whole scenario. He is doing something very, very special here with some very, very vulnerable people. Woe to you if you mess this up, woe to you if you have to answer to Him for hurting any of His special plans right now."

Agent Boyd left Pastor Billings and went to her hotel room. She watched the videos from the internet after conducting an internet search on Scott Mann. Agent Boyd couldn't believe her eyes. This Scott Mann is a wonderful kid going through some very tough times. Then for the first time, she got very nervous, and goosebumps formed on her arms. She realized that she had been threatened three times today; professionally, personally, and spiritually about this case. Agent Boyd determined that she did not want to contact the Mann family or Cindy at all.

She will recommend that she would conduct clandestine surveillance only for the purpose of collecting information on Cindy in order to let the Royal Family know of her activities and to provide a security detail for her safety.

Boyd contacted the Deputy Secretary of State and informed him of everything she was able to collect today.

She forwarded copies of the CPS reports and all of the information on Scott Mann to be sent to the Swedish government. He agreed with her recommendations on how to proceed.

Agent Boyd went to bed that night thinking, “This is not going to go as I thought...”

Chapter 17

Gold Country Family Services
Case Name: Scott Mann
Case File: #4237
Case Worker: Amanda Peters
Date: October 2019

This case is closed from an investigatory standpoint. I will conduct continued follow-up visits to the family to see if there are any further needs the county may assist them with and to ensure they continue to thrive and heal. Cindy Mason has begun to form deeper bonds with each member family. The girls rely on her as a mother figure in many ways. Cindy embraces this role and seems to want to fill the emotional needs of each child. Cindy and Scott continue to grow in affection for each other, but both of them are determined not to cross any lines that distinguish improper behavior for the employee, employer relationship. The children are thriving and the home seems very stable. Naomi spoke her first words.

It was Monday morning, Scott's first day of work at his new job with the department of public works. Cindy could hear Scott in the kitchen very early before anyone else in the house was up. She decided to get up and go out to join him in the kitchen. She could smell the coffee brewing in the coffee pot, and eggs cooking on the stove. Cindy felt so cozy with the smell of hot coffee and breakfast cooking and of course seeing Scott alone without kids. She had hoped to spend some alone time with him.

Scott looked up adoringly at Cindy as she walked into the kitchen. "Good morning Cindy, it's so nice to see you. For some reason, I don't like to be alone in our home. There is some coffee in the pot if you want some" "Thanks Scott", Cindy replied as she poured herself a cup of coffee. "I heard you from my room and decided to see if you needed any help." Scott finished the omelet he was making and started buttering the toast. He used a butter knife and spoon to make a happy face with the jam over the buttered toast. "Nope don't need any help, but, here is your breakfast."

"Scott! I can't take that, that was for you", Cindy replied.

"No, see the happy face, I made it just for you. Because I am so happy to make you breakfast."

He stared at her as she happily sat down at the table to eat. He drank in her blond hair as it flowed down her thin shoulders and her perfect blue eyes. He was amazed that she wanted to eat with him. Scott felt a little insecure again and wasn't sure what to say. Cindy quickly noticed that he was staring at her, admiring her. She was flattered that he was unable to hide his attraction. Cindy quickly said, "What?".

"Oh" Scott embarrassingly answered. "I was just so happy that you joined me for breakfast. I enjoy your company."

Scott quickly cracked and scrambled up another three eggs in a bowl for his own omelet. Cindy thought for a moment that she could not remember anyone ever making her breakfast or any meal for that matter just because they wanted her company. They talked for about forty minutes until Scott had to wake up the kids before leaving for work. Scott decided to allow the girls to sleep in because they had a school holiday today. Cindy thoroughly enjoyed her breakfast with Scott. They talked about everything, from what each of their favorite colors was to favorite activities they liked to do. Sometimes talking about simple things was so comforting. Cindy felt so close to Scott and so safe around him as if she had already known him for ages.

Every word he seems to communicate and the actions coming from him were always positive, encouraging, and kind. Cindy decided she liked being alone with Scott and would try to spend as much alone time with him as she could.

Just as Scott had all the girls at the table before he left for work he made an announcement. "Ok everyone, this is my first day at the new job. Cindy will be home with all of you to take care of you until I get home. Then, we're going to the park for a bike ride!!!" "Yeaaah" the girls yelled.

Scott packed his lunch and left. Cindy then went into the living room to turn on the TV and noticed three envelopes with each of their names on them, on the top of the table near the TV.

Cindy called each of them into the living room and put Naomi in the wind-up baby swing. Cindy handed Annabelle and Maryanne their envelope's and she looked at her envelope. Before she could open it, Annabelle asked Cindy if she would read them their cards. Cindy was touched that the girls wanted her to read them their cards.

"Ok, let's sit down", Cindy said. Cindy got Naomi and placed her in the baby swing next to the couch and wound it up. Cindy and the girls then sat down on the couch squished up next to each other. "Let's start with yours, Annabelle."

Inside Annabelle's envelope was a simple piece of pink colored paper along with some stickers of fairy princesses. The paper had a simple poem on it:

Annabelle, Annabelle, the truest little maiden in the kingdom.
You're so wonderful you cast everyone under a spell.
From the tip of your toes
To the top of your head
You're as pretty as a rose...

Maryanne's envelope also contained the same contents along with the poem:

Maryanne, Maryanne, the fairest girl in the land.
You're so amazing there is no equal who could stand.
If you look all around
There is no-one as sound
As you, the fairest little girl in the land.

Cindy's envelope also contained a pink piece of paper with a poem:

Cindy, Cindy, you are wonderful too
Surely as the sky is blue,
You are too good to be true.
As they say in the fair kingdom,
"Thank you for you"

Cindy marveled that Scott seemed to take every moment to let the ones closest to him know he was always thinking of them and trying to leave them with words of encouragement and praise. Cindy's father or mother never took the time out of any day to leave her a simple note of praise or encouragement.

Scott couldn't stop thinking about Cindy all day it was quite distracting for him. Scott had an easy enough day on his first day on the job. They assigned him with another employee to show him around.

Scott worried as he realized he gets off work several hours later than when school gets out for the girls. It's hard to think far in advance, being a new parent. He wondered how he would be able to pick them up once they started school. He took comfort in knowing there was another adult in the home with him to think problems through as a team. He didn't want to shake the boat with his new employers and ask for special hours either.

In a moment of doubt, he pondered the prospect of quitting if things got too hard. He debated the pressures and demands of work versus his own family needs. Scott knew he wasn't in a terrible financial need for work at this time in his life. He really only needed medical insurance.

Scott had a sizable amount of savings in the bank after the modest inheritance from his parents along with the payout of his father's retirement. He also received a sizeable amount from the donations due to that viral video someone posted of him and Naomi on the internet.

He owned the house outright. Real estate in California was expensive, but he didn't have any mortgage payments to add to his monthly overhead. He almost prided himself when he added the full assets of the house and savings combined, he was worth around a million dollars, at least on paper. Although that wasn't much in today's world. Any disaster could come and wipe out his resources in a day. Deep down Scott would need to continue working.

Scott got off work and went straight home. He wanted to spend time with Cindy as she consumed his mind all day. However, he promised the twins before he left for work that he would take them bike riding in the park.

Scott was greeted at the door by everyone in the house as soon as he arrived home from work. Cindy was holding Naomi in the entrance way, Annabelle and Maryanne were also standing by the door jumping up and down. They were all so happy to see him, even Naomi googled with glee. Scott felt like he was being welcomed home as a victorious warrior.

Cindy spent all day playing with the twins, "dress up dolls" with the girls' dolls and doing arts and crafts. Cindy enjoyed their company and tried to learn to tell the difference between the two girls. They were identical twins with no visible differences between the two. How could Scott tell the difference so easily she wondered. The girls couldn't stop talking all day about their bike ride in the park that Scott had promised them.

Naomi was just starting to crawl, and it was so exciting for everyone to see how excited she became when she could scoot over to you on her own in order to clamor for your attention. Cindy felt she was fast becoming a part of this family and did not want anything to change.

Scott prepared the bikes for everyone and even fastened a baby bike carrying trailer on the back of his bike, for Naomi. As soon as Scott and the children got on their bikes, Annabelle yelled out, "What about Cindy? She needs to come with us too". Cindy felt flattered that they wanted her to come, but there was no other bike for her. Scott was also disappointed because she wasn't able to join them. He had been anticipating hanging out with her all day. Scott kept this matter in mind as they rode through the park. He had to think of a solution because this was a popular activity for the girls. However, he also knew it would be good for Cindy to have some time alone, away from kids since she had been with them all day.

Cindy stayed home after the others went on their bike ride and searched the internet for news about her own family. She watched the video again of the news footage of her father and mother pleading for her return, and of the news conference with the Mexican Ambassador. Cindy was glad she was able to get a message to her parents, without them finding out where she was.

After Scott returned Cindy helped him put the bikes away and placed Naomi in her crib as she was fast asleep. Moments later, Cindy heard some loud banging downstairs with the walls shaking intermittently. She ran downstairs and could see the pictures bouncing on the kitchen walls. Cindy opened the garage door to see Scott working out on a heavy bag hanging from the garage ceiling on a long metal chain. He punched it two or three times and then a hard roundhouse kick which forced the bag up and then as it fell back down on the end chain rocking the house.

He repeated the same punches and kicks over and over again as if he were working some specific drills. Cindy was mesmerized watching, she had never seen anything like this in real life. Scott's back was facing her and he didn't know she was watching. Each kick was very powerful as it lifted the bag up into the air. She also noticed for the first time since he was wearing a tank top, that he was very muscular and in shape. She admired his shoulders and trapezius muscles on his neck and back and his biceps were amazing. Scott turned around to continue with a different kicking drill when he noticed Cindy.

"Hi Cindy, I'm sorry I didn't see you. Am I bothering you?"

"No, you're fine Scott. I was worried the house would fall down".

"My mom always worried about that too when my dad and I came down for our workouts. This is my first work out since they died. I guess I need to move on with my life. You are helping me a lot with that Cindy."

"Scott, I haven't done anything. You guys are doing a wonderful job yourselves."

"Cindy you don't realize how much kindness and peace you have brought to us. We all feel comforted greatly with you here, actually, I am so happy that you are here. Everyone feels that you are becoming one of us."

During dinner they discussed how they would be able to pick the twins up after their kindergarten class since they ended school around 1:00 in the middle of Scott's work day. Cindy offered to take the bus over to the school to pick the girls up. However, he would talk to his boss, and see if he would be able to get them during his lunch break and take them home. Cindy felt like she was becoming part of the family as they tried to solve the new challenges together.

The following day Scott's boss allowed him to pick up the girls in the company work truck which saved him even more time from going back to the yard to get his personal vehicle. He didn't want to keep taking advantage of his employer so he would think of a better way to get the girls after school.

Scott finished work and stopped at the Rockville Bike Works after work. He thought he would surprise Cindy and buy her a bike after all the girls wanted her to go with them on their bike rides too. Honestly, Scott thought to himself, he just wanted to buy Cindy a present because he was really starting to like her a lot.

Scott picked out a nice purple women's touring bike. He picked out a bell and a basket for the front handlebars. He also bought a light set for the front and rear of the bike and had the mechanic install each of the items before leaving the shop. Scott then picked out a nice purple bike helmet to match the color of the bike along with a pair of bike gloves.

Scott arrived home that night a little later than usual but, like yesterday everyone ran to the front door to greet him. The twins were so excited and jumped up and down yelling "Scott's home". Naomi seemed to feel the same excitement as he walked into the front door, then she spoke her first words "Da Da".

Scott couldn't believe his ears. "Did you hear that? You're such a sweet baby" Cindy was still holding on to Naomi but, she leaned over toward Scott and held her little arms out to him, and said, "Da Da" again. Scott took her into his arms and fought back the tears. Cindy also teared up. Scott composed himself and said I have a surprise for everyone out in my truck. They walked out to the driveway.

Cindy looked in the back of the truck and saw the bike leaning over the tailgate. "Is that for me?"

"Yes, it is", Scott answered. "The girls wanted you to come riding with us so bad yesterday, but we didn't have a bike for you. So, I picked this up for you today". He lifted the brand-new bike out of the back of the truck and held it up for her. Cindy excitedly took the bike by the handlebars and admired the basket and, said, "Look it even has a bell". Scott also retrieved the bike helmet and gloves from the cab of the truck and gave them to her as well.

Cindy couldn't believe her eyes. No-one ever bought her a bicycle before. She felt like a little girl on her birthday.

She didn't know what to say. All Cindy could do was blurt out, "You shouldn't have. You hardly know me".

Scott quickly answered, "I should have, and I did". Cindy hopped on the bike and rode it out into the street ringing the bell. She felt so happy, so welcomed as a part of this family. She excitedly yelled out with glee, "I can't wait to go on a bike ride with everyone!"

Scott said, "Lets' go!" They got the other bikes, and everyone went on a ride to the park.

That night during dinner, Cindy told Scott that she had a great idea, for them to work out the transportation problem for everyone. "Scott, if I got a driver's license, I could drive you to work in the morning and then take the kids to school.

Later in the afternoon, I could pick them up, and then get you from work after that. I just need to practice driving that big truck of yours. Will you teach me and let me practice in your truck?"

Scott thought about it for a minute and agreed with her. Besides, there wasn't much of an option any other way. "I can take you to the church parking lot when I get off work and let you practice in the parking lot."

Cindy being from Europe had only driven smaller luxury cars or sports cars when she visited friends on their estates. But she had never had the opportunity to actually get a license to drive as she had her own personal driver her whole life.

Scott then asked Cindy another question changing the topic altogether. Halloween was coming up. He was worried about how the girls would react to the holiday season without mom and dad. What about Thanksgiving and Christmas too? How was he going to cope with the holidays without his parents?

“Cindy I’m a little worried about the holidays as we get closer them. I still feel a lot of pain when I think about how I am going to celebrate the holiday season without my parents. I worry about the children too”. How are we going to do it? We can’t just stop celebrating them, right?”

“Scott I am here for you. I am here for the girls. Let us just start with the first holiday and take each one, one at a time. I don’t think Halloween will be as bad emotionally as the others. Your older, and haven’t trick or treated in a while, right? “No”, he answered.

“Ok, let's just make this a fun event we’ll dress up the twins in fun costumes and take them out together. I think the girls will be fine because they are both still pretty young and haven’t developed a long tradition in celebrating Halloween with their parents. They are both going to be excited just to dress up and get candy. It's going to be harder on you to take them out Trick or Treating remembering your parents doing with them last year.”

“I know”, he answered.

“Scott, I will be with you and I won’t leave your side. We’re going to do this together.”

Cindy felt good about herself that Scott trusted her with his feelings and valued her advice on how to endure such great emotional fear in his life. She had never had anyone confide in her with such blanket trust before.

Halloween came and went without stirring up much grief in any of the Mann children. Scott was mesmerized by being with Cindy. They loaded Naomi into a stroller and took the girls together, as a family unit, so to speak. Cindy seemed to enjoy it as much as the kids. It was very nice for her to walk through the neighborhood meeting so many neighbors. It gave her a great sense of family and community just being here. The girls were simply so excited to get dressed in costumes and go trick or treating. Thanksgiving was also coming up, but Scott was greatly comforted knowing he would figure it out with Cindy.

Chapter 18

Gold Country Family Services
Case Name: Scott Mann
Case File: #4237
Case Worker: Amanda Peters
Date: November 2019

Cindy obtained her California driver's license to assist the family with running errands and transportation issues for Scott and the girls. Cindy is now volunteering at the girl's school during the day and has been playing piano on the worship team at the family's church. The Mann family is taking all appearances of a healthy normal nuclear family. Cindy and Scott have maintained a professional relationship with each other at home and have not allowed their closeness to develop into a physical or an outward emotional relationship. However, it is apparent they are each in love with each other.

Scott devoted most of their free time to helping Cindy practice driving in his truck. He realized she would be able to help him a lot with the children if she could also drive. It would also give her freedom of her own in order to pursue hobbies or interests if she just had wheels. Scott decided this was an important game changer for all of their lives once Cindy got a driver's license.

The only uncomfortable moment was on the first day of practice when she first sat in the driver seat in the truck. Cindy readjusted the seat and mirrors, to Scott's look horror. "Did I do something wrong?" She asked. Scott then smiled and reassured her, "No it's just me, it is ok. I just remembered something". Scott never told her that he had left the seat adjustment settings as his dad had left them before he was killed. It was just another small way for him to remember his dad. However, the more time Cindy spent with this family, the more they all seemed to overcome their grief.

Scott was feeling more and more that he could comfortably let go of some things reminding him of his past life and start embracing a new and exciting future.

They had set up several cones he borrowed from the public works yard and practiced driving, backing, and parallel parking drills. She seemed to be handling the bigger vehicle ok. The key Scott told her was to always back your truck into the parking stalls. The parking spots are smaller in California, but the big trucks maneuver better if they are backed into the stalls.

He also warned her not to rely on the front and rear parking sensors in the bumper or the rear back-up camera, but always use her mirrors and turn her head to look back.

Cindy knew she was ready, she studied the DMV booklet and practice the written test every day on Scott's computer.

After a couple of weeks of practice driving in the church parking lot, Scott agreed with Cindy that she was ready to take her driving test. Scott took the afternoon off from work and drove her to the Rockville DMV for the big day of the test. He sat down and waited with Cindy in the lobby until her number was called. Cindy approached the clerk at the desk where her number was flashed up on the monitor. Cindy had overheard the clerk speaking in Spanish with the person in front of her, and naively started speaking Spanish when she approached the clerk.

Lucinda Vasquez was working her shift at the DMV counter when a tall beautiful blond girl with dark blue eyes approached her desk. She spoke in perfect Spanish with a slight European accent. The girl said, "I would like to apply for a California driver's license, please. I only have my passport and a library card, but the passport is sufficient is it not?" Cindy presented her false passport in the name of Cindy Mason.

Lucinda answered," Actually I do need your birth certificate for your first license. Are you from another state?"

Cindy answered, "I'm from Minnesota."

"Why are you speaking Spanish with me, especially if you're from Minnesota?", Lucinda asked.

"I heard you speaking Spanish with the woman before me, I thought I was supposed to." Cindy still had not figured out the cultural differences here in America versus how things were in Europe. In Europe, it was not unusual for one to hear a collage of languages in any public place. No one thought it was strange if you spoke English, French, Dutch, German, or any other language for that matter. Most people are bilingual at least.

Lucinda smiled and answered, "We can speak English if you like."

"No thank you", Cindy answered. "I am a little nervous about taking the exams and feel more confident speaking in Spanish". Cindy grew up speaking Spanish in Spain with her relatives in the Spanish royal family. She spent many summers there and only started speaking English regularly when she went to college.

Lucinda checked the Minnesota database to see if Cindy had a prior license or ID there. As soon as she typed her name into the computer a US State Department red flag popped up on the screen with a number to call.

Lucinda told Cindy, "I'll be right back, let me see what I can do to help you with that birth certificate problem." Lucinda went to her supervisor's office and called the number from the State Department warning advisement. A State Department official answered the line and immediately transferred her.

Moments later, a female voice answered the line. "This is Agent Samantha Boyd with the FBI how may I help you".

"I am Lucinda Vasquez with the California DMV. I have a Cindy Mason in our office right now and was given an advisement warning on the computer that I need to contact you".

"Yes, I know, I am in your parking lot right now, we followed her to your office. Can you tell me why she came into the DMV?"

Lucinda explained the circumstances of her contact with Cindy. How Cindy applied for a driver license but did not have all the needed documentation. She also explained how odd, it was that she wanted to speak only in Spanish because she was nervous.

"Ok, Lucinda, this is not a criminal circumstance, and we are not investigating a crime. However, we are involved in a special investigation of sorts. You do not need to worry about your personal safety around her, nothing like that. But this is of extremely sensitive national interest. If you indulge any of this information to anyone else you could be arrested for obstructing a federal investigation. With that being said what I want you to do is stall her for a few moments. Give her the written test if you need to. I will get all of the necessary requirements to your supervisor in order for you to issue her the driver's license."

Lucinda went back to the counter and gave Cindy the Spanish version of the written exam.

While Cindy was taking the written test, Lucinda's supervisor came over to her and whispered. "Lucinda, I just spoke with our main director, the head kahuna, in Sacramento, make sure Cindy Mason gets the license, as long as she passes both the written and the driving test of course. I've been instructed that we do not need a birth certificate, that's been taken care of. I want you to personally give her the driving portion as well, I do not want anyone else from our office having contact with her today."

Scott watched while Cindy walked up to the counter, he could have sworn he overheard her speaking in Spanish but realized maybe it was other people nearby since the office was very crowded. Cindy finished the written exam and passed with flying colors. Lucinda asked Cindy to escort her to the vehicle she will be driving for the driving test.

Cindy walked with Lucinda outside to Scott's truck. Lucinda thought this was surely the weirdest customer ever, usually, everyone brings the smallest compact car so they can get around back and parallel park easy enough for the driving test. She didn't bother asking Cindy why she brought a huge 4-wheel drive truck in for the test. She just took her out for the driving test just like she did for everyone else.

Cindy completed the test with no problems. She came back into the office with a huge smile on her face. "Scott, Scott look I got my driver license!" Cindy thought to herself with satisfaction, she is probably the only crown princess in Europe with a California driver license.

The following morning Cindy got up early with Scott again for breakfast. He made her oatmeal, scrambled eggs, and sausage. She was beginning to seriously enjoy eating alone with him in the mornings without kids. After the kids ate their breakfast Scott and Cindy loaded them into the truck to take them to school.

Cindy said, "I'm driving". She drove Scott to work and dropped him off first, then took the kids to school in Granite Beach.

Cindy parked in the parking lot and saw Linda Maxwell, Cheryl Adams, and Beth Klingson in the parking lot. They each stared at her as she drove up and backed into the nearest parking spot. Cindy felt a little insecure as she exited the truck and helped each of the kids out. She placed Naomi in a baby stroller so she could walk the twins to their class.

Cheryl, loudly stated, "look at her, now she's driving Scott's truck and carting his kids around. I wonder what else she is doing for him?" Cindy briefly overheard Cheryl's cutting words but was so excited she got to take the kids to school that the insult didn't phase her much. Besides she's been trained not to show emotion in public. Beth and Linda didn't comment this time. Perhaps they felt that Cheryl's characterization of Cindy was in bad taste.

Cindy walked the girls to their class and hugged them both before saying goodbye.

As Cindy walked through the halls toward the exit, she overheard the school principal, Janet Stilwell, talking with another woman in the hallway near the front foyer. "Sandy Evans is getting married and will not be able to play piano for our school Christmas play rehearsals. What are we going to do? Do you know anyone that can play the piano?"

Cindy interrupted the two women, "Excuse me, ma'am. I can play the piano. I have since I was a child."

Janet Stilwell, asked, "Who are you again?" "I am Cindy Mason. I am helping Scott Mann with his children. I will be bringing them to school every day and I have the free time to help with piano."

"We will need to hear you play, can you play for us for a moment right now?" Janet and the other school administrator escorted Cindy and Naomi to the music room.

Cindy played several very nice classical pieces from memory. She also played from the songbook that Janet Stilwell provided.

"Excellent "Janet said smiling. "You're in".

Later that day, Cindy picked up Scott from work and drove everyone home. Scott spontaneously stated, "Bike rides to the park?" Everyone shouted "Yes!" in unison. The twin girls were so happy riding bikes with Scott and Cindy. They seemed like a real family. Cindy could see how the girls looked at her as they rode together, they were so adoring of her. It's no doubt the girls were becoming attached to her. Cindy wondered to herself about this new family of hers. This is her family, right? What about her parents in Sweden, and her own siblings? What about her position in the royal family?

She is the oldest child, the crown princess, she is going to be the next queen of her country, where does that fit in with this new family here in California? There is no doubt that she is bonding with each person and she knows she is falling in love with Scott, but how does he feel about her? So many questions that do indeed bring fear with each potential answer. Cindy decided that for now, she is going to continue every day with all of her heart. She thought to herself, “If I was meant to be here, then I need to give myself fully to this family and not be afraid of my feelings. Maybe I need to start considering that I am part of this family too. We are one. I need to trust in something bigger than myself.”

Sunday Morning arrived with the family leaving for church. Cindy thought to herself that she would have never in a million years thought she would be so eager to go to church when she secretly traveled to America. Everyone was so welcoming and friendly from the minute you walked into the foyer until you left.

It was so different than her church back home in Stockholm. She only went for official functions or to be seen publicly with her family on holidays. No-one just talked about their everyday lives with one another or made plans to go out for lunch afterward. She laughed as she found herself almost late for the service every single time even when they arrived for church early. Everyone kept visiting in the hallways, the bookstore, the coffee shop, and the childcare rooms until the music started in the sanctuary. It was so different to see such excitement these people had in just being together.

However, Cindy decided she still needed to talk to the Pastor about how things are developing with Scott and the girls and to seek his advice as soon as she can.

The following morning Cindy brought the girls to school after dropping Scott off at work. She was met in the parking lot by Linda Maxwell and Cheryl Adam's again. Cheryl asked her, "Who do you think you are? Are you barging into Scott's life just to have access to his house and truck because he's young and vulnerable? Do you have some agenda? What's up with you at the School? Your no-one's mom. We see your playing piano for the school play now too. It looks like you're working on some selfish plans of some sort. Are you trying to take him?"

Cindy's feelings were hurt, but she kept her composure, something she was trained to do in the elite society of the Royal Family. She also refused to answer their suspicion with insult. "No, Cheryl, I'm sorry I may seem suspicious to you, but I assure you, I just want to help here with the school and with Scott." I care about this family deeply, it's obvious to me that you are very protective of Scott, and I appreciate that."

Linda didn't say anything and seemed embarrassed by Cheryl's bold accusation. Cindy wondered if the women were simply jealous because she was helping so publicly with the school play. Cindy knew she had an opportunity to be involved which gave her recognition of some sort. Besides Linda and Cheryl's kids were also in the Christmas play. Linda and Cheryl were not asked to help. Maybe that is the reason why their aggression seems to grow more each day.

Or perhaps maybe it possible the other women was angry that Cindy had a more visible role in Scott and the children's lives? Maybe the women were being protective. Cindy wasn't sure why they were acting this way. She had never been challenged by anyone in this manner or frankly disrespected in this way.

Cheryl's words might have been off, but the potential danger to hurt Scott is there. They are vulnerable. Cindy worried because she is afraid. She didn't realize how vulnerable she is too. She knew how deep her own feelings of attachment to the Mann's were.

She had no idea she would become so deeply attached to each of the children and to Scott most of all. Is she just selfishly taking and getting her emotional needs from them in order to satisfy her own neglected heart? She knew that eventually, she must leave them to return to Sweden and fulfill her role, her life calling, as the Crown Princess. Why is she here then if she knows she has to leave someday?

Cindy felt a searing tinge of guilt after Cheryl's words. She doubted herself and feared that her selfishness may be putting each of the Mann's at risk. Can she allow herself to get even closer? Will guilt cause her to become distant? All these questions caused a new panic in Cindy. She only knew one place to go for help.

After Cindy dropped the girls off at school, she went to the church to meet with Pastor Billings. She walked into the administrative offices and asked the receptionist if Pastor Frank was in. The receptionist advised her that he was currently in a meeting with the church music director, but she would let him know Cindy was there to meet him.

A few minutes later, Pastor Frank invited Cindy into his office. She noticed that he had a large clear glass window on the front door to his office. Pastor Frank saw her looking interestingly at the door. Hi Cindy, "What a surprise seeing you today. Do you like the door? That's so anyone outside my office can see what goes on inside my office. It's an accountability thing. However, I assure you everything is confidential and soundproof. No-one can hear the content of our meeting."

"I understand", Cindy answered. "It's wise in this day and age I think."

"What brings you here today Cindy?" Cindy shared how things have been going with her and the Mann's, and how she is helping out more at the school. Then she explained about the confrontation she had with some of the women at the school and their accusation against her that she was essentially a gold digger.

Cindy continued, "I was so hurt. I have never tried to take anything from anyone nor have I ever needed anything. Those women do not even know me or anything about me. How could they say such a destructive thing to another person without even knowing them?"

Cindy started to cry as she continued, "Pastor Frank, this confrontation caused me to doubt and wonder if I am taking something from Scott and those beautiful girls. What if I am only here just to receive their emotional support, love, and attention for my own needs? What if those women were correct, and I am the selfish one? I would feel horrible Should I just quit now and leave before they get even more attached to me? I am worried that I'll always feel guilty whenever I am around them now. Will things ever be the same?"

"Cindy", Pastor Frank answered, kindly smiling at her. "First of all, those women don't know you, that's true. However, my first impression of you was probably the same as theirs. Honestly, they are intimidated for sure, and most likely probably jealous too. You see, you can't hide the fact that you are incredibly refined and polished in your manners, your speech, and even your posture is almost perfect. You were brought up this way your whole life and taught how to function in the highest levels in society. You see, you give off this very regal vibe so to speak. Those women can't pay for that kind of training. They see it and know deep down there is something about you that intimidates them."

"The fact that you are worried about Scott and the kids reassures me that you are just fine and not selfish at all. Let me ask you a few questions. First of all, are you falling in love with Scott?"

Cindy immediately panicked and looked at Pastor Frank fearfully. “Yes”, Cindy couldn’t believe the words coming out of her mouth. “I started falling for him the same day we met. He is the most wonderful guy. Every day he continues to surprise me with something new I find out about his character or how gentle he is with his sisters. He has the most loving heart I have ever seen in another person. We talk alone together every morning at breakfast before the kids get up. We talk every afternoon. We talk at night after the kids are in bed. He is never afraid to tell me about his feelings or his fears. I have never had any person open up to me about so much of their life. He makes me feel that he wants to be with me, he values me as a person. Frankly, I love being with him.”

Pastor Frank didn’t comment on her last answer but asked yet another question. “Cindy do you love the children?” “I do, oh so much, they are the most precious and loving little girls. They have treated me with love from the minute I entered their home, and baby Naomi is so sweet her smile and giggles are the most wonderful thing in the world. I could never imagine my life anymore without Scott and the children.”

Pastor Frank continued, “What do you think Scott’s feelings toward you are?”

“I believe he loves me but is too afraid to say how he feels. I believe he is desperately trying to keep his family together and does not want to initiate any controversy regarding me living in his house.”

Pastor Frank asked, “So Scott would do anything to hold onto those he loves?”

“Yes, he is the most passionate man I have ever met when it comes to his family”.

Pastor Frank continued, “So you believe Scott Mann would do anything, change jobs, or even move to keep his family if he had too for those he loves, those he holds dear in order to hold them all together right?”

“Yes absolutely”, Cindy answered.

“Would you be ashamed of him back in Sweden?”

“No Never!” Cindy answered”.

“Ok Cindy thanks, I don’t have anything to say or ask. I think you answered all of your own questions about your fears. I encourage you to return home and enjoy this wonderful time in both of your lives. Enjoy getting to know Scott and enjoy the children, enjoy each wonderful act of love and fun that you experience. Let God do the job he brought you here for. Let happen what is meant to be.”

“By the way Cindy, I noticed you mentioned that you were going to play piano at the girls’ school. How would you like to play the piano here at our church for the Sunday Service?”

“I don’t know”, Cindy answered, “I’m not sure I’m that good.”

“Well, Cindy our piano player is out for a while for medical reasons. We can pay you a small honorarium for each Sunday you play with our worship team.”

Pastor Frank called one of his assistants into his office to see if the music director was still in the church. Moments later, she entered his office.

“Hi, Pastor Frank you called for me.”

“Yes Paige, this is Cindy Mason, she plays the piano very well and can fill in for you as an interim pianist until Sandra gets better. Of course, as long as she can pass your tryouts.”

Paige turned to Cindy, “Hi I’m Paige Wilson if you have some time, let's go see what you got. Just give me a minute alone with Pastor Frank, I’ll meet you in the sanctuary up on the stage ok.” Cindy thanked Pastor Frank and left to practice on the piano before Paige arrived.

Paige asked Pastor Frank, “Are you sure you want to give her this opportunity, we don’t know much about her. Is she going to represent the values of our church?”

“Paige, I know her, and I know her family. She is good people. Listen, I wanted to offer her this opportunity for more than just filling an empty spot on the team. I wanted to bring her closer to someone in our leadership for accountability, and for an opportunity to help her out financially. You know she is the girl Scott Mann hired to help with the childcare. I’m sure she is not making much in her role as a child care helper. I think that I may be able to help a little just to make sure all of her financial needs will be met. Besides, I want to keep an eye on her too since she is living in his house. Listen, I want to give her a $100.00 honorarium for each Sunday she plays.”

“Pastor Frank!” Paige exclaimed. “This is a voluntary ministry, a way for people in our church to serve God, we don’t pay anyone on the team.”

“I understand, please trust me on this one. I promise you this will be for only a short time, and when the time comes you will fully understand why we are doing this for her.”

Paige left the office and walked into the sanctuary just in time to hear Cindy playing a beautiful melody. Paige listened as the music seemed to draw her into a deep sense of peace. She could feel certain parts of the piece evoking strong emotion in her as well. Cindy stopped playing as soon as she noticed Paige watching her.

“Wow, that was beautiful Cindy”.

“Thank you, that is something I have been working on since I was in college. I am working on the lyric’s now. It’s a song for my parents”.

“Would you ever consider playing that in church?”, Paige asked.

“I can’t”, Cindy answered. “This is something I wanted to play just for my father and for my mother.”

"I understand Cindy. Since you wrote that song, I take it you can read music then?"

"Yes, I do Paige. I have formally studied the piano since I was a little girl."

"Cindy I will leave you with these songbooks. We practice one hour before church each Sunday, and once a month we meet on Wednesday evenings to learn new songs and for a time for our worship team to fellowship and bond together."

Cindy thought it was a great idea for her to join the worship team for now, as it allowed her an opportunity to help Pastor Frank. She finished her tryout with Paige and started to leave the church office.

Pastor Frank caught Cindy in the hallway before she left. "Cindy, I have a quick question. I know you contacted your parents earlier. I saw them on the news. I wanted to make you another offer. I feel it's vital that you continue to reach out to them to reassure them that you are ok and haven't forgotten about them. You need to tell your parents that you love them. Now If I promised you that I could get a message to them anonymously. Without anyone finding out where you are. Would you consider recording a message here in my office? I will send get it directly to them in confidence."

Cindy thought about it for a moment, and realized, that they have to be terribly worried about her. Pastor Frank was right. She remembered seeing her mother crying on live TV during their news conference. That's a big deal because it is forbidden for royals to even show personal emotion in public. Cindy knew that her parents were doing everything to find her. She knew they were desperate. "Ok, Pastor Frank, I'll do it. No one will know where it came from right?"

"Cindy, I promise you they will not look for you here because of the video. They won't know where it came from".

She agreed, and they went into his office to record a simple video. Pastor Frank assured her he would transfer the video to a CD so that it wouldn't be traced from his cell phone or internet IP address and get it to her parents through a private courier, an anonymous source. Cindy trusted pastor Frank.

Cindy sat in a chair against a plain wall for the backdrop. Cindy took off her glasses and motioned that she was ready for him to start the recording.

Cindy started speaking in Swedish: *"Dear Fader, I wanted to get another message to you to inform you that I am quite well and healthy. Pappa, I love you and Mamma. I miss you so much." Cindy began to cry as she spoke, "Pappa I confess that I left the palace for selfish reasons. However, God has steered me to a new path. I believe that I am doing something very important right now and cannot come home yet. I am coming home, I promise you. I am coming home, and I will be a better princess when I return. I realize now how much you mean to me. I will never hurt you like this again. Please forgive me."*

"Maman", Cindy started speaking in French this time as her mother was from France. "I miss you so much I never realized how much you mean to me until I left. I miss being with you to talk about all my fears and worries. I miss your help and advice through life. I simply can't exist without the care of my mama with me. I am coming home soon. I promise. I will be the daughter you always wanted. I cherish you." Cindy paused then continued, "I am very safe here and well provided for. I am with very wonderful people and am doing good works that would not dishonor the crown. Please trust me and be patient. I love you both."

Cindy started crying as she repeated that she loved both of her parents to conclude this short video.

Pastor Frank stopped recording.

It seemed that as she made this video the whole concept of what was happening just hit her hard. The way that she left home causing both of her parents to panic. Cindy knew that they would be seeing this video shortly. There was such a vast range of emotions running through her heart. Guilt, because this was her choice to leave home and she didn't take into consideration how much panic she could cause both of her parents. Sadness, because she didn't realize how much she would miss her home and family.

Then finally, fear and embarrassment, because eventually she would return home and will have to face the media, her government, and her family for taking this huge venture of her coming here to California.

Cindy finished and regained her composure. Pastor Frank stared at her in amazement but didn't say anything out of respect. She quickly left his office without saying anything to him.

As soon as Cindy left the office, Pastor Frank looked for Agent Boyd's business card with her cell phone number she provided for him. "Hi Agent Boyd, I have something of interest to you and was wondering if you could come by my office".

Agent Boyd answered, "Thank you pastor Billings, it just so happens that I am in your parking lot right now."

"Why am I not surprised, Agent Boyd?" Pastor Frank gave her the CD of the video recording and once again admonished the FBI agent about interfering with the princess.

Chapter 19

Gold Country Family Services
Case Name: Scott Mann
Case File: #4237
Case Worker: Amanda Peters
November 15, 2019

The family is thriving now. It appears the trauma of losing both parents is waning on Scott and the children. Cindy continues to take on a larger role in this family and is forming deeper bonds with each family member. Cindy has also volunteered to assist in the worship ministry at the church the family attends. She has also volunteered in the girl's school with several projects. I am witnessing the fact that love is a powerful universal force. Love can heal and overcome the deepest of pain and emotional trauma.

Cindy returned to the girl's school after meeting with pastor Frank. She picked up the girls from school without incident with the other women, and then later picked up Scott from work. The family took a bike ride in the park when they returned home. They parked at Scott's favorite spot near the wooden bridge. The girls played in the nearby playground, and Naomi slept in the bike trailer behind Scott's bike.

Suddenly, Cindy blurted out to Scott, "Scott I met with pastor Frank today, and he asked me to join his worship team to play the piano."

"That's great Cindy! That's so cool, I am excited for you that you get to help out."

"Well, that is not the only reason I talked with him. I confessed to him that I like you."

"Cindy", Scott answered, "I like you too very much".

"Really?" she asked in an attempt to pry more compliments from him.

"Yes Cindy, I like you a lot. I like you so much that I don't want to meet anyone else, to like."

Cindy loved the attention and flirty small talk but didn't realize how much she meant to him until he continued.

"Cindy when I first met you. We were all in a very deep emotional crisis. The girls were mourning the loss of mom and dad but losing mom was hardest for them for me too. Mom was their foundation their security. She was mine too. There is something about a kid's bond with their mother. When mom died, I inherited all three of these girls. Then I inherited fear, stress, loneliness, and grief. Those four emotions ruled my life every moment of every day. I woke up in the morning and the instant I was awake grief met me hard. Reminding me that mom wasn't going to say good morning to me. Not now or ever again."

Scott started crying as he continued, "I felt a deep sadness all the time, I couldn't escape it, I felt there was no remedy. All I could feel was a negative emotion, dark oppression. I never told anyone person about all of the fullness my sadness, because it was so powerful that it would overwhelm any single person that I confided in. I split my grief up and shared portions of it with different people each day. But it was still so dark, even that didn't help. I couldn't get away from that pain. Then one day, I walked into the coffee shop and saw you. I saw a light inside the room for the first time. You were so pretty, so stunning, but there was something else. Just being with you soothed my sadness."

He paused and then stared directly into her blue eyes.

"Every day we were together I felt more peace, I regained more joy to life. More gladness. Good things started to take over from the bad. You are my light, my angel Cindy. Not just for me but your light comforted each of the girls dramatically.

You walked into our home and brought peace and comfort that rushed over each of us. Cindy, you are an amazing human being. You mean so much to me to all of us. I have to watch myself really. To be honest, I am worried because you're working for me technically, and living in my house. I don't want for you to become an item of controversy. In other words, I don't want you to ever have to deal with prying eyes and wagging tongues of cruel people. I care about you Cindy, I really do."

Cindy was very flattered that he was so open and able to articulate and express his feelings to her and to show a protective side as well.

The following morning, Cindy arrived at the school with the girls. She escorted them to their class and then waited outside of the auditorium for the drama teacher to begin working with her on the school play. Moments later, Cindy saw Cheryl Adams walking toward her in the hallway.

Cindy gritted her teeth expecting another judgmental insult. Cheryl had just dropped off her kids at their respective classrooms and was leaving rather quickly. Cindy then noticed that Cheryl seemed to shy away from her as she neared. Cindy greeted her warmly and asked how she was doing today. Cindy thought it was odd that Cheryl was wearing sunglasses inside of the building, then she noticed a large dark purple bruise on the left side of her left eye and face that the sunglasses could not cover or hide. Cindy was horrified when she realized what happened.

In that split moment, Cindy realized why Cheryl seemed so mean. She was abused at home and couldn't help acting out against others that were easy to pick on. Cheryl noticed Cindy's unwanted attention and blurted out, "What are you looking at?"

Cindy stopped in front of her and said, "No-one has a right to hit a woman. You are the queen of the home and the mother of your children. You have a dignified and honorable place in life. You must be treated as such."

Cheryl wanted to walk away and keep her secret. But something seemed strange about Cindy, she seemed to speak with an authoritarian but caring demeanor. Cheryl couldn't put her finger on how strange Cindy seemed at times, but somehow Cindy always gave the impression she was in charge of life itself. Cindy always had that strange vibe, that's what intimidated Cheryl.

She immediately started crying and thought of some way to leave without attracting any more attention from Cindy. "Thank you, Cindy, I'm fine".

"You're not fine Cheryl, you have been unfairly hurt. This is unacceptable. You deserve to be treated with all respect every day all the time. You need help with this problem and cannot solve this on your own."

"Have you ever called the authorities about this?", Cindy asked.

"No, I was afraid. What if he wants revenge?"

Cindy responded, "You have to call the authorities because there is never an instance where this behavior should be allowed. He needs to know that he cannot hit you without consequences and it can never ever be tolerated not even once."

Cheryl answered, "I know, but I would be embarrassed if the police came over to my house".

Both women then saw Janet Stilwell and another teacher walking in their direction. There was no escape for Cheryl's dilemma now. She would have to explain to the school staff about her bruising, and of course, they are required by law as mandated reporters to report it.

"Look, Cheryl, let's go to my house you can make your report and I will not tell anyone about this so you don't have to explain to all the other staff or the moms here about what's happening with you. This will be my secret with you I promise. I will help you. We can go over to my home and call the police. I know some very nice and helpful police officers that are friends of the family. You will be treated with dignity and respect, and most importantly you will get help. Your husband will get help, he really needs it. He needs counseling to help control his anger and how to treat a woman with respect and love. You have to act now Cheryl, or this will continue or even get worse, it will escalate. I believe with the proper help this whole issue can be redeemable in your marriage."

Cheryl, realizing there was no way out said, "Ok let's go, can I go in your truck with you?" While quickly walking away, Cheryl continued, "I'm sorry for picking on you. You see, you seem so refined and dignified, somehow above the regular problems of life. I couldn't help acting out against you, it's because I was intimidated. You never judged me, you never responded to me in anger, and now you're trying to console me. I really don't deserve your friendship."

Cindy drove her to Scott's home and they called the police together. Later that day Cheryl's husband was arrested at his place of employment, and she was granted a 3-day emergency restraining order.

Agent Boyd was able to access the call for service when the police arrived at the Mann residence, she was also able to get a copy of the police report for the domestic violence incident. She documented in her report how the Princess intervened to assist a victim of domestic violence.

Later that same afternoon, after everyone arrived home from work and school, Scott decided to cook dinner for the family from his mom's recipe for her famous baked chicken and vegetables for dinner. Scott found her recipes in the kitchen cupboard after she passed away but rarely looked at them. The recipes were handwritten on scrap papers and stuffed into an envelope. It was a simple dinner that really didn't take long to make.

However, once he started, Scott started to cry when he thought he was alone in the kitchen as he looked over the recipes and studied his mother's cursive writing.

He meditated on the notes and looked over each one wishing there was another note stuffed in that envelope from her, just to him, telling him how much she loved him. He missed her so much, he couldn't stop crying at the moment. Cindy and the girls were all in the living room when they heard Scott crying. She told the twins to watch Naomi for a second while she looked in on Scott. Cindy saw him holding the scrap papers and walked over to him and gently placed her arms around him.

Scott didn't push her away, rather he just said, "I miss her so much Cindy. I don't want to 'not have my mom' in my life anymore". She held him for just a few moments, enough to realize how hard and muscular his arms and shoulders felt as she embraced him. Scott thanked her and said they should check on the kids.

As soon as they both walked back into the living room all three kids were staring at them. Anabelle and Maryanne ran to Scott to hug him. Naomi was sitting on a baby blanket spread out on the living room floor with several baby toys strewn about nearby. She held up her arms toward Cindy and said "Ma-ma", and then again, "Ma-ma". Naomi's second ever spoken words startled everyone. Cindy picked her up and laughed with the girls. However, she instantly got butterflies and goosebumps. It was at this moment that she knew she had a new family, her own family, a family besides her parents and siblings. Cindy knew that this was where she was meant to be. She would put this family first before anything else in her life.

She believed Scott felt the same about her and decided she would just take comfort in knowing that at the right time they would eventually become that family in a more official capacity sometime in the future.

Cindy helped Scott prepare the rest of the dinner that night and decided she would take on a larger role in helping him prepare meals for the family.

Scott started calling Cindy regularly from his work during his lunch breaks just to talk to her. He enjoyed the fact that Cindy never seemed to get tired of hearing from him. Scott worried at first that he would seem clingy, that his daily phone calls would chase her away. However, Cindy seemed to look forward to their phone calls. This made him want to be with her even more. It gave him a deep sense of security knowing that she seemed to enjoy talking to him. He loved hearing her voice, her vocabulary was so formal and the accent drove him crazy. They simply talked about anything. Cindy also realized that Scott was calling her more and looking for the opportunity to be with her. She loved the fact that he wanted to be with her just because he liked her and not for any other agenda.

Things seemed to become quite routine for Cindy and Scott. Their days were filled with work and evening college classes for Scott. Cindy taking the kids to school and practicing for the school play as well as worship practice at church with Paige and the rest of the team. Of course, the best part of the days were bike rides in the park and family time in the evenings when they were free. Sgt Weathers still met with Scott on Saturdays and Amada Peters still came by every now and then to visit with everyone.

Sgt Weathers invited Scott, Cindy, and the girls over for Thanksgiving with his family. Scott and Cindy agreed that it would be best to accept their invitation this year. It helped just to be with other people. It would be very hard emotionally on Scott to be alone in his family home for that holiday without his moms cooking or the joy that his father always brought into the home. Perhaps in the years to come, they will begin to develop their own traditions and memories. But for now, Scott wanted to simply get past this season without a terrible outpouring of grief and depression. Cindy for that matter dedicated herself to being there for him. She had never celebrated Halloween as a child and also being from Sweden had never celebrated the American holiday of Thanksgiving either.

~~~~~~~

King Ludvig Bergfalk of Sweden and his wife Queen Amelie received the latest report from the American government regarding their daughter. “These reports from the Americans are very thorough Amelie”. They cried as they both watched the video of Princess Charlotta that pastor Frank recorded for them.

“I can't believe this is our daughter. She is helping out at a school and a church. I would never believe she would ever want to be so involved in the community”. She even helped a woman through some difficult family problems. She is becoming quite a remarkable woman.”

Amelie answered, “It's because she is in love with the boy. It looks like he and the children are also equally falling in love with the princess.”

“This is hardly what I imagined or dreamed our daughter would find in a man”, Ludvig answered. He is not poor by any means, but he is still just a gardener for the city government. He hasn't completed college yet, but at least he is trying to finish school.”
~~~~~~~

"King Ludvig! You shouldn't judge him just yet! He looks like a very honorable man, you must agree. He is extremely committed to his siblings, and he is from an honorable family. However, I agree, it is troubling that we only know about two generations of his family past".

They continued reading the report including surveillance photographs and also pridefully watched another recent video that an FBI agent recorded of her playing piano in the worship group at the church.

Chapter 20

Gold Country Family Services
Case Name: Scott Mann
Case File: #4237
Case Worker: Amanda Peters
Date: December 1, 2019

Cindy has provided a positive sense of stability for this family. She is involved in their church and the girl's school. Cindy has made new friends at the school and is becoming popular with several of the moms and staff. The family is thriving and each member of this family seems to have overcome much of the grieving process from earlier months. The children are now looking at Cindy as a mother figure.

Cindy received a pleasant surprise this Saturday. Sgt. John Weathers and his wife came over for their weekly visit. Sgt. Weathers took Scott to the police department shooting range for him to shoot some of his dads and grandfather's guns. Mrs. Weathers told Cindy that she would watch the three children while they were gone. This gave Cindy some alone time. She decided to go for a drive to explore the Sacramento area.

Cindy exited the freeway heading downtown to look at the shops. As soon as she pulled off, she saw a vehicle turn left at the intersection in front of a single motorcyclist and continued on without stopping. The motorcyclist purposely laid his bike down in order to avoid colliding into the car. Cindy immediately stopped her truck to aid the motorcyclist who went down. She recognized the male rider as the leader of the group of men from the motorcycle club she saw in the restaurant dinner the first night she met Scott. He appeared to have a broken leg in the accident. Cindy started to call 911, but he stopped her immediately stating he did not want to involve the authorities.

"Miss", he tersely stated, "Just give me my cell phone to call someone else to come to pick me up".

“No, you’re not, I’m taking you to the hospital right now, and I will take care of everything.” She spotted a landscaping truck and hailed the driver and passengers to assist in loading the injured motorcyclist into her vehicle.

As he was being loaded into her truck, he could have sworn he overheard her speaking Spanish to the bystanders assisting her. They used several long planks of wood from their landscaping trailer as a ramp to load his large Harley into the back of her truck.

Cindy entered her vehicle and started to the hospital. “Miss, you don’t understand who I am, (He grimaced in pain as he continued speaking) I am the president of my club, we are very dangerous people. I’m telling you to take me to my clubhouse”.

“Young man!” Cindy replied harshly, “I decidedly outrank you, and at this moment I’m ordering you to come with me to the hospital at once! Now, I will take care of everything”.

Hank Jones, was shocked at Cindy’s take-charge reply, besides she was at least twenty years younger than him. He also noticed her lack of fear, after all, he was wearing his full patch, his colors so to speak, identifying himself as the president of his motorcycle club. She didn’t even seem bothered by his full-sleeve tattoos on his arms or the large tattoo of the pistol on his neck. He had never met someone like her before and was slightly intimidated, but he wasn’t sure why. “My name is Hank, he said”.

“I’m Cindy, I was with Scott Mann that night you bought us dinner at the restaurant. This is the least I could do for you to repay your kindness. What you did for him that night means more than words.”

Cindy drove to the nearest hospital emergency room entrance. She ordered him sternly to stay put inside the truck until she could get assistance. Cindy walked inside the entrance, and moments later, two male nurses exited with a wheelchair. Cindy listened as Hank gave the admissions clerk a false name for himself. She interjected, and once again spoke with authority. I will be the responsible party for the bill. You must put my name on the paperwork. Hank couldn't believe his eyes. This very young petite blonde girl spoke in a manner that carried the authority of a general. This was something he decided was not learned, but must be an attribute from her genetic make-up, leadership was in her DNA. Cindy stayed with Hank for the duration of his treatment.

After an hour or so, they were released from the hospital ER with a cast on his leg. Cindy followed Hank's directions to his clubhouse. It was a large building in West Sacramento with a very large parking lot attached. There were no other buildings nearby just some unsightly empty lots piled with junk cars and motorcycle parts adjacent to their clubhouse. Cindy noticed dozens of motorcycles and other assorted vehicles parked in the parking lot.

Several large tattooed bikers exited the building as she drove up near the entrance, to some, this greeting would be extremely intimidating or rather fearful.

Cindy exited her vehicle and started giving orders immediately to gently help Hank out of the truck. Hank yelled out. "It's ok, she's a friend and she's with me. Someone get my bike unloaded from her truck."

Cindy followed them inside. She saw several pool tables, booths lined the walls and chairs were scattered everywhere. There was also a large bar in the back of the room near a kitchen area behind the bar. Cigarette and marijuana smoke clouded the room. There were empty beer bottles and beer cans cluttered on every table and on the floor. The room appeared as if it was meant to be a large dance hall or reception room originally. There were dozens of Bikers, even the females in the room were very intimidating. However, at Hank's orders, everyone kept their distance from Cindy. Hank was assisted by several of the Bikers into an office.

Moments later, Cindy was escorted inside. Hank introduced her to his lieutenants, his club treasurer, and the Sergeant of Arms. Cindy graciously greeted each one. The men inside the office also recognized there was something different about Cindy, she had a regal posture and a military bearing. Her accent along with the unusual formal speech was in a way, commanding of respect from all the person's present.

Cindy assured Hank that she also kept his name confidential on the hospital admission forms along with the bill which was to be paid by her. He started to object, but she gave him a stern look which quieted his resistance immediately. Cindy answered, "Your kindness to Scott Mann was priceless and meant more than you can realize sir."

Hank asked Cindy, "How are things going with Scott, are you his girlfriend or something?"

"I am his nanny", She answered. "I needed to make some money. So, I answered an ad that he posted at his church. He is a quite remarkable young man. I feel privileged to help him to be honest with you. I don't deserve this opportunity."

"There is no doubt that he is a tough kid that's been given a crappy hand in life.", Hank answered. "The fact that he never gave up on his own, speaks a lot to people like us."

Cindy continued with a gleam in her eye and starting to blush, "I think he is something very special too." Hank smiled when she added that information.

Cindy continued, "He's tough too, just like all of your tough men. Scott works out in martial arts and works hard in his job every day. It's interesting though because he is never too tired to spend time with the children. He is like a father to them now. You know, Cindy continued to blush as she spoke, I am falling for him. I don't feel worthy of him."

Hank just listened and smiled as Cindy continued for some time about how wonderful she thought Scott was, and all the new and wonderful feelings she had for him. Cindy then embarrassingly realized. She was pouring her heart out to an outlaw biker. But deep down she knew that he would never speak a word of this to anyone.

"I'm so sorry!" she then stated. Who would have thought, a strange girl would be here in your office telling you she is falling in love. I'm probably boring you to death."

Hank answered, "I am honored you wanted to talk. As far as I am concerned you are one of us."

They offered Cindy food and asked her to stay awhile, but she stated she had to leave to get back to Scott and his children.

Hank immediately got up and hobbled to the door with her, and as they entered the main room Hank barked out loudly, "Everyone, bow to the queen of California".

He stated this in a slightly uncomfortable gest since he didn't know exactly how to show her the honor that her character demanded. Hank bowed at the same time in which the entire room, dozens of people, instantly quieted from speaking and each person bowed. Cindy stood and looked around at the room. She was impressed by the instant respect Hanks authority commanded and his leadership.

She turned to Hank as he bowed his own head low leaning over his crutches. Cindy leaned over and kissed the top of his head. “Sir, in another age, you would have been the lord of a great host.”

Hank instantly had an epiphany that this was the missing Crown Princess. “Your Highness, he asked? Are you the missing Princess?”

Cindy gasped “I am, how did you know?”

“I just did”, he answered. It’s just your demeanor I guess.”

Cindy contemplated that he did not know her family nor had probably ever seen a picture of her. He recognized her solely by her attributes and character alone. “Hank, you know you are the only person in this country that knew who I am simply by my character alone and not by how I look. You are a remarkable man.”

“Please I beg of you though, please do not to tell anyone who I am. I fell in love with Scott. I love his family, I love being with them. I don’t want to leave him now, and I don’t want anyone to interfere with my life right now until I can figure things out”.

Hank smiled. “Ma’am we are the king of keeping secrets, each person in my organization would never, ever, not even at the pain of death, speak of our business to an outsider”.

“Your Highness”, Hank continued, “You showed me, my club, and each of us a great respect today. I tell you no government authority has ever done this. We have always been treated as outlaws. Well, maybe we are outlaws, (everyone in the room laughed) but never treated as respected people of value. We are forever in your debt”.

Cindy turned to leave, several of the bikers escorted her to her vehicle, the others bowed, some smiled and stated, “Your Highness” as she passed by.

Ten minutes later after Cindy left, a plain sedan entered the compound with a single female driver. Special Agent Sandra Boyd exited her car and was immediately surrounded by several Bikers. She identified herself as an FBI agent and politely asked to meet with Hank Jones. Agent Boyd assured them she was only there in peace, and not to cause any trouble.

Moments later a Biker, who identified himself as the Sergeant at Arms arrived outside and escorted Agent Boyd inside the clubhouse and to Hank's office.

Hank was seated with his lieutenants around a large table. They motioned for her to have a seat. Hank knew that the FBI was not after him on this occasion or they would have sent in a SWAT team, not a single female agent.

"How can we help you?" Hank asked.

"I am Special Agent Sandra Boyd from our Washington DC bureau, (she said as she handed him her card) This is my personal cell phone number on the back. I am working a case for the US State Department of extreme national sensitivity. No one is in trouble and this is not a criminal investigation. Actually, I ran a records check, and I had your existing arrest warrants dropped and any current cases expunged from your record before my arrival here. I am not here to make any deals with you or insult you in any way. We are simply and humbly asking for your help."

Hank interrupted, "Thanks for your humility, as for the warrants, as you know, I don't accept your help nor recognize the favor. I am in no way indebted to you or the government." Hank was impressed however, that she had the juice to have those warrants dropped.

Agent Boyd continued, "I am here on a personal matter first and foremost. There is a young woman gone missing from her family. They are, extremely tore up with grief over her disappearance and are worried to death about her safety.

“OK, Agent Boyd, let’s cut to the chase. I know that you followed us here or you would not have suddenly and randomly just walked into my house. I also know you have a team of agents outside scattered throughout the neighborhood, we’ve already identified several of your units. Since we all know who were talking about, we are aware of this young woman and am aware of her circumstances. Boyd looked shocked at his answer as Cindy has been so careful to conceal her identity.”

“So, then you know that this is also an international matter as she is the next head of state for a major European power. It would be a huge embarrassment for the United States for anything to happen to her on our soil or to embarrass the Royal family while she is in our country.”

“OK,” Hank answered, “I don’t care about international matters and politics. I only care about this so-called ‘girl’ you speak of. We’re not going to help you in any way. We’re not going to interfere either. If you're worried about embarrassment due to some bad behavior on her part, this is insulting if you really knew her character. She helped me as a good Samaritan and treated us with deep respect. She is honorable people.”

Hanks tone became even more serious, “You know that we have a huge influential reach, able to extend our decisions and authority anywhere on the planet if needed. I will tell you that if anyone harms her or Scott Mann, then the full force of all the violence that we are capable of will be brought to bear in a public and loud manner. It would be a very clear brutal act of vengeance.”

"Oh, one more thing Agent Boyd that you need to be aware of as you continue on with your case. I resisted her help at first, she knew who I was, but had no fear of me at all. Rather she sternly looked me in the face and said, 'Young man, I decidedly outrank you, and I order you to do what I say.' I didn't know who she was at the time, but there was this regal stature an aura of authority about her. I don't know how to quite put my finger on it, but she put a natural fear into me when she spoke. Listen, centuries of kings and royalty reside in her DNA. As far as we know, people from her own bloodline may have ruled over many of our own ancestors. She is the real deal, a true world leader."

Agent Boyd stared at Hank for a moment and then thought hard about how she is handling this investigation. She realized the true scope of who Cindy Mason really is and the growing footprint that the Princess is now starting to leave here in California. "Hank, let me ask you a question, off the record. How do I deal with this? How do I do the right thing here for everyone involved? I mean, you're right, she isn't a spoiled royal princess just here for a good time. This is huge, more than I or our government ever realized."

Hank thought for a moment and sympathized with the Agent. "OK, I believe you want to do the right thing. We all do. Somehow, we have all been roped into this together. I think, simply just leave them alone. I mean just keep doing what you're doing and keep your distance. Trust her and let what is meant to happen in her life happen. This is no coincidence that she is with Scott Mann. In the end, I think we all get the privilege to be part of something very big and very exciting. Something that we don't see very often in this dark and sad world we live in today".

Agent Boyd thanked them for their time and left their clubhouse. She quickly returned to her Hotel and wrote a detailed report about her meeting with Hank Jones and Cindy Mason's good Samaritan activities. She quickly sent it off to her superiors at the State Department. She hoped they would all begin to see the gravity of this case, that this is much bigger than they all realized in the beginning.

Cindy Mason is now beginning to make a huge impact in many peoples lives in her new life here in California. Eventually, the truth is going to come out who she really is. Even Agent Boyd feared that it would not go well.

Cindy returned home that afternoon and became the same old love struck little girl again. The family sat down together for dinner including Naomi who graduated to a high chair at the dinner table. Cindy stared at Scott throughout much of the dinner admiring everything she could about him. The way he fed Naomi so carefully to the way he smiled and made funny faces at Annabelle and Maryanne. After dinner, Cindy helped Scott do the dishes. She continuously and purposely bumped into him to feel her arms against his arm, or against his shoulders several times. Scott seemed to understand and accept her flirting which made her feel that he enjoyed being with her. This made Cindy feel all the more excited to be with him. Just as they finished the last of the dishes, Scott looked at Cindy and said, “You are so nice to be with, I don’t ever want you, to not be with us. We’ll ok honestly, I just always want to be around you, Cindy. I like the fact that you don’t ever get tired of me.”

Cindy blushed and told Scott. “I don’t ever want things to change between us. I think there is becoming an ‘us’.”

Scott smiled and caringly looked into her eyes, “I agree Cindy, there is an ‘us’ now, I like it, and I want you to like it too. Cindy, I want you to like me.”

“I do like you Scott, a lot”.

Chapter 21

Gold Country Family Services
Case Name: Scott Mann
Case File: #4237
Case Worker: Amanda Peters
Date: December 15, 2019

Scott and Cindy are growing closer together as well as their relationship with the children. Each of the children is now accepting Scott and Cindy as parent figures now. Cindy continues to make more friends at the school. Most of the moms are a decade or two older than her, yet despite her youth, the women continue to flock to her to help friendship and guidance.

On Monday morning Cindy arrived at school after dropping Scott off at work. She met Cheryl Adams and Linda Maxwell in the parking lot. Cheryl was hugging Linda, as Linda seemed very distressed. Cindy quickly dropped off the girls at their respective class and went back to the parking lot. Both women were still in the parking lot crying together. Cheryl asked Cindy if she could help Linda with rides for her kids after school.

"Cindy, Linda is in a bit of a crisis right now and needs us to come alongside her to help out. Her husband left her last Friday night for a younger woman. Can you believe he did this right before Christmas too!"

Cindy gasped and said, "I'm so sorry Linda, you don't deserve this. You are an amazing mom, an amazing woman. Whatever I can do to help."

Linda cried and said she also had to leave her job because she worked in the same office as her husband. "I am worried that I won't be able to pay the bills. I can get my old public relations job back, but it doesn't pay as much and I may not be able to pay for the tuition for the kid's school. My husband never agreed to their private schooling and said a public-school education was just as good.

I believe he just didn't want to pay this extra expense. Cindy, I won't have the flexibility to get off work early in the afternoons to pick up the kids from school. Can you please help, just with some rides?"

"Of course I will", Cindy answered, and hugged Linda. Cheryl looked at Cindy and thanked her too.

"Cindy you're such a good friend We should never have been so rough toward you early on in our friendship. You know we just were protecting Scott. We didn't know what to think when you came along."

Cindy smiled at each of them and said, "I didn't notice a thing, you both have always been such a big help and encouragement to me."

Later that afternoon, Cindy picked up all the kids from school and headed to Linda Maxwell's house to drop off her two boys. Cindy noticed Linda's car was in the driveway as she arrived. Linda invited Cindy inside of her house and seemed very despondent.

"Cindy, thank you so much for helping me this is such a bad time in my life. It seems everything is falling apart in my life right now. I just got home from my job interview, and my old company is going to hire me back, unfortunately, my salary will be decidedly lower than my last job. I never saw this whole nightmare coming. I thought we were happy in our marriage.

Cindy sympathized with Linda and held her hand. "Linda, I have always looked up to you from the first time we met when I answered your advertisement for babysitting. You seemed so professional in your demeanor, and you have never changed. I know that this is hard right now for you, but these problems do not define you. I will help you in any way that I can. You're my friend Linda, and I will not leave you to do this alone."

Linda cried, "I can't believe how much you have grown on all of us, Cindy. There has always been something different about you. You're very polished you know. But you have changed, much more, ever since I noticed you moving in with Scott. I noticed you have a much brighter disposition, you're always happy now. Almost as if your walking on the clouds. Are you in love with him, I won't tell anyone?"

Cindy smiled and looking Linda straight in the eye, and said, "I have to get going to pick him up from work."

Cindy picked up Scott and immediately started telling him about her day, "You wouldn't believe how things are going at the school. The women that were making problems for me before were so nice to me today. Scott, one of the ladies is having some serious problems at home with her marriage and with her finances. I hope you don't mind, but I offered to drive her two boys' home from school every day because she had to change jobs."

"Cindy, that's fine, I am so glad that you are making friends at the school. It's exciting to see how much you are getting involved at church and at the school. I am so proud of you. Besides, I was getting worried that you would become bored with just taking care of our family."

Cindy looked at Scott and smiled, "Our family?"

"Yes Cindy, Scott answered, "You are part of us. Cindy, you're a huge part of my life, I can't think of having a day go by now without seeing you at breakfast with me, or riding bikes, hanging out at the wooden bridge in the park. Just having you pick me up in my dad's truck means the world to me you make me look forward to coming home."

Cindy started quietly crying as Scott told her how much a part of his life she was. She had never felt so attached to a person and so needed in someone else's life before. Cindy quickly changed the subject so she didn't get distracted from driving home.

“I was wondering Scott if we could have a picnic for Cheryl Adam’s, Linda Maxwell and their children in the park this Saturday? I’ve known Linda before I even met you, she is a wonderful woman. I think it would be so good if they could meet you in person and see why I’m so happy every day.”

“That would be a great Idea, Cindy, that would be so much fun, just plan it and I’ll help with all the food.”

Cindy contacted Janet Stillwell in the School office first thing Wednesday morning after dropping all the children off at their classroom. Cindy handed her an envelope with cash. It contained most of the savings from the monies she had earned working for Scott, and for the honorariums, she earned playing music on Sundays. Cindy demanded that this be an anonymous gift toward the tuition for Linda Maxwell’s two kids. Cindy hoped it would stretch at least helping them for a little while. Cindy said it wasn’t much, but hoped it would get her through the tough times until she got a better job.

Janet Stillwell stared in disbelief, almost moved to tears that Cindy, a mere live-in babysitter, would give up all of her earnings to help a parent at this school. Janet being greatly moved by Cindy’s sacrifice took the funds and promised Cindy that the school would also provide a scholarship if needed, and waive future monthly tuitions until Linda Maxwell recovered from her current situation.

“Afterall”, Janet said, “It’s the holiday spirit. We all need to do out part to spread as much cheer and love and comfort as we can”.

Saturday arrived soon, Cheryl and Linda also thought it would be a great idea to get their families together before Christmas for a nice and peaceful day in the park, it would be a pleasant distraction for all the worries they have been facing lately. Besides, they both wanted to officially meet Scott Mann and get to know him better. Scott canceled his plans with John and Sandy Weathers for the day. They were both very excited to see Scott socialize more with other adults outside the home. Especially an activity that was recreational for him and not counseling or mentoring.

Scott and Cindy got up early for the day and spent the whole morning planning their meal. They poured over his mother's recipes together and decided to make baked chicken with crumbled crackers as a breading, along with homemade potato salad and coleslaw.

For dessert, they would make his moms famous pumpkin pie. Scott remembered how she loved pumpkin pie. She often made pies for their friends during the holidays. She even made them just for his father's co-workers and brought them into work as a surprise.

Cindy thoroughly enjoyed working together with Scott all morning. They talked about food and cooking, but they also talked about everything else. It gave her a true sense of belonging since they had a project to work on together, a goal of preparing to meet and socialize with other people. This was far more exciting to be with her friends now because she was actually preparing everything for them herself. She eagerly waited to see the looks on their faces to know that she and Scott prepared their entire lunch at home. This was completely different than any social planning she was accustomed too. This was going to be the perfect afternoon. Since they lived right next to the park they could drive right over to the picnic area before the food got cold. Cindy was quite surprised, but she was most anxious in simply showing off her man Scott to the other women. She realized at that moment that he was her treasure!

Everyone met in the park for the picnic. Scott brought all the food items and arrayed them on the picnic tables so Cindy could visit with her friends.

He placed Naomi in the baby stroller to keep an eye on her, but she always wanted to get out and crawl around much more these days. Scott ended up carrying her while he set up the tables so she didn't crawl off. Cheryl, Linda, and Cindy sat at the tables and visited while Scott worked and the other kids went to the nearby playground where they can all keep their eyes on them.

Cheryl admiringly noticed how much Scott doted over Cindy. He often gave Cindy the most loving and adoring looks while they talked. Scott made it a point to make constant eye contact with Cindy each time they spoke with one another.

She whispered to Linda, "Do you see what I'm seeing?"

Linda whispered back, "Oooooh Ya, they absolutely seem like a young couple in love."

Scott finished setting things up and sat down for a moment before calling the children over to eat. Cindy introduced Scott to the two ladies. "I know you guys know Scott from school, but I don't think you've formally met." Cheryl and Linda saw how gently he held Naomi. Cindy tried to take her from him for a moment, but Naomi held on tightly and said, "da, da, da, da, da". It was obvious that Naomi wanted some dad time. Both women teared up seeing how lovingly the older brother cared for his little sister. He never prohibited her from having his attention when she wanted it. It also broke their hearts to think that the baby's mom and dad were gone. Scott is now the dad for this little one there was no doubt.

Cheryl whispered in Cindy's ear, "So this is your boss huh?"

Cindy shook her head, yes, and Cheryl continued, "Kind of like working in a candy store".

Cindy laughed looking at Cheryl, said "YES!"

Linda wondered what was going on between Cheryl and Cindy. Cheryl looked at her and said, "I'll tell you later".

They called the children over from the playground, prayed over the meal and had a great lunch. Both women were amazed that everything was home cooked. Cheryl couldn't believe they even made the coleslaw from scratch.

She commented, "You made coleslaw, who makes that? Normally you just buy it from the deli. I would never think a couple of millennials would cook anything unless they could put their cell phones down long enough."

Linda answered, "Ya but these are not normal millennials look at how Scott is parenting those babies, he's made them feel as if they are his own children. He's on survival mode. But what's your story, Cindy? Why are you so different from all the other young blonde California girls?"

"I met Scott" she answered, "He makes me want to be a better person."

"Cindy!", Cheryl blurted out, "You make all of us want to be a better person. Honestly, there is something about you that we haven't figured out yet."

Linda left early from the picnic in order to get home to start work on a work project that was due on Monday. Cheryl helped Scott and Cindy clean up after the picnic and load things into his truck to go back home.

Moments later, as they stood in the parking lot to say goodbyes, Cheryl's husband exited a car parked nearby. He yelled profanities across the parking lot at Cheryl and appeared very threatening and angry. Cheryl's husband was a very large man and was unkempt. He appeared intoxicated as he spoke and walked. The man became more irritated as he drew near his wife. He clenched his fists and walked even faster toward Cheryl.

Cindy was the first to recognize what was happening and spoke out immediately warning the man to leave.

His anger diverted instantly to Cindy, "Who are you bitch? Are you the one who talked my wife into calling the cops in the first place? I'm going to make you pay for interfering into something that's not your business."

He turned toward Cindy, Scott instantly pushed him back to protect Cindy. "You SOB" he yelled at Scott, "I'm going to kick your ass first right in front of your girlfriends."

Scott knew the man was larger and very angry, he was also slightly intoxicated. Scott heard his fathers voice in his head which calmed his fear. "When you face a larger more dangerous opponent, do what you know son." Cheryl's husband charged at Scott, Scott in one fluid motion, performed a simple striking pattern drill as he had so often done hundreds of times in his garage.

He sidestepped out of the man's path and threw a hard roundhouse kick into his rib section. The instep of Scott's shin and the arch of his foot made hard contact with his ribs. As the man doubled over Scott instantly followed up with a hard-right uppercut into his chin, a left hook into his jaw and a right cross directly to his nose. The larger man fell straight down and was knocked out cold. A professional trainer would have recognized that he was out with the uppercut. There was no doubt his nose was broken as it was bent to one side and bleeding heavily. Scott swore he also broke a rib with the roundhouse kick.

Cindy and Cheryl stared in total disbelief. Scott quickly ran over to Cindy to see if she was ok. He hugged her and held her to comfort her after what had occurred. Cindy could see the deep concern Scott had for her.

The kids were crying and several people ran to their direction. One man checked Cheryl's husband and stayed with him until the police and paramedics arrived. He reported to the police that he saw the whole incident, simply stating that Scott was protecting the women and himself. The man who reported the incident seemed to speak with the police for a long period of time and seemed to know some of the officers.

Cindy stared at Scott in a new manner of amazement. No-one had ever stepped into the way of danger to protect her before. Cindy also couldn't believe Scott was able to defeat the larger and angrier man. She knew that Scott would protect her forever no matter the threat, that he would stand by her side and never leave her alone just as he has done for his own sisters.

Agent Boyd and her team of agents were getting ready for another quiet day of surveillance at the park. Each agent had already picked out spots where they could easily watch Scott and Cindy without being noticed. They settled into the monotonous duty of watching a family picnic.

Just at the end of the day when they were walking to the parking lot, they noticed a vehicle parked in the lot near Cheryl's car. The subject in the vehicle stayed in his car and watched the party for some time. One of the surveillance agents was able to identify the subject from his license plate as Cheryl's husband.

They conducted a record's check and found he had a current restraining order on file preventing him from having contact with Cheryl of their kids. Agent Boyd called the local police anonymously to have him picked up before he caused any disturbance. Before the police arrived, they saw him charge Cindy with Scott pushing him away. Agent Boyd directed several of the nearest team members to intervene immediately. Before they could exit their vehicles, Scott dropped him.

Agent Boyd and her team could not believe their eyes. She quickly called them off, except one agent was directed to stand by Cheryl's husband until the police arrived.

They would make sure the full details of the incident were reported correctly as Scott was acting in self-defense. Interestingly, none of the officers interviewed Cindy after the incident occurred. Cheryl's husband was arrested for violating a restraining order, public intoxication, and assault.

Agent Boyd laughed to herself thinking about her conversation with Hank Jones. Scott most likely saved Cheryl's husbands life. If he would have harmed or accosted Cindy in any way, there was no doubt in Agent Boyd's mind what would have happened if the motorcycle gang heard about it.

Later that afternoon, Amanda Peters came by the house to speak with Scott about the incident in the park. As usual, Amanda spoke with each family member in private in the family den downstairs.

Amanda smiled as she began her talk with Scott. She really wanted to get to the nitty-gritty, Amanda could tell Scott was falling deeply in love with Cindy. It was so romantic to see him blush about her all the time.

"Scott, I heard you are quite the hero."

Scott thought to himself at Amanda's first question regarding the day's events. He had so much fun planning this picnic with Cindy. It was so nice to do something together. He loved spending time with her, but also enjoyed showing off his girlfriend to the others. Yes, Scott kept that definition in his secret thoughts for now, but he considered her his girlfriend. If only he could tell Cindy how he felt really about her. Then this crazy guy interrupted a perfect day and came rushing upon them and cussed at Cindy. Scott had to stop him no matter how big he was. Scott was only so glad to send him sleeping to the pavement.

"Amanda", Scott answered, "I'm not a hero. I just couldn't stand to see anyone threaten Cindy. She means a lot to me".

“Scott, do you love her?” Amanda asked. “Amanda, I have to admit. I am falling very much in love with her”. Scott couldn't believe his outside voice. He was just admitting in his thoughts that she was his girlfriend, now he outright voiced his true feelings about her to Amanda!

“Scooooott,” Amanda asked again, “Do you really love her?”

Scott was embarrassed, but somehow admitting it out loud and saying the words about his true feelings for Cindy was very freeing to his spirit. If only he could tell Cindy.

“OK, yes I do, I am crazy in love with Cindy. Actually, I liked her from the first time I saw her and I just kept liking her more and more every day. Is this going to get me in trouble?”

“No Scott, just because you have custody of your siblings doesn't mean you can't have a love life.”

“I was just worried that any appearance of an improper relationship would give me a bad reputation with your office and endanger me having the kids.”

“Scott, I have to say, I think you have a very lovely young woman that is a big part of your family and she needs to know how much you do care about her. She is probably dying for you to make a very big statement about your relationship with her. The kids love her, you love her.”

“Ok, I'll think about it”, Scott answered.

Amanda asked to speak with Cindy in private after she spoke with the twins. “Cindy that was an exciting day for you today. How are you feeling about what happened?”

“It started so wonderfully”, Cindy answered. Scott and I made this wonderful lunch together. It was so fun working with him in the kitchen. I felt we made a great team and prepared this great picnic for two of the women from the school.”

Amanda listened in shock as Cindy spoke, she couldn't believe this was the crown princess of Sweden boasting about making a picnic and serving two women from the children's school.

Cindy continued about her day, "The picnic was so fun, everyone loved our food. I was so proud of my achievement then this crazed man approached us in the parking lot. I have never been so afraid in my life. I have never been threatened by anyone before. I panicked and froze. Before I could blink Scott stood up and protected me. I couldn't believe it. No one ever physically protected me before. Scott was so brave. This man was huge, and he was so angry. I thought for sure we were all going to get beaten. Before I knew it, he was knocked out and the police were coming."

"How did that make you feel Cindy when Scott protected you? I only ask because I worry you may think Scott has a violent streak in him"

"It made me feel safe, it made me feel that he cared about me. I know he is a true gentleman and is not a violent person. I'm kind of proud of him too that he fearlessly faced a much bigger older man. It's good to know that no matter what danger, he would be there for me."

"Cindy, how do you feel about your relationship with Scott. I want you to be honest with me. Trust me, he is not going to be in trouble. You are both allowed to have feelings for one another."

"I am frustrated, Amanda. I am very much in love with Scott. I feel that he is in love with me too as well. However, my life is very complicated and I am afraid of where we need to go from here for us. I want more of him in my life. I want a bigger relationship with a commitment from him. But you see, as much as I love our lives here, I will have to make some changes soon. I have some very important family issues that may require me to go home soon. More than anything, I want to have Scott in my life. I love him so much and I love his sisters each of them. I want to be with him and his family forever. I am just worried that nothing is going to change for me and I won't get to have my dreams."

"Cindy", Amanda answered, "I want to encourage you. I have a feeling that Scott feels the same way about you. If that is so, you don't need to worry. I think Scott proved to you today that he will do whatever he needs to do to be with you. Cindy, I think you are Scott's whole world honey."

With Amanda's encouragement, Cindy decided to be a little more assertive toward Scott just for the Christmas Holiday.

She knew it would be tough for him and the girls, but wanted to make this a special holiday for everyone. She talked with Scott about not trying to replicate the Christmases past that he enjoyed with his parents. She encouraged him and the girls to give of themselves to others this Christmas instead. Cindy thought it was best and most healing for the kids and Scott to look to help others rather than to mull over what they wanted for themselves. She also encouraged them to make new traditions unique to the new family that they are now.

They baked cookies and other pastries for the Gold country children's receiving home, the police officers at Rockville PD, as well as the deputies at the Gold Country Sheriff's Office. The family went Christmas caroling at retirement homes, and the children's receiving home.

They also decided to make some new traditions for themselves which included going driving through neighborhoods to see Christmas light display's, and binge-watching Christmas movies on TV with the children. These activities gave them all a sense of bonding and family. Not replacing family lost, but looking forward to having each other.

Chapter 22

Gold Country Family Services
Case Name: Scott Mann
Case File: #4237
Case Worker: Amanda Peters
Date: January 2020

Scott and Cindy worked together on preparing a picnic for two other families. Cindy was very proud of preparing the food and hosting her friends from the children's school. However, during the picnic, a male subject accosted one of the women and threatened Cindy. Scott physically defended her from any danger. The male subject was eventually arrested after he received medical treatment for his injuries. Cindy was quite smitten by Scott's chivalry. Scott and Cindy both told me directly in our last meeting that they are both in love with each other. Cindy is frustrated in the current speed at which things are progressing in their relationship. She mentioned that she will need to return to her family soon for reasons she did not share with me. Cindy is very worried that somehow this unknown family business could threaten her relationship with Scott.

The King and Queen of Sweden read the most recent reports from America about their daughter Princess Charlotta.

King Ludvig Bergfalk sat in silence as he meditated on what he had just read then he turned to the Queen. "Can you believe that our daughter befriended a violent Biker gang? Did you see that the leader of this gang said he would violently defend our daughter?"

"We'll" she answered, It seems that Scott is capable and able to defend her. She is quite safe in America. I can't believe all the lives she is touching and the woman she is becoming now. However, I am very alarmed about her relationship to Scott now."

"Yes, me too the king answered. I don't know about him, this young man is not what I pictured for my daughter."

"What are you talking about. What I meant was that I am alarmed that things are not going forward in their relationship. They are both afraid of the next step. He is the best thing that ever came into her life. There is no better man for her, if you had a romantic bone in your body you would see this too. I am very worried about her right now. I think it is time for us to intervene. I think we need to come to America right now. It's time, I know it is really time for us to come to our daughter, she needs our help."

"I don't think we really need to go", the King answered. We can send for her now if you like, the American government would be more than glad to contact her and get her to come home. This Agent Boyd seems like she is capable of the task."

"Under no circumstances! I am her mother. A Mother knows what her daughter needs. She needs her parents there in California with her now more than ever. We are leaving for America at once!"

The King saw the importance of what his wife had to say and how much this meant to her. "Ok," he said, "I see we are leaving for America. I will inform the Prime Minister to make all the proper arrangements with the American government. However, if we are going to help her, we should go discreetly until we make contact with her to see how we can help her and Scott."

Agent Boyd had just started her day and was enjoying her morning coffee when her phone rang. "Hello agent Boyd, this is Mike Samuels from the US State Department. stand by for the Secretary of State…."

Agent Boyd contacted her surveillance team and briefed them about the arrival of the King and Queen of Sweden. They were to meet with them at the Sacramento Airport.

The King and Queen would be accompanied by a team of four Swedish security agents led by Agent Lucas Wilbrink. They were to coordinate with the royal entourage and bring them to the Princesses' location to reunite the Royal family. The operation would continue to be covert until the Royal family decided when to inform the media.

Agent Boyd assigned the majority of her team to stay with Scott and Cindy in order to lead the arriving party to Cindy's location. Agent Boyd then went to the airport to meet with the family. She was directed to a US Customs hangar where the royal family would be arriving.

There were two dark SUV's provided from the State Department in the hangar. The Swedish airliner taxied directly to the Customs hangar. Agent Boyd waited nearby for the royal entourage.

"Your Highness, I am agent Sandra Boyd. I have a team of FBI agents watching your daughter right now and will lead us directly to her. However, I think it would be prudent first to have one of your agents identify her, just to make sure it's her before we bring you to them. I believe in taking every precaution to avoid any possible problem. I have information that they are preparing to leave from a meeting at the children's school. It should only take us about 30 minutes to arrive at Scott Mann's residence, which is where we believe they should be going. I have notified the local police department to send two marked police units to stand by in the area in case if we need them. They have not been briefed about the nature of our operation at this time."

As they neared Rockville, they could overhear the surveillance team following them over the radio. Agent Boyd radioed the team to inform them they were in the area. One of the FBI agents then broadcast that they are arriving into the target neighborhood now.

“I have eyes on our target, a male, female, and three children just arrived at the residence. They have exited the vehicle and entered the target residence.” FBI Special Agent, Sandra Boyd, then spoke into the radio, “We’re rolling up to the residence now.” A three-car convoy of dark SUV’s quickly entered a quiet middle-class neighborhood subdivision and stopped at a plain, but well-manicured house on the block. Agent Boyd continued, “I want the surveillance units to hang back at the perimeter and bring in the two marked police units at each end of the block in case if we need them for security.” Agent Wilbrink and I will make contact with the female now, standby...”

~~~~~~~

On Monday morning immediately after the weekend of the picnic, Scott went to the den and retrieved his mother’s wedding ring from the safe for a lunchtime visit to the Jewelers. The jeweler promised he would have the modifications completed on the ring ready by Wednesday afternoon.

This was a busy week for Scott as he had class on Wednesday evening and on Thursday, he had a parent-teacher conference at the girl’s school. Regardless of how busy things were he still made Cindy breakfast in the morning and called her often just to talk throughout each day.

Scott also asked Cindy if she would join him Thursday for the parent-teacher conference because he wanted her to feel that she was more involved in the family.

Annabelle and Maryanne were so proud to have Scott and Cindy both come to the parent conference to meet with their teacher. They both proudly held Cindy’s hands as they walked down the campus to the classroom.

Scott whispered in Cindy’s ear, as they walked. “The kids feel like we're a family. I do too. I am so glad you’re with us, Cindy.”
~~~~~~~

Cindy stopped walking and turned to face Scott. He looked at her, made direct eye contact, and stared momentarily drinking in her beauty. Cindy could feel his adoration and waited for him to make his move. He leaned in to kiss her at just that exact moment. The girls each read the moment as well and watched in silence and awe. Just then, Linda Maxwell walked out into the corridor and yelled, "Hey guys. How are you doing?", and interrupted the whole scene.

"Were fine Scott, looking embarrassed turned as he spoke with Linda. I heard about you last weekend Scott. You're a hero. I am so proud of you."

"Thanks, Linda. Well, we're on the way to meet the girl's teacher now."

"OK, I'll let you guys go. Thanks again Cindy for picking up the kids after school. You are a real, lifesaver."

They finished the conference with the girl's teacher, Mrs. Bell. Cindy felt so part of this family. Even Mrs. Bell recognized and praised Cindy's efforts in helping the girls this year in school. Cindy felt the deepest satisfaction that she was really part of this loving family.

They left and went straight home. Scott promised everyone that on Friday after work they would do something special since he had finished his semester and had one more class down.

Just as they arrived home, Cindy took Naomi upstairs to change her. Scott and the girls were talking in the living room when the doorbell rang. Scott opened the door and immediately a professional looking woman held out her wallet with a gold badge and ID with giant letters "FBI". "Hello sir, are you Scott Mann?"

"Yes, I am."

She held out her hand to shake his hand in an effort to appear non-threatening and continued. “I am Agent Sandra Boyd with the FBI. This is Agent Lucas Wilbrink with the Swedish government. Is Cindy Mason here?” Scott looked very surprised and wondered why they would be here looking for Cindy.

Just then Cindy walked downstairs carrying Naomi. Agent Wilbrink immediately gasped, bowed and stated, “Your Royal Highness”. At that exact moment, Agent Boyd broadcast on a portable radio. “It's her, our target is confirmed stand by....”

Scott didn't know what to think. He stared with his mouth wide open. He was struck with a moment of disbelief in this surreal moment.

Cindy looked so surprised and walked Quickly over to Scott and handed Naomi over to him immediately. “Lucas Wilbrink”, she gasped, “What are you doing here?”

“I am here with the King and the Queen, your mother and father, they are outside and want to see you now.”

Cindy turned to Scott and trembled with her knees buckling. “Please forgive me, Scott. But, I promised you one day you would find out about my family. That day is here. I couldn't tell you before. I don't know why I just couldn't. Please forgive me, I'm still me. I am still the girl you have always been with. I still feel exactly as before about you and the girls. Nothing has changed.”

Scott had to make a quick decision, he saw the panic on her face, and instantly realized he needed to de-escalate her fear. “Cindy, please bring your parents inside. I want to meet your family. It's OK we will get through these problems together. I promise, don't worry. Remember, ‘We're all of us there are’. We stick together and you're one of us.”

Scott gathered the children and went outside to the back yard to play with them to allow Cindy to meet privately with her parents in the living room. The girls seemed scared. Scott tried to comfort them and reassured them that Cindy was not in trouble.

He couldn't believe this turn of events. Scott laughed to himself and thought If her parents are a King and a Queen then she is a real princess! He never saw this coming.

He thought he heard the FBI agent introduce the other guy as an agent with the Swedish government. "Girls", Scott blurted out. "Cindy is the missing princess from Sweden!"

King Ludvig Bergfalk and his wife Queen Amelie were waiting in the SUV. He stared outside in disbelief at the neighborhood he was parked in. That this row of cookie-cutter houses was where his daughter the crown princess of Sweden had become a domesticated house servant.

He decided, however, that he would hold his thoughts and keep his opinions to himself for the time being until he could properly discern everything regarding his daughter and what led her to this life.

At that moment, one of the Swedish agents opened the car door for them and said, "The Royal Highness is ready to see your Majesties."

They walked up to the front door of the house…

Chapter 23

As soon as the royal couple entered the residence, Queen Amelie saw her daughter and instantly started crying very hard. Princess Charlotta also started crying very hard. Agent Wilbrink quickly grabbed Agent Boyd's arm and said, "We must leave outside at once".

Agent Boyd was shocked after Wilbrink grabbed her and so abruptly stating they had to leave in this great urgency to go outside. He saw the annoyance in Agent Boyd's eyes, and tersely stated, "We must not be present when Royal's are having a private family moment. We will not be needed inside the residence for now."

There are certain protocols the American's were just not used too. Agent Boyd got her first lesson in Royal protocol.

Amelie hugged her daughter and sobbed for a long moment. The king also teared up and hugged his daughter when Amelie stepped aside. Charlotta motioned for them to sit down on the living room couch. Charlotta removed her eyeglasses because she no longer needed to keep up her disguise.

They each sat together on the couch with Amelie holding on to her daughter's hand very tightly and refused to let go. Speaking in French, the queen said, "I love you so much, I missed you so much. My life would have been over if something would have happened to you. I don't understand what happened, or why you came here, but I sense there is some powerful force in the universe involved."

Charlotta could not believe her eyes and ears, but the tight squeeze of her mother's hand in her hand reminded her that her mother loves her. Charlotta never expected to see this type of emotion and feeling from her own parents.
She started to cry.

Her mother answered, "We came for you, child. You are our daughter, and I couldn't stand knowing that you were half a world away from us. I love you, and I missed you too much."

The king added, "I am so sorry this whole thing happened, that you would go away from us. I was so afraid for your safety the whole time. I worried every day and couldn't sleep at night. I also worried about your struggles too. I knew it must be hard to come to a different country with a very different culture and try to adjust your life. But mostly I was sad for my own failures. Because we could have been better parents to you, to show you all the attention and love you should have had from us. For that, I am so sorry."

Charlotta started crying again, "I left for selfish reasons there is no doubt. I will accept full responsibility for my decision. I missed you both so much. I never realized how much my own family meant to me until I came here. However, God brought me here for another purpose. Something I cannot fully tell you in words, but you will soon see with your own eyes what has happened."

Amelie answered, "We have been fully briefed and read all of the US government reports in thorough detail about your life here in America with Scott Mann. We can see there have been some wonderful things happening between you both. He is quite an amazing young man is he not?"

"You mean they have been following us all along?" Yes, ever since you went to the Mexican Consulate, the FBI followed you. We received all of the reports and also all of the reports from the children services. We saw a video of you playing piano in church. You have done so many things here in this country."

The king humbly interjected, "Charlotta, we are very proud of you. It seemed you have helped everyone you ever met here. You have become the ideal example of a true royal servant."

"Mother, Father, there is something else. I need you to meet this family. They are the most amazing people I have ever come to know. To come to love."

Charlotta walked out to the back yard to bring Scott and the children to introduce them to her parents.

The King and Queen looked around inside the living room and admired how immaculate the house had been kept clean. The queen showed her husband a photograph in the living room. Look, Ludvig, this must be the boy's parents. Look how handsome his father is in his police uniform. And his mother is so regal and beautiful."

The king looked at the picture and admired the portrait but kept his silence. She then commented, "I think I feel a very loving atmosphere inside this house. However, I think we're going to be waiting for a while. Our daughter may have some explaining to do with the family of this house."

"I am in no hurry, my love. I am so happy to see our daughter and see her healthy. I believe this is a time she needs us both as her parents and not as a King. I have all the time in the world."

The girls were both shocked and weren't sure what was happening. Scott reassured them again as they played on the swing set in the back yard that Cindy was meeting with her parents and needed some alone time.

Scott meditated as he pushed the girls in their swings, thinking about the fear he saw on Cindy's face. This is a potential crisis for his family. If only he had time to figure this out. Could this new piece of information even take Cindy away from him? Scott decided he would try to think fast and not give up without trying.

Charlotta walked outside to the back yard and started to panic. "Scott, please forgive me. I left my home and came here to get away from my life from my family. But I know that God brought me here to you."

Scott could see the fear in her eyes and interrupted her, smiling as to reassure her. "Cindy so you're a princess?"

Cindy sobbed slightly and said, "I'm so embarrassed, I'm the Crown Princess Charlotta. Yes, in fact, I'm next in line for the throne of Sweden."

"I have to admit", Scott answered smiling, "You were always my princess."

Annabelle interrupted, "You're my princess too!" Cindy looked at Annabelle with the most love in her heart and hugged her. "You're such a sweetheart. I can't say how much I love you two. You guys are my family. I don't know what to do now."

Scott reached over and held Cindy by the hand, "To start let's go meet your parents Cindy. Can I still call you Cindy?" He asked. Charlotta laughed through her sobbing and said yes please do.

She then explained a simple protocol. "Before you can meet my parents there are some rules. I'm truly embarrassed and ashamed now to say, but it's important that we follow these rules."

Scott interrupted Charlotta again, "Cindy, listen when you first came to us. We were not a normal family. There were very unusual circumstances along with a lot of emotional baggage. There was a tremendous amount of grief in this house. I guess you could say it required you to relate to us very differently than with other people, yet you didn't hesitate. You embraced us and brought all of your love and compassion into our home. I will never forget that. Cindy, your other family's rules are nothing for us to embrace. What do we need to do, were in, right girls?" "Yay", They answered in unison.

Cindy showed the girls how to curtsey. "Whenever you publicly meet my parents or even me, you need to curtsey. I recommend you do this tonight in our home for the first time just because it shows respect and proper protocol. But in private they are just like regular grandparents."

"Scott you just need to stand at attention and bow your head. Don't reach out to shake their hands or touch my parents unless they initiate the physical contact. You cannot turn your back on them. Oh, and You have to walk behind me" (Charlotta grimaced as she said that part).

Scott looked at her lovingly, "Cindy this isn't new, my mom always taught me that a gentleman never walks in front of a lady anyways."

Cindy couldn't believe how kind Scott was being. He was so understanding. She wondered what he must be thinking. She knew he loved her but was terribly afraid he would turn away at any moment. That, the sheer magnitude of who she is and who her parents are must be incredibly intimidating for him.
Any young man would turn and run right? Cindy worried and thought that her worst nightmare was about to come true. Scott would be out of her life forever.

Scott said, "I need to change Naomi before we go in go ahead and introduce Annabelle and Maryanne."

Charlotta then said, "Ok girls first, are you guys ready to meet a real king and a real queen?" Annabelle and Maryanne then walked behind Charlotta and followed her to the living room.

Scott quietly made his way upstairs to change Naomi, while the girls were meeting with Cindy's parents. He tried to grasp the fullness of what he is facing here. If Cindy is a princess, she cannot just continue on as she has been here. Everything changes now.

What if her parents demand that she return to her country today? Scott panicked briefly, at the thought of losing yet another person he so deeply loved. Yes, he thought, he admitted to himself he loves her. He wished he wouldn't have been so scared before and told her how he felt. But now these new circumstances were a possible threat that might take her away. He couldn't stand to lose another person from his life. After losing his mom, his dad, and even Julie. But how could he lose Cindy? Cindy, it seems, has become the most important person to him he has ever had in his whole life. Flashbacks of riding bikes with her in the park. Being with her in the evenings and just talking. Having someone to call during the day, every day just to talk about the day's events. Memories of having breakfast with her in the mornings flooded his mind. He loved sitting across the table from her staring into her deep blue eyes and seeing how she adored him back in return.

"Yes! That's it she loves me too! I know she does.", Scott thought to himself. Scott knew what needed to be done and he was ready.

Cindy entered the living room with her parents. "Papa, Mama, this is Annabelle and Maryanne". Both girls entered the room and curtsied. Ludvig and Amelie saw the two most beautiful identical twin girls enter the room humbly and graciously. It was obvious they had been raised with love. Amelie almost cried when she saw the girls.

She spoke in French with Charlotta interpreting for her. "You two are the most precious and beautiful little ones ever".

Turning to Charlotta, she asked, "How do you tell them apart?"

Charlotta answered, "I don't know, after living here for a while you realize everyone is unique and has unique feelings, fears, and joys, different ambitions, a different sense of humor, even children. I could tell them apart blindfolded, just by hearing them talk."

Ludvig looked at his daughter with amazement. She seemed so materialistic before coming to America. The typical young person, only out for fun and excitement, and void of responsibility.

Here now his daughter had bonded to these children so much that she knows them by their character attributes alone and not by their appearance. He realized that he still needs to suppress his thoughts about Scott at the moment. There is something quite different about these people that have completely changed their daughter and transformed her into a woman of character, but he's not able to put his finger on anything yet.

Moments later, Scott entered the room carrying Naomi. "Pappa, Mamma, this is Scott and Naomi." Scott bowed his head and the King quickly walked over to Scott and shook his hand. He introduced himself and thanked Scott for taking care of his daughter and providing a safe and good home for her while she was in this land. The queen smiled at Scott and smiled bigger at Charlotta, almost a sense of approval.

Amelie then surprised everyone and walked over to Scott and kissed him on the checks. She spoke in broken English, "It is good to meet you". Charlotta gasped, it wasn't that the queen was so affectionate right up front with a complete stranger, but the princess had never seen her mother speak English. She knew her mother had some issues with some American soldiers when she was in college and vowed not to never speak English again, but her parents never spoke of what happened.

The king addressed Scott, "We are honored to actually sit in your home. Scott, I have read so much about you and your family. I feel like I know you."

Scott thinking quickly, handed Naomi over to Charlotta, and politely asked the King, "Sir, with respect, may I please speak with you in private. This is a matter of extreme importance?"

The manner of his request shocked everyone in the room, Ludvig answered, "Son we just arrived let's visit awhile..."

Scott interrupted to Charlotta's horror, "Sir I assure you this is a matter of extreme importance, I cannot yield."

Ludvig smiled, thinking to himself, this is where Scott will make his mistake to provide the opportunity for him to begin the process to remove the princess from this environment. There was just too much controversy with Scott Mann and these children.

This wasn't the normal way a Crown Princess was to meet her new Prince. He was uncomfortable after reading all of the reports from America in how close his daughter was becoming with this boy. But at the same time, he did not want to hurt Charlotta either.

He wanted to build new trust with her and repair the father-daughter relationship that was broken enough that she left her own family and country. He needed to be careful too, not to hurt the boy. This boy was very looked up too in this country for the heroic way he protected his own family.

Ludvig thought yes this is a good opportunity. If he is a hasty and immature lad, this might prove an opportunity to gather the Princess and go home in peace.

"Yes, son. Where shall we go." Scott escorted the king into the den and closed the door. Charlotta stared in disbelief about what just happened. Amelie motioned for them to have a seat on the couch. Amelie didn't seem to worry at all or was surprised about what just happened. Charlotta sat down with the two girls sitting next to her, one on each side exhibiting a sort of shyness. Annabelle cuddled into Charlotta's shoulder. Charlotta, still holding Naomi whispered baby talk to her in order to keep her pacified and to distract herself from the fear of what just happened.

Amelie looking at her daughter with these three children smiled and commented again, “These children are so beautiful, but how do you do it, Charlotta, how do you manage to care for three small children all day long?”

Before she could answer, Maryanne leaned over into Charlotta and whispered something into her ear.

Amelie looked curious and asked, “What did she say?”

“Maryanne wanted to know if she could learn the ‘mommy language (French)’ so she can tell you directly how pretty you are.”

Naomi then tried to wiggle out of Charlotta’s lap and giggled, “Mama mama mama”. Amelie teared up instantly and looked so lovingly at the girls on the couch with her daughter.

Charlotta started to cry instantly. “These are my babies now, I don’t know what to do?”

Amelie answered, “Oh my sweet baby girl, they are yours, aren’t they? I see that God brought you here. I could see that months ago after reading all the reports. Your father, on the other hand, is doubting.”

“He’s doubting what mama?”, Charlotta asked.

“Doubting that you two are in love. Doubting that the universe brought you here to meet Scott. Doubting that Scott was meant for you. As your mother, I could see these things clearly. However, I could see that Scott is also, like a typical boy, slow in knowing and sharing his true feelings. As a woman, I knew the time was right, I knew that you needed immediate help. I knew that our coming here would force Scott to do something. I just didn’t know it would be so quick.”

“Do what mother?”

“Just wait. He’s doing it right now with your father. Soon you will see.”

Chapter 24

Scott invited King Ludvig Bergfalk of Sweden to have a seat in his father's den. Scott sat behind the desk.

"Sir", Scott began, "Please forgive my haste, however, I can foresee that haste is quite necessary now due to the recent events. Sir, I understand a little about certain protocols for European royalty. If I am correct, I believe no-one in the royal family may wed unless permission is granted by the ruling monarch. Sir, I did not know who your daughter was or her position, wealth or title when she came into our family. I did not know her true identity until this very day. Although she has always been a Princess to me. She came at a moment of extreme crisis for all of us and gave of herself. So much she won all of our hearts. More importantly, I have fallen deeply in love with her. I cannot bear to be without her, nor can I bear to think of my sisters being without her. I already consider Princess Charlotta part of my family. Sir, I am completely in love with your daughter and I believe she is equally in love with me. I believe I can support her and not be a distraction in her role as the Princess. Yes, I believe I will add to her in her duties in the future. I will never leave her side, nor will I ever fail to protect and honor her. From the day she came into my house to this very day, I have honored, provided for, and protected your daughter. I believe I have proven I would make an outstanding and honorable husband. This matter is urgent due to the nature of your arrival in my country. I foresee her departure soon and return to Sweden to resume her responsibilities as the crown princess."

The king concentrated on Scott's words. It is hard now for him to disrespect such a request on a whim. No, King Ludvig knew he needed to think this through first.

One thing for sure was that Ludvig Bergfalk was a man of patience and prudence. He didn't know much about this young man at all. The king meditated thinking to himself for a second, "Wait, I do know a lot about him. I have been reading about him regularly for months with all the reports coming in". They have conducted extensive background checks on him and his family. Everyone they have interviewed attests to this young man's character. The king stared directly into Scott's eyes as he pondered further. His own local government trusted him to keep the children. The condition of this house is immaculate. The children are doing so well. There is quite the evidence all around him that he is a fine young man of character. There is much more than meets the eye with this person.

Perhaps he may delay things and look for another way to sidetrack this relationship until everyone can slow down and carefully look at this without so much emotion involved right now.

"Mr. Mann", the king replied, "I am honored by your request. But, do you believe you are ready for the very question you presented me with today? I mean you cannot ask her to marry if you don't have a ring. Do you even have a ring?"

"Yes sir, I do" Scott replied. Scott opened the safe next to his desk. As soon as the large safe door opened the king's attention was quickly diverted to the guns inside. Scott retrieved a ring box from inside the safe.

The king thought, "That tactic failed…"

Scott opened the box and handed it to the king. The king was instantly surprised and did not expect the boy to present him with this amazing ring. Scott explained, "This ring first belonged to my grandmother, and then it was passed on to my mother.

This ring represents generations of love sir. Last week, before you came, before I knew you were coming before I knew Cindy was Princess Charlotta, I took my mothers ring to the jewelers and had two, identical one-carat sapphire stones, added. One stone positioned on each side of the two-carat diamond on the engagement band. Sapphire's to represent her beautiful blue eyes. I also turned in the wedding band for cleaning and polishing. You see I was going to ask her to marry me even before I knew who she was."

The king was impressed with the ring. He was also impressed that the ring was a priceless family heirloom. Scott loved Charlotta enough that he was going to give his own mother's ring to his daughter, the princess.

The king looked into the gun safe again and asked. "Please tell me about your guns. Hunting is a very popular and respected pastime in my country. I myself am a member of the Stockholm gun club and own my own hunting rifles".

Scott began with his grandfather's guns and explained the story about each rifle and how it was passed down to his father, and now to him. The king was especially very impressed with the M1 Garand. He was also impressed with how careful Scott was to present the king with a safe weapon and to gently handle each weapon as if it was priceless. He used a rag applied with light gun oil and wiped the fingerprints and oils from their hands off of each gun before replacing it back into the gun safe.

"Please tell me about your father Scott and your grandfather". Scott retrieved the Law Enforcement Medal of Valor from the safe and explained the story of how his father earned the medal. Scott explained how his Grandfather was also a hero in the war. How his grandfather passed down the family values to his father and how his father had continued to instill those very values and traditions that were from his grandfather.

Scott said his dad had always used every opportunity as a teachable moment for him to become a man. He explained the Mann mantra as a rallying cry to do the right thing, "We're all of us there are."

The king realized this was indeed a special and honorable family that valued good character traits. Scott was an honorable man. He was quite humbled, after seeing and hearing the things Scott shared. He realized that he couldn't stop this wedding, that it would be a sin against heaven if he tried. However, the king worried though that Scott may not be up to the life of someone in the public spotlight. But, he would have to deal with those worries on his own.

"Scott you have my blessing".

"Sir, may I ask her now? I have this special place in the park, it's our favorite place. I would like to take her there, right now. I will not be very long." Scott wanted to immediately ensure he would have a place in Cindy's life.

"OK son", the king teared up as he realized the gravity of the situation now. He is starting to understand that there is something special about the entire totality of events from when the Princess first came to America until now with the circumstances before them all at this moment.

They walked out of the den into the living room. Scott had secretly placed the ring into his pocket before leaving. Amelie, Charlotta and the girls each stood up as they entered the room. Everyone present knew that this was an important moment and no-one knew what was going to be said.

The king spoke, "My dear daughter, please go with this young man. He has somewhere to take you right now".

Charlotta started a high-pitched whimpering cry as she began to understand what is happening.

Scott placed her hand into his hand at that moment and asked her, "Please walk with me to the park to the bridge, to our favorite spot."

Charlotta continued her high-pitched cry and held tightly onto his hand.

Amelie stated in French that she and Ludvig would watch and play with the children.

Scott and Charlotta stepped out onto the front porch. The King spoke briefly with the security personnel on the front porch to inform them of what was happening. Agent Boyd discreetly assigned several agents to follow them into the park at a distance but keep an eye on them.

Princess Charlotta continued crying in a high-pitched tone as she walked with Scott. Agent Lucas Wilbrink overheard her as she walked out of the front yard toward the park and smiled.

Agent Boyd asked Wilbrink if she should offer to help the King and Queen with the children. Wilbrink thanked her but stated, "No this is their family now, they will want to be alone with the children".

It was the perfect afternoon for Scott to propose. It was a warm 70-degree afternoon typical for California at this time of year. Not a single cloud in the sky was present to throw any shade on the events to unfold. They continued to walk through the neighborhood and could hear the sound of children playing on their bicycles and people in their front yards.

Scott meditated on what he was going to say when he proposed. They walked past the gates and into the park and could hear the sound of more children playing in the nearby ball field. Scott still held Cindy's hand as she continued to wept very gently.

He then told her, "Cindy I really like your parents. I think they are wonderful people. Your father is a man of honor and integrity that's for sure. I respect him. Cindy, I also like your mother, there is a special kindness about her, I think the girls see that too."

Cindy nodded and still meditated on the moment, not sure what is about to happen. Scott continued, “You know, I sort of have some things figured out. I am very encouraged. By the way, I like holding your hand.”

Cindy started crying again as they approached the bridge and then she stopped crying very abruptly when they arrived, almost as if she expected something. They stood silently by the handrail overlooking the water. Scott paused for a moment in order for them to listen to the water as it ran underneath the bridge. He released the princess’ hand. She turned to see where he went and saw Scott kneeling on one knee before her. Scott held out his hand with the ring.

“Cindy, I like you so much… I love you. I love you, I love you. I love you more than anything and anyone. I love you so much that I humbly ask If you would marry me. I will always be yours, and always give all that I am for you. We have already been a family, and you are already so much a part of all of our lives. I could never imagine a life now without you. I want to invite you to not only be my wife and best friend but also to be the mother of my sisters. You know they love you to pieces and want only you to be their mom. I promise you, you will always be treated like a princess. But I want you to know. I will leave my homeland for you. I will go anywhere for you. I will support you in any way. I accept all who you are, and all the duties and responsibilities that you will do, because I love you.”

Princess Charlotta stared momentarily in disbelief, and then quickly said in between sobbing, “Yes! Scott, I am so lucky to have you. I love you too. I loved you ever since I first moved in and saw you with your sisters”. She held out her right hand at first, but Scott took her left hand and placed the ring on her ring finger and stood up.

Scott placed his hands into both of Cindy’s hands and gently kissed her. The butterflies in Scott’s stomach were stronger than anything he had ever felt.

She smelled so good it was pure heaven having her this close to him. Scott felt his world in slow motion as they kissed. He could vividly feel her long fine hair against his face as they kissed. Her lips were so soft and so smooth, he couldn't believe she was his. Scott stopped the kiss for a moment and pulled away a few inches to look into her face to check for her approval. Her deep blue eyes were powerfully hypnotic. Scott was lost, but he mouthed the words, "I love you so much".

Cindy smiled back at him and wrapped her arms around him and kissed him much stronger than their first. Scott loved the sweet smell of her breath and the taste of her mouth as they kissed again.

Charlotta couldn't believe her life. How could Scott win her fathers approval to marry her so quickly? It didn't matter. She was fully convinced that she was the lucky one, that she was marrying far beyond her status. Charlotta knew that there was no better man in Europe, no better man anywhere. He was perfect, and he was hers, all hers alone.

Their next kiss lasted much longer. They held each other close and felt the warmth and heartbeats of each other's bodies. Scott then asked, "Do you think your parents are waiting for us? They are alone with our kids..."

Cindy looked at Scott and said, "Our kids?"

"Yes Cindy, I know you love those girls as if they were your own. We're young there is no doubt, but God has given us these little ones to care for and to love. After we marry, would you adopt these three as our own with me?"

"Yes Scott, YES YES YES! Now I really want to go back and tell everyone were engaged Oooooh I can't wait! But this ring, I have seen it before, but it's different."

"It was my mother's ring Cindy. I changed it by adding two sapphires on each side of the diamond to represent your blue eyes. I had this ring done last week, I was still going to ask you to marry me even before your parents came."

Cindy smiled and cried, celebrating this fairy tale moment.

Agent Boyd waited outside with the Swedish agents as they listened to the surveillance team on the radio. “They are at the bridge….”. “The male subject is on one knee….” “The female said yes…” “They’re kissing….” “Ok”, Boyd interrupted, “Stop all radio traffic unless it’s necessary.” She turned and saw each of the Swedish agents almost dancing in the front yard with glee.

Boyd seemed surprised why they were so ecstatically happy. After all, it’s just a young couple getting engaged? She asked Wilbrink, “Why is this such a big deal to you?”

“You don’t understand Agent Boyd”, Wilbrink answered. “Your country is a democracy, we are a monarchy. Our very same royal family has ruled over our country for hundreds of years. Your president is a citizen of your country who becomes elected to lead for four years, and then he becomes a citizen again. Our ruling monarch is not just a citizen of Sweden, our monarch is Sweden. Princess Charlotta will become the head of state for her entire life. Her personality will shape the general direction of our entire nation. Her life will be our example. Her life will also be the showpiece to the world of who we are as a people. When there is a good monarch on the throne a person of character he/she leads our nation forward in a good manner. Everyone follows this example. We rejoice today because the Princess will be marrying very well. Sweden will be doing well indeed!”

Agent Boyd then immediately called the US State Department to inform her supervisor of the news, and the recent good turn of events.

Chapter 25

Scott and Charlotta returned to the residence. Each of the Swedish security team bowed their heads as they walked past them in the front yard. Wilbrink stated, "Congratulations your royal highness!"

Princess Charlotta replied, "Thank you, Lucas, I will tell you all about it later."

Scott asked Cindy, "How did they know about us already?"

"Scott, we have eyes on us, everywhere, apparently it's been the FBI for some time now."

"Ooooh, he answered, I would have never guessed. Do you know who watched?"

"I guess your government knew about me for a while Scott. They assigned people to follow us to make sure I was ok. Kind of like how Amanda and Sgt. Weathers checked up on you and your family all the time. They were making sure you were ok."

They opened the front door of the residence with everyone standing in the entranceway.

"Mama mama mama" Charlotta cried out instantly, "He proposed!" She held out her left hand to show off the ring. Both women started crying.

Scott leaned down to Annabelle and Maryanne, "Cindy and I are getting married, we're going to be a real family and she wants to be your mom!" Both girls started dancing in the hallway much to the joy of the king and the queen.

Amelie turned to Ludvig, "Darling look, this is why our daughter stayed here so long."

"I see Amelie, I see, I want to stay too."

Charlotta ran to her bedroom and retrieved the photograph of Scott's parents while everyone returned to the living room. She showed the picture to her parents and said, “Look mama this is the ring.” Holding out her hand to Amelie.

Her parents were very impressed with the photograph. “That is a beautiful picture of your parents. They seem like lovely people, and it is a huge honor for Charlotta to be given your mothers ring. It’s a beautiful ring. Please tell us more about the ring and your mother Scott”, Amelie asked in French with Charlotta interpreting.

“That ring was originally my grandmothers. My grandfather picked it out with a single carat diamond in a raised setting on a plain yellow gold band. It was a lot back then for a working man to buy such a ring. But he loved her. My dad told me stories about their romance, and how he was so much in love with her. He adored her every day they were together. My dad said he tried to love my mom and give her the same adoring attention the same way my grandfather did. He figured if it worked for him and they were married for their whole lives, this type of love will last a lifetime in any marriage.

Later, when my grandpa could afford it, he changed and upgraded the diamond to a two-carat stone. When my grandma died, the ring was passed down to my dad. He changed the wedding band and added seven ¼ carat diamond stones on the wedding band before he married my mom”.

Scott showed the family the wedding band that was still inside the box.

“Oh so beautiful”, Amelie stated. You have quite a history of long loves in your family Scott. I’m beginning to understand why you fought so hard to keep your sisters. This is a true family of love.”

Scott continued, "I knew I wanted to marry Cindy for some time." The king and queen smiled at each other when Scott called her Cindy. So, I took my mom's ring to the family jeweler's where my parents always went. I wanted to add more color to the ring because Cindy brought so much joy and peace into our lives at a time when we all needed it the most. I picked out two, one-carat sapphire stones, as beautiful as Cindy's blue eyes and had them added on each side of the single diamond".

"Well done Scott", the king added.

Amelie held Charlotta's hand and admired the ring for some time. She also held the photograph of his mother and admired at how loving the couple in the photograph was. Amelie told Charlotta, "I couldn't be happier as a mother."

Moments later, there was a small commotion outside at the front door.

Agent Wilbrink entered the residence to inform the family that a Sergeant Weathers from the police was at the door causing a scene and demanding to see the princess whom he only knew as "Cindy". He was worried she was in some sort of trouble with the FBI.

Scott asked Cindy and her parents if it was ok to let him in and tell him what is happening. He was his father's closest friend.

"Of course," the king said, "We have read about him in our reports. I am very interested to meet this man who has been such a part of your family Scott" Let's just tell him and any others not to inform the media or any other public medium of the Princess' identity until we can schedule a press conference.

Agent Wilbrink escorted Sergeant Weathers inside the residence to the living room and walked back outside. Sergeant Weathers (was on duty and in his full police uniform) walked straight over to Cindy and asked her in a very nervous tone, "Cindy are you ok? What's going on, what can I do to help? Just tell me."

It was obvious he was terrified, “I saw on our CAD (Computer Aided Dispatch) screen that two of our marked units were here assisting the FBI. I contacted the officers and all they could tell me it was something about you, Cindy. I contacted the FBI agent in charge in front of the house, an Agent Boyd, who wouldn’t tell me anything. Well, no one is going to stop me from helping you. I let them know that.”

“John”, Cindy said in a calming tone while placing her hand on his shoulder. “I’m not in trouble. Actually, the FBI assisted my parents to find me. I would like to introduce you to my father and my mother. King Ludvig Bergfalk, of Sweden and Queen Amelie”.

He stared open-mouthed for a second. Then asked, “Then you’re the missing princess?”

“Yes, I am the crown princess of Sweden, Princess Charlotta”.

“Wow”, John gasped, “I knew you were special. But this, wow, I can’t believe it!”

He turned and nervously apologized to the monarchs and said, “Please forgive me, first of all, I’m shocked by the news. Secondly, I am not sure how to properly greet you. However, I am pleased and honored to meet you. Your daughter, Cindy, has touched all of our lives and has become such a huge part of this family and our entire circle of friends.”

The king answered, “It is an honor to meet you as well sir. It is amazing for us to see such a large support system of friends, you and so many others in place helping our daughter, helping this family. I am honored that you would actually barge in on United States federal agents to try to come to the aid of the Princess. Now I am beginning to see more and more, why she loved being here, and how much she must have felt loved and protected and accepted here.”

"John", Scott said, "I have an announcement." The Princess walked over to Scott's side and held out her hand to show the ring. "John, Cindy and I getting married."

Sergeant Weathers teared up, and said, "Congratulations, it's about time. I know your young, but we could all see this coming. Did you know she was a princess?"

"No"

"Wow" Sergeant Weathers answered, "This is the biggest secret ever. Now I have so many questions for both of you. I never saw this coming. We had the official missing person photographs in our briefing room. I mean she was in the system for us to locate her. I never recognized Cindy either. Everyone was looking for her".

The king interrupted, "Sergeant Weathers, it is my pleasure to ask you personally to remove her from the missing person registry in your country, but we need to wait until we can conduct a press conference to announce all the good news."

"It is my honor, sir."

Sergeant Weathers turned and leaning down to the girls. "Hey, little ones how do you feel about Scott and Cindy, oops, I mean the Princess getting married."

Maryanne said, "This is the best day ever! Annabelle in her excitement spoke right over Maryanne, "Ya and she's a real live princess!" Maryanne then yelled out, "We wanted them to be together. I prayed for them. I think they should be a mommy and a daddy."

Scott said, "We'll we have more news everyone. Cindy and I have decided to adopt the girls as soon as we get married." The whole room went silent. Scott continued, "These precious little ones need a real family with a real mom and a real dad. With every diligence and strength in me, I want to make that happen."

Scott turned to the girls. “How do you feel about that, it’s your final decision? Would you like Cindy to become your real mommy and me to become your real dad?”

Annabelle ran over to Cindy and hugged her saying “Yes, I dreamed she would be my mommy.” Maryanne said, “I did too. But she’s not Cindy she’s a princess!”

Cindy cried after hearing the girls express their love for her as a mom, Amelie also started crying. The queen turned to the king saying, “We're going to be instant grandparents.”

“I know,” he said, “I believe this is a special moment today under heaven.”

Sergeant Weathers politely reminded everyone that he was on duty and had to return to work. He promised he would not say anything to anyone until the press release and left the residence.

The king said, we have two problems, “I’m starving we need to go have a celebration dinner, and we need to somehow schedule a press conference at once.”

Cindy immediately said, “No problem, I have just the right people that can work on both of those problems. However, I will need them to come over here in person right now so we can work out the details.”

Cindy couldn’t wait to call her two best friends that she met while living here in California. She really wanted them to meet her family, but most important she was dying to tell them that Scott proposed.

“Father, I have a good friend who works in public relations. Her name is Linda Maxwell. She can help with the media and schedule a press conference. I would also like to call my other good friend, Cheryl Adams. I really would like both of them to come over right now. Cheryl knows all the best night spots and restaurants in the area, she can help us decide on dinner for tonight.”

"Oh", the queen replied, "We will be so glad to meet them. We read about both of them in the reports we received from America."

"Yes Mama, I want you to meet them too. I really like them both, although at first, we didn't get along so much. But when you get to know people, they can surprise you."

Cindy called Linda Maxwell, "Linda its Cindy, I need you to come to my house right now. It's an emergency!"

"Are you alright?", Linda gasped.

"Yes dear", Cindy continued. "I need you right now to drop what you are doing and come to my house, please. This is the best of news, and I have a professional offer for you that will be a life-changing opportunity for you, but you need to come at once!"

"Tell me, tell me."

"I can't over the phone." Cindy stated, "You have to come in person."

"OK, I'm on my way."

"Oh, and I need you to pick up Cheryl too she needs to hear the good news. Do not let her decline your invitation no matter what, she must be present too."

Cindy sent Cheryl a text message to tell her that Linda Maxwell was on the way to her house to pick her up. Cheryl replied, "What for". It's an emergency of good news, you must come with her to our house at once!"

Linda and Cheryl arrived into the neighborhood, both excited about this secret good news, and nervous about such a strange and cryptic request for them to come right now.

"Look, Linda, Cheryl gasped.

There were two police cars in the neighborhood and several dark SUV's parked out front of the Mann residence, along with several men in suits standing near the vehicles and on the front lawn. One of the men, with an accent similar to Cindy's, approached the women as they exited the vehicle. He asked if they were 'Linda and Cheryl', and said he needed to escort them inside the residence.

Both women stared at each other in disbelief. "OK, this is an emergency!", Cheryl stated.

They entered the residence, and Cindy met them at the entranceway, "Thank you, Lucas.", she answered, "We'll be fine from here."

Cindy began, "Ok first of all my parents are here, before we go into the living room to meet them, I need to tell you, I am not Cindy Mason. So much has changed, I have so much to tell you both. First of all (holding out her ring finger), Scott proposed".

All three women screamed, with Cheryl jumping up and down in the hallway. The king and queen smiled and laughed as they listened from the living room. He turned to Amelie, "Our daughter has sure made so many good friends here as she not?"

"Yes Ludvig, she has, I am so proud of her, these are all very good and hard-working people."

"OK", Cheryl gathered her composure, "You said your not Cindy, then who are you? The next thing you're going to tell us if you're some famous movie star or something."

Cindy removed her glasses, "I am, the Crown Princess, Charlotta Bergfalk, of Sweden." My parents, the king, and queen are in the living room right now, I want to introduce you to them. Ooh, and Linda, I have a job offer for you that you will find quite lucrative, I kinda need your help now."

Both women held their hands over their mouths in shock and disbelief. This was stunning information, and neither of them had a chance to process anything. Charlotta took Cheryl by the hand and said, "Come."

They entered the living room and stood frozen with that last piece of information.

Cheryl feeling uncomfortable, but true to her form saw Scott and yelled out, "Congratulations! What a beautiful ring you gave Cindy, Ooops the Princess." She hugged Scott and continued, "We knew it was coming, as much as you two kept eyeing each other and doting over each other at the picnic, it was obvious."

Scott thanked her and added, "Were also going to adopt the girls as our own." Linda and Cheryl both started crying when they heard the announcement.

Linda said, "I don't know how to process all of this. This turn of events is complete life changing spectacular news."

Princess Charlotta then said, "That's where You come in. You work in public relations. My family would like to hire you specifically to manage the media for the duration of our stay here in America for starters. You will need to organize an immediate press conference in a large meeting hall, I know there will be a huge media firestorm with every major media outlet in the US and in Europe needing to be present. Can you handle this Linda?"

Linda still shocked about the first piece of news, and now this, just shook her head slowly yes. "Linda, we would like the press conference first thing, perhaps tomorrow sometime."

The king cleared his throat as a polite way to interrupt. He asked, "Will you please introduce us to your friends."

“Yes papa”, Cindy introduced her friends to the king and the queen. King Bergfalk, graciously thanked Linda for giving good references for the Princess to get her first job. Charlotta and Linda looked surprised.

The king noticed their surprise and confessed, “Ladies, we knew everything about your complete lives here and all of your friends. Yes, right after you went to the Mexican Consulate. Everyone involved with our daughter was investigated. It just comes with the territory. We were warned, however, by the US government, your pastor here, the social workers, and even a biker gang to leave you all alone. But we followed up on you and every aspect of your lives.”

The king turned to the Princess, “You’re my daughter and I was worried, I needed to know you were safe.”

Queen Amelie holding hands with both Annabelle and Maryanne made the announcement in French that she was going upstairs to see the girl’s bedroom.

“Mama”, Charlotta asked, “How are you communicating with the girls?”

Amelie released Annabelle’s hand momentarily and touched Charlotta’s face. “My child, there is a magic that allows a grandmother to speak clearly with her granddaughters.”

Charlotta instantly started crying and hugged her mother. “I love you mama so much. I love you for loving these babies too.” Amelie started crying too, and said, “Of course I do.” She grasps her chest and continued, “Heaven is involved with all of this. I am not a religious person, you know this, but I have never seen anything like this in my life. You were clearly brought here for these babies, there is no doubt in my mind. I cannot deny the hand of God.”

Linda Maxwell and Cheryl looked at each other in amazement. Cheryl stated, “Can you believe Cindy is speaking French?”

Scott replied proudly, "She speaks five languages".

"Lucky you", Linda laughed "She can argue with you five different ways.

Cheryl excused herself in order to find a nice restaurant for the family to have a celebratory dinner. Somewhere the media will not have access.

Amelie walked upstairs with Annabelle and Maryanne still holding their little hands. They walked past the doorway to Scott's room first. Amelie stopped for a moment and looked inside. Maryanne said, "That's Scott and Naomi's room".

She noticed what appeared to be a normal middle-class boy's bedroom, then it struck her hard. There was a crib at the foot of his bed, and a diaper changing table against the wall. The sight picture spoke volumes. This was a sight normally reserved for a child's nursery or a mother's bedroom.

Why else would a crib be next to his own bed? Now she could understand the pain of loss, fear, and grief in this house for the first time. It was one thing to read about the circumstances in a report, but to see this first hand.

This was a bedroom adapted to accommodate a family crisis. It spoke volumes of Scott's love, dedication and sacrifice for his sisters that he did what he needed to do to keep his family together. Amelie was sure there was still a whole lot more to this family yet for them to learn about. She held the girl's hands even tighter now just beginning to realize the pain these little ones endured together along with Scott.

Chapter 26

Amelie returned downstairs to a mini-crisis in progress. Cheryl tried to get the King and his family into an exclusive French restaurant in Sacramento. However, it was fully booked and reservations are made weeks in advance. The King demanded to come there regardless because he feared the media would possibly spot them at a diner-style family restaurant open to the general public. The king has the final say so. The family all loaded up into the SUV's and headed into Sacramento.

Linda Maxwell immediately went home with Cheryl to begin working on the next big several projects. The first order of business was to schedule a meeting with Amanda Peters first thing in the morning.

The royal family entered the restaurant and spoke with the staff in the front foyer. They were very polite but told the newcomers they didn't have a table. They were booked tonight. The king said, "Sir I am the King of Sweden, surely you could make room for the royal family. Imagine the bad press if you turned us down?"

The gentleman said, "Let me go get the manager".

He returned shortly with the manager, who also advised they couldn't turn any of their other customers away. "Your majesty, our clientele are all very distinguished people like yourself. We would face equally bad press if we turned any of them away for someone who did not make a reservation."

At that moment, the manager caught sight of Scott Mann while Naomi started fidgeting in his arms. He politely asked, "Sir, are you, Scott Mann?"

"Yes sir", Scott answered.

"Wow! It's an honor to meet you, Scott. I think we can bring a table out from our storage area and make room for your party. Just wait here for a moment please."

The manager left the foyer. Returning shortly later, he escorted the royal family to the back of the restaurant. The entire staff, including the chef, were standing in a line near the table to meet Scott Mann. "It is an honor to meet you sir", the chef said, "Dinner is complimentary tonight including our special dessert, we will make special just for your sisters", as he leaned over and smiled at Maryanne and Annabelle who giggled in return. "I will be right back with a high chair for your baby sister".

Scott made funny faces at his sisters as they sat down seemingly unaware of what just occurred. Ludvig and Amelie stared at each other open-mouthed.

Charlotta whispered at her father, "You see this is what I have been living with. Scott has been such an encouragement to so many people just like the staff here at this establishment. He is quite the celebrity, isn't he?"

Ludvig whispered back, "It appears the boy has more pull for getting into an exclusive restaurant than a king."

They discussed the plans for the next few days while eating. Moments later, one of the other patrons approached their table.

"Excuse me your majesties, may I have a word with Scott?"

Scott stood up and shook the gentleman's hand, "Sure".

"I am Roger, Martinson", he stated as he handed Scott his business card. (The king stared in shock and disbelief)

"My corporation is in the process of coordinating this year's corporate leadership retreat for all of our top management officials worldwide. I would be honored if you would be our keynote speaker at our conference."

Scott thought about it for a moment, and said, “I would also be honored, especially if I can help anyone going through a crisis. However, I cannot accept any monetary payment. It wouldn’t be right to make money from what I went through with my family.”

Roger answered, “Scott, but we couldn’t just have you speak for free, it just not right in the business world.”

Scott said, “OK I have a compromise, how about if you take the honorarium for my time and donate that amount to the Gold Country Family Services. That would be the honorable and right thing to do.”

“I can’t tell you how pleased I am to meet you, young man. I’ll have my personal secretary call you with the details. Wow! Thank you!”

Ludvig turned to Amelie, “Do you know who that man is, he is one of the richest men on the planet, he owns half the internet”.

Amelie asked, “Do you know this man?”

“No, I have never met him but he is well known in the business world.”

No-one said anything else about the discussion that just occurred. Cindy just smiled, knowing that her family is just starting to get to know how magical Scott really is.

After dinner, the King and Amelie visibly surprised at the surreal events of the day sat together with everyone at the table before leaving. The king said, “OK I am making an announcement. We’re not leaving America for some time.

I am so glad to be back with my daughter, who was lost and is now found". He teared up while speaking. "I love you, Charlotta, I am so proud of what has happened with you since you came to America. I can't believe the person you have become. I want to meet all of your friends, go to your church, go to your school, see all of the places you go during the day. I want to experience your life as you lived here to see what has become so important to you that has shaped and changed you so much. We as parents have often fallen into the trap of running our family like a business and focusing on protocol and not love. I am giving you my time now my daughter, I am very interested in your life. I am so sorry for lost years. I will call the prime minister right away to inform him of our plans."

Charlotta was so shocked she didn't know what to say. "I love you papa more than you could know."

The king and Amelie returned to their hotel room for the night. He meditated on the day's events, and stated, "I am shocked. I am starting to get the picture that I was wrong the whole time about Scott. He is every bit capable of handling public life, and he does it so innocently. He is a very wonderful young man, perfect for our daughter. I am starting to feel that we are the lucky ones to have him. Our daughter definitely chose beyond her social status in that young man."

Amelie answered, "I see the hand of God in all of this, I am getting goosebumps every time something else happens or we meet someone else involved with our daughter."

Amanda Peters received the phone call from Linda Maxwell last night. Linda explained she needed to come over to the Mann residence first thing in the morning for an urgent meeting. Amanda nervously drove into the neighborhood, and the first thing she noticed upon arriving at Scott's house was the three SUV's parked in front of the house with several men standing near the vehicles and others near the front porch.

Amanda wondered what the emergency was about. A gentleman stopped her in the driveway and asked her who she was. Amanda noticed he spoke in a similar accent as Cindy. He politely told Amanda that the family was waiting for her, and he would escort her inside.

Amanda thought herself, “This is it, the cats out of the bag.”

She was escorted inside the residence. Charlotta met her in the entranceway, and thanked Lucas, “Your welcome your royal highness” he stated and walked back out into the front yard.

“Amanda, you knew who I was all along didn’t you?”

“I am so sorry, yes, I found out who you were just after we went to the Mexican Consulate. I saw the story on the news.”

“Why didn’t you tell me you knew?”

“I saw something happening between you and Scott. I was afraid it would mess things up if I changed the dynamic. Besides the FBI approached me at work and told me not to tell you that we knew about you. I was threatened with federal obstruction charges.”

“I heard that you made some serious threats yourself Amanda.”

“I did Cindy, Oooh Princess Charlotta, I was so afraid the government would mess things up too. I couldn’t stand by and see Scott get hurt anymore. I couldn’t take the chance. This family means so much to me, you mean so much to me too.”

Charlotta hugged Amanda and said, “You too”.

“I have good news”. Charlotta stated as she held out her hand showing off the ring.

“Oooohhhh” Amanda started crying. “This is all too much, I can’t believe this. I can’t believe all that has happened these last few months. This is such good news! Such good news.”

Cindy then said, "There is more good news. Please come to the living room, I want to introduce you to my family."

Everyone stood as the two women entered the living room. Amanda noticed Scott was holding Naomi, but Annabelle and Maryanne were sitting on the couch with Queen Amelie, quite happy, laughing and playing with her hair.

Scott then told Amanda, "I'm sure Cindy told you that we're getting married."

"Oooh I know, I know, I am sooooo happy for you both. You both deserve each other. Look at you now, you deserve a Princess!!"

Scott said, "I never knew who she was until her parents arrived at our house. Cindy can keep a mean secret."

"Haha, that's funny. I noticed, you still call her Cindy?"

"That's who I fell in love with, that's the girl I met. She's always going to be 'Cindy' to me."

Cindy laughingly interrupted, "I like it I think it's cute. Besides, it's what I get for taking a false name and identity. I think the universe is paying me back, and I worry I will forever be identified by the name Cindy. I can't complain because the man I love will forever call me by that name."

"Amanda we have another surprise for you", Scott interrupted. "Amanda as soon as we get married, we want to adopt the girls.

"Ooooh my, that is precious", Amanda stated as she started crying again. "Oooh, I can't believe how God has so blessed this family Scott. I could never have dreamed this would be the outcome back on that first very sad day when I met you in the hospital.

The King of Sweden then thanked Amanda for her work with this family, for her role in taking care of his future grandchildren. He stated that she is a true example of how all family services social workers should be. He acknowledged that she was the true hero in this story.

Chapter 27

Linda Maxwell arrived at the residence to inform the family of today's press conference. "You won't believe it", Linda stated. I got the school auditorium at our school free of charge. I told Janel Stillwell that this was a surprise press conference that would also indirectly impact the school and some of the students. When I reassured her that this wasn't anything bad but it was a true fairytale, truly good news. She said it was ok, I also informed her that parents and staff were invited as well. It's set for 3:00 this afternoon. She did seem a little suspicious when I advised her that Annabelle and Maryanne would not be in school today."

The queen then added (with Charlotta translating), "This gives me time to take my daughter and my grandbabies out to get new dresses, shoes, and their hair styled. We're going to have a girl's day out!"

The royal family along with Linda Maxwell, and Scott and the children arrived early at the school to meet with the principal. Scott didn't think it was fair to surprise her publicly about Cindy or the nature of the press conference. Scott had arranged to meet her and some of the school staff in a conference room due to the size of the entourage. It was quite a scene with Cindy and the girls, dressed to the nines, along with the 4-man Swedish security detail walking through the halls of the school. Several of the teachers and staff curiously poked their heads out of classrooms to see the unfolding scene. Janet Stillwell also heard the commotion as several of the office staff ran to the windows to look out at the arriving party wondering what was happening. The news quickly spread to the entire school and several of the parents that something big was about to happen at the school.

Janet walked into the conference room along with Mrs. Bell, the girl's kindergarten teacher. She saw the entourage sitting at the table already and the four security agents who stood nearby. Each of them stood up when they entered the room.

Janet Stillwell didn't know what to think at first so she greeted everyone in the room with a friendly hello.

Scott said, "Mrs. Stillwell, Mrs. Bell, I am going to be very direct with you. I need to introduce you to Cindy's family. Actually, Cindy's real name is Princess Charlotta, she's a real princess. This is her father King Ludvig Bergfalk of Sweden, and her mother queen Amelie."

Both women looked stunned and were too shocked to speak. They couldn't believe how beautiful the Princess was and how regal she looked in her dress.

Mrs. Bell then said, "I knew Cindy was different, her whole bearing and presence was so formal. I knew this wasn't normal for a 21-year old girl in today's age unless they came from a very refined and trained background."

Mrs. Stillwell commented further, "Yes but she was so eager to get involved at the school, Cindy, I meant the Princess, never felt helping out or getting involved was beneath her." She told the king he should be proud of his daughter. She cared about the school and everything she was involved with at the school. Mrs. Stilwell also told the king and queen how the Princess volunteered much of her free time to play piano and help out with the school Christmas play.

Linda Maxwell then thanked the principal for allowing them the use of their auditorium. She apologized for the media attention that will no doubt affect the school after their press conference. Once they understand that the princess had volunteered at this school. Many media outlets will probably seek information from the school staff about the role the princess had at the school.

They waited in the conference room, until the appointed time. It appeared every media outlet, local news, cable news, and internet news and blog sites were present in the auditorium. There was a huge excitement once they were informed that the king of Sweden was giving this press conference.

The whole world was dying to know any new information about the missing princess. There was also a large crowd of parents present in the auditorium. Most of them arrived after seeing the news vans in the parking lot. There was definitely a huge interest to find out what is going on.

Linda Maxwell stayed with the children in the conference room, while everyone else filed out into the auditorium. There was a noticeable gasp in the crowd as many of the parents recognized Cindy and Scott as they walked out to the stage and took a seat at a long table that was set up along with several microphones at each seat at the table. Cindy was dressed differently and did not have her glasses on. The media, as well as many others instantly recognized her as the missing Swedish Princess Charlotta.

The crowd quieted as soon as they took their seats on stage. The king, began in Swedish, while the princess interpreted each sentence for him into English. Many of the parents and school staff stared open-mouthed watching Cindy.

Once the king started speaking it was obvious that he was struggling holding back his emotions. Queen Amelie, breaking royal protocol, was not as successful with her emotions and openly cried while he spoke.

"I am here to announce to the world, that we have been reunited with our daughter, the Crown Princess, Charlotta. The princess left Sweden and came straight to America. At no time was she ever under duress or in any danger. She left on her own accord and became involved in this community here in California. The Princess assisted Mr. Scott Mann with raising his three sisters and volunteered at the children's school as well at a local church. She has become very involved with her community and has made many new friends here. However, the crown princess will not be abdicating her title and will be returning to Sweden with her family. I am also pleased to announce that Princess Charlotta is engaged to be married to Mr. Scott Mann."

At that announcement, the entire crowd erupted in commotion. Many of the reporters began shouting questions to King Ludvig.

Linda Maxwell interrupted and asked everyone to quiet down and they would take a few questions at the end of the press conference.

King Ludvig continued this time speaking English, "I am very proud of our daughter the princess. She has conducted herself in a royal manner, in integrity and honor. I am proud of the young man she has fallen in love with and will marry. There is no finer young man among all the noblemen of Europe."

The king then turned to Charlotta and continued, "We will return to Sweden after some time however, we will be staying indefinitely here in America. The queen and I are very interested in our daughter and her life. We will stay until we get to know all of the new friends she has made here in California, as well as all of her interests. We will not leave until she is ready to return to Sweden, and then we will return as a family, together. The wedding will take place in Stockholm on a date to be announced later".

Charlotta could not believe her ears, her father was making a public statement that she meant something to him. That her life was important to her parents and they were putting their lives on hold for her. This is a dream come true.

Her mind rolled back to the time when she first left Sweden thinking she just wanted to get away and to be her own person. She didn't think that her parents cared so much for her or would even worry that she was gone.

Then all the struggles of adapting to life in America, this new and strange country. The loneliness of living out of a hotel room. She remembered how she felt doing her laundry in the bathroom sink and hanging her undergarments to dry on the shower curtain rod. She remembered being hungry and counting leftover change hoping there was enough to buy a granola bar in the hallway vending machine so she would have something to eat before going to bed. Then the joy she felt when she met this wonderful boy and his sisters. How accepted she felt when they welcomed her into their home and their lives.

She bonded so deeply with them and never thought she could find that same love and bond in her own family. Now her father is declaring to the world that he loves her.

The Princess was jolted to the present with the sound of her father's voice speaking at the Press conference. Linda Maxwell then announced they would take some questions.

The first reporter from a major cable news network stood and asked. "King Ludvig, is it true that the princess was pregnant and came to America just to hide this fact? Did she move in with Scott Mann to assist with the cover-up and make it more believable?"

This particular reporter thought he would stir the pot with an outrageous question and perhaps shock the royal family into admitting something salacious. Not even the tabloids had written any unfounded rumor or accusations this egregious about the Princess.

The parents in the crowd aggressively erupted in a very loud and angry outburst. Many of them even shouting threats at the reporters. It took several minutes for Linda Maxwell to regain control of the crowd.

As soon as they quieted, Janet Stillwell stood up from her seat in the audience. She angrily addressed the reporter, "I am Janet Stillwell the principal of this school. I am not in charge of this press conference, but this is my auditorium I have a right to say what I need to say in it. You will not insult the Princess, Scott Mann or his children. Questions like that are nothing but sensational garbage. What you are seeking to stir up with a question like that? This is also insulting to a good woman who gave up her life bringing little Naomi into this world. You insult Scott Mann who faced endless days of tears with the death of his family and the fear and the stress in taking custody of three babies. You insult the good name of this community that so lovingly stood by this family when they faced this worst nightmare anyone could imagine. The Princess came to us as Cindy Mason. She neither knew who Scott Mann was nor did we know who she was. She innocently came humbly to serve. She sacrificially and lovingly came and served this family helping them through the darkest and worst of times ever imaginable."

At that rebuke, the room became very silent. Linda Maxwell reading the moment, decided to conclude the press conference.

The King then thanked the media and the parents for showing up. He also added, "We are all here today for an innocent and beautiful story. A story of a stranger traveling to your country and being welcomed with care and love by everyone.

The love the Princess earned here is genuine. The very protective nature of her friends here today proves this fact. I am honored by all of the parents and staff of the school here today and thank you all."

Chapter 28

The very next morning, the King and Queen arrived at Scott Mann's house for the beginning of the day's events. There was a huge media presence at the front of the residence. There were several news vans parked in the street with many reporters standing in the front lawn. This is a huge news story being played out on every news outlet in the world. Since the press release was cut so short yesterday, there were still so many unanswered questions that everyone wanted to know. Besides, it's not very often that a real-life princess comes to America and gets engaged to a commoner. Not just a commoner but a young man with three children.

The family met in the living room and discussed how to handle the problem with the media. Cindy told Scott, "This is what I left behind when I left Sweden in the first place. I am so sorry, but now this is even worse than I have ever experienced."

"It's not that bad Cindy", Scott answered. "We don't have anything to worry about. Honestly, Were all here today because of love. Your love for us and our love for you. My love for you. There is no fear in love."

Cindy smiled appreciating his affection in the midst of this crisis. She still worried about what they should do next and if they would be hounded for the entire duration of their stay here in America. Cindy then asked her father what he thought they should do.

No-one noticed that Scott left the room. Scott walked into the garage and grabbed a fold up tent style awning and went into the front yard. He set up the awning to the stares of the reporters. He returned to the garage and brought out several chairs placing then underneath the awning. Scott then went into the garage and filled a large ice chest with ice and several brands of soft drinks and brought it out to the front yard near several of the press vans.

Everyone stared at him wondering what he was doing. Some of the reporters asked him questions in an attempt to get information from him as well as a sound bite.

Scott then stood in their midst and asked everyone to please listen. “I have an announcement to make. Turn off your cameras for one moment, I promise I will give you all everything you want. Each one of you. Now I brought sodas out for everyone since I know it’s a hot day. I’m sure we may be here a while. Is there any way I can compromise with all of you?”

“What do you mean Scott?” One of the reporters asked. Well, I would like my privacy, and I’m sure Cindy would like hers.”

“Scott you still call her Cindy?”, someone else asked.

“Look I promise I will answer all of your questions, I’ll even let you know some of the things we want to do here in California before we leave, mostly boring stuff I promise. We just want some privacy. However, if one of you really needs to know something I’d prefer you call me instead of showing up at any of our events or at my house. I’ll give any of you a personal interview. Actually, I set this tent up because I want to give you all a full interview right now. Let’s get it over with, right? Or, I’ll answer any question by phone if you want something clarified. Is that a fair deal?”

Some of the reporters laughed, they talked amongst themselves for a second. Each of them agreed that they would have an interview/press conference in the tent right now.

The king moved the living room curtain aside when they noticed Scott was gone. He froze and asked, “What is that boy doing? Does he know what he is doing?”

The Princess, answered, “Don’t worry Papa, let's turn on the TV and find out. I think Scott is taking care of everything for us. I have a feeling that he will solve the media problem once and for all.”

They turned on the TV to the sound of "*Breaking News, Interview with Scott Mann*".

The reporters agreed that there would be two interviewers from different media outlets as well as anyone else that wanted could ask any questions at any time during the interview. Many of them knew about the negative publicity they would receive if they insulted Scott Mann again. They all knew about his viral videos earlier, but by now each news station had run several programs about Scott's bio. People wanted to know who the princess was going to marry and who captured her heart.

"Scott, can you tell us from the beginning, about your family."

"My grandfather served in the Marine Corps during the second world war with Carlson's Raider Battalion. He won a silver star medal. He was a hero. He taught my dad that family meant everything. He never told me or my dad where his family was from. We think he was from back east somewhere because he had an accent. He made sure we would always stick together because there were not many of us. My Grandpa Jack was the one who invented our family saying "We're all of us there are".

"My dad was a cop with the Rockville Police Department. He was killed in the line of duty not long ago, during a traffic stop. My dad taught me everything. He was the best man I ever knew. He was so giving and was always there for me to help me figure out life. We worked out together, we hung out. He always encouraged me to do the right thing. He taught me that a man never has to be afraid if he is doing the right thing. He was a hero and won the medal of valor when he stopped a school shooter."

Mom was pregnant when dad died. I believe the sheer pain and loss of his death was a contributing factor in why my mom died. She had serious complications with her pregnancy and died during childbirth. Before she died, she begged me to keep our family together. Mom was my everything. Mom listened to me even when I had stupid things to say. She made me feel that my feelings were important. Whenever I had problems at school or anything. She just listened. She made me feel valued and loved because she was always there for me. When she died, I decided I needed to provide that same love and care to my sisters. They needed to know our parents. The only way they could know our parents is for me to live out the same kind of life they lived as an example before them.

When Naomi was born, I demanded to take full custody of my sisters. I named Naomi to let the state know that this is my family my blood. But it was hard. I didn't know how to be a mom and a dad. I struggled, with everything on top of the sadness and grief we all felt, I was afraid I couldn't go on any longer."

"Then Cindy came along…"

One of the reporters in the crowd interrupted, "Scott why do you still refer to the Princess as Cindy?"

"I don't mean any disrespect to her true name and title. I am honored who she is and that she would love someone like me. Rather, it is out of respect that I will always call her Cindy. You see Cindy is the humble and kind girl who came into my home. She saw all of our pain, she reached out with all of the love she had to nurture all of us. She never grew tired of our grief but was patient. She was so patient and gentle to my little sisters who were so broken. This is the girl I fell in love with. The title and wealth were a secret from me. I was and am still attracted to the person she is, not her position and station in life."

"I want her to always know, forever, that I am in love with her for the person she is. You see the name Cindy represents who she is to me. It is always important to respect your leaders. It is important to respect people in honored positions in life. But, I feel that is much more honorable and respectful to view a person on their capacity to love. 'Cindy' represents someone who has the greatest capacity to love more than anyone I know or have ever known."

The royal family stood in awe as Scott continued to speak. The Princess was overwhelmed and cried when she heard Scott publicly declare to the whole world how much he loves her. Moments later, she disappeared from the room.

Queen Amelie grabbed her husband's arm. "Can you believe it? Have you ever seen something so romantic or chivalrous?"

"No, I have not." answered the king.

They continued to earnestly watch the interview on live TV when suddenly, Princess Charlotta could be seen coming from the garage carrying a folding lawn chair and joined the interview. Each of the reporters stood when she walked over to the tent. No-one shouted questions, but rather respectfully assisted her to place the chair next to Scott.

"Amelie", the king said, "I can't believe these are our children. She was right, Scott can handle the media. I have never seen anything like this. I don't know what to say. Only, we are so lucky."

Chapter 29

The media left shortly later after their interview with Scott. It was an exceptional treat for the Princess to come outside to join them, although they primarily spoke with Scott. It appeared they were content with their time with him. Charlotta assumed they were light and easy on the questions to her due to the harsh treatment they received from the crowd at the last press conference at the school. Perhaps they were nervous, afraid of a possible negative public reaction if they were to malign her in any way.

King Ludvig asked Charlotta if she would show them around and give them a tour of the area. Ludvig wanted to have some time for him and his wife to spend some alone time with their daughter. He wanted to use this as an opportunity to bond with her as her parents and to express an interest in what she has accomplished here in America.

She excitedly made arrangements with Scott to watch the kids while she borrowed the truck. She wanted to show them the area and things she has done when she stayed here as Cindy.

The king and queen were very shocked when she told them she was giving them a tour in Scott's truck. The King was exceptionally surprised when they climbed up into the vehicle, as it was a lifted truck and they had never been in such a vehicle. He asked, "Are you sure you know how to drive this monstrosity?"

"Yes papa", she answered.

They left with the four Swedish agents following in one of the governments issued SUV's. They entered the freeway heading East to the small historical gold mining town of Auburn nearby.

At one point, the security vehicle pulled alongside Scott's truck. One of the Swedish agents snapped a picture of the entire royal family driving in the 4WD truck. The agents were all laughing and smiling as they slowed back down and dropped in behind the truck to follow. This appeared to be a surreal novelty to them. Later, the royal family jovially asked to see the photograph of the crown princess driving the king and queen around in this huge truck. They all asked for copies of the photo and said they didn't mind if he posted it on his social media page thinking it was in good fun and harmless. Little did they know that the royal family was becoming quite the media darlings while they were here in America.

The picture went viral.

Amelie was surprised that her daughter became so involved in the local community and developed a life for herself, or rather leisure activities to unwind by herself outside of the family. She had her favorite shopping areas, coffee shops, and hangouts. She also showed them the hotels she originally stayed in and other local points of interest. The king and queen both admitted that disappearing into the American middle class did seem quite appealing. Charlotta also told them about all of the serious struggles and hardships she endured before she met Scott.

There is always a price to pay for any cozy life she thought to herself.

The following morning the king and queen took the three children shopping in Sacramento in order to free up the Princess while Scott was at work.

She had a scheduled interview at Scott's residence with a leading European tabloid based in Germany. The reporter, Sophia Richter, was well known for writing not so favorable articles against all the European royalty.

She felt the monarchy's today are obsolete. That they were spoiled and entitled people that didn't deserve any public attention or respect. She was going to ask Princess Charlotta the hard questions. Charlotta knew she was going to have a hard interview, but she remembered Scott assuring her and telling her to be honest to be herself.

Charlotta was home alone, besides some security personnel outside, when Sophia Richter and her photographer arrived. Charlotta invited them inside the living room to begin the interview.

"Your Royal Highness, let me ask you. Did you know Scott Mann, or have you heard about Scott Mann before coming to America?"

"No, Sophia, I have never met him until I came here. I didn't know who he was until the first day he interviewed me for the job. I also wanted to know more about him before working for him. So, I searched his name on the internet and watched the videos."

"Then why did you come to America?"

"I was selfish honestly. I felt sorry for myself because I wasn't happy with my family at the time. I felt they we were always too formal. I wanted to be free, a real person. I just graduated from college, and I wanted nothing else but to have fun, to break the constraints of the protocol so to speak. My original goal was just to go to LA and live the party lifestyle."

"Ok, so what happened, why did you end up here?"

"I ran out of money. Most young people fail to plan when they leave home for the first time. They don't realize how expensive life could be. Neither did I."

"Is that why you started working in childcare?"

"Yes, this is a difficult profession. It doesn't pay enough, and I realized I needed to find a job with a live-in position that provided room and board."

"Why didn't you just go home at that point?"

"I was afraid, I was ashamed. But there was something else in my spirit that said stay. I felt and believed I was meant to be here for something else. Something bigger."

"So, you met Scott and fell in love?"

"There is so much more to that question. This family was in such a crisis when I came to them. But they still loved each other so deeply even in so much pain. Then there are the children, they are so special. This family has this special bond between them. This bond started two generations ago. They even developed a family mantra, "We're all of us there are", that seemed to cement them closer together. This is what changed me. I would never change the fact that I left Sweden, even if I had to do it all over again."

"Princess, let me ask you is it possible, after you arrived in America that when you originally found out you were running out of money, and as you said were embarrassed. You came to this family and realized they were an opportunity, a way out for you to save face with your family and with your country?"

Charlotta became very upset at that last question but knew she should not answer in anger. "No that's not true. My life here is evidence of the contrary. With that said, I need to conclude this interview."

Sophia smiled and thanked the princess she confidently knew she had the article she wanted to print. Charlotta was no different than any other royal. She made a bad life choice and tried to make the best of a bad circumstance.

The reporters got up to leave, but Charlotta noticed the photographer couldn't stop yawning during the interview. They were jet lagged from their flight over from Europe.

Charlotta asked. "Have you had anything to eat since you arrived?"

"No, we haven't", the photographer volunteered. Sophia interrupted, "But we'll get something after we get back to the hotel. We have a flight out the first thing in the morning."

Charlotta insisted, "You must come into the kitchen. I will make you some lunch. I cannot send you away hungry."

"That's ok", Sophia started to say, but Charlotta cut her off.

"No, the woman of this house would never allow a guest to come here and leave hungry. I must keep the tradition in order to honor this woman."

Sophia smiled and said, "Yes then we would love to have lunch." Thinking she could catch another embarrassing moment for the royal princess. After all, no-one ever heard of a princess serving someone lunch.

Charlotta let them into the kitchen and made them each a chicken sandwich from leftover baked chicken. She also provided fresh fruit for them and iced tea to drink.

After they finished their meal the photographer accidentally spilled his tea on the table. "I am so sorry", He stated.

Charlotta immediately retrieved a kitchen towel to clean the mess. Sophia then spotted the engagement ring on her wedding finger. "Is that your ring? It's so beautiful. Can we take a picture everyone will want to see your engagement ring?"

Charlotta held out her hand to show off the ring for the photograph. Sophia looked carefully at the ring and said, "May I, your highness?" She wanted to position her hand in the light for the best picture. As she held the princesses hand she stared at the ring, and at her hand. She instantly noticed her fingers were swollen and red around the knuckles, chapped and callouses on her fingertips. Her fingernails were trimmed down to the fingertips.

Sophia's eyes filled with tears. She recognized those hands. Those were her mother's hands, those are also her own hands as she has three small children of her own. Those hands are special loving hands made from changing diapers all day long, washing your hands constantly, doing the dishes, cooking, laundry in and out of the water all day in a dry environment. Those are the hands of a woman caring for those she loves. The evidence is indisputable. Charlotta loves this family and her red, chapped, and swollen knuckles prove it.

She turned to the princess and said, "I am so sorry for being so rude and curt. You have truly given your life to these people. There must be a lot of love in this house. I do not doubt that he loves you, and you love him. You love the children too. Please tell me the story about the ring. I didn't see it on your hand. I was looking on your right hand when I first came into the house."

"He's an American, they put rings on the left hand here. This is the hand that he put my ring on me, on this hand, it will forever stay." Charlotta also told her all about the story of the ring and how it was passed down to her from Scott's mother and grandmother."

Sophia was so humbled by this amazing story of love. Scott gave the most precious thing belonging to both his mother and grandmother to Charlotta. The Princess has found true love.

The following day the story hit the presses. The picture of the princess' hand with the engagement ring was on the front cover. Titled "A Royal Love Story". Every woman in Europe that saw the article could now identify with Charlotta.

She is no different than regular people in society. Charlotta does not slack in caring for those she loves. She is not a pampered rich girl living this secret elitist party life that some people would assume all royals enjoy.

She truly lived as a mom taking care of the basic needs of three children and a young man. The magazine sold out. Everyone couldn't get enough news of the life the Princess lived in America. She is normal like everyone else. She was proud of being normal and thrived in this lifestyle. Europeans were equally proud of Charlotta to represent what it means to be a real mom regardless of your status.

~~~~~~~

King Ludvig answered the phone in his hotel room that night. "Yes, Prime Minister."

"Your Royal Majesty, whatever you and your family are doing in America is amazing. Everything all over the news and every TV show all day long are about the Princess. Every aspect of her life and her story is constantly being talked about on every talk show and news program. Every Swedish person is transfixed on the Crown Princess. There has never been so much pride in our country and in our royal family. Take your time in America Your Majesty This is a time of tremendous national pride."

"Yes, Prime minister, there still are several events we need to go to and people that I still need to meet. I have also been told the President of the United States will be hosting the royal family at a State Dinner in Washington. It is also very important for me to meet all of the people Princess Charlotta had contact with. I still need to meet her friends, and to thank them for their kindness as well. It is quite amazing here for us too."
~~~~~~~

"There is no doubt this is an amazing story. To be honest with you I am watching all of the news programs myself. I can't believe that young man Scott walked out in his yard and set up a tent for them. Who heard of such a thing? But, he handled the media by himself. I must say he is quite an amazing man to listen too."

"Prime minister, the reporters have left us alone ever since that interview. I have never seen anything like it. We are free to go anywhere without paparazzi bothering us."

Chapter 30

Sunday was a big day. Charlotta wanted her parents to meet Pastor Frank. Linda Maxwell had spoken with the church staff earlier to prepare them the royal family would be in attendance and to prepare for a large media presence.

The Royal family arrived an hour early before church to meet alone with Pastor Frank. Charlotta came early to meet with Paige Wilson and to practice music before the service. Scott and the girls would come later, just before the service.

Pastor Frank was in his office when the royal family arrived. He graciously invited them inside. "Good morning your majesties."

King Ludvig instantly shook the pastor's hand and then hugged him warmly (which was completely out of protocol for a reigning monarch, but not for a grateful father).

"Pastor Billings, I am so grateful, I cannot tell you how indebted I am to you. You looked out for my daughter and became her covering the moment she came into your house. I understand fully, the counsel you gave her, protection, even spiritual accountability. I am also to understand that you paid her money for her help with the music band. However, I have also been informed that is not your policy. I guess you wanted to ensure all of her financial needs as well. Sir, my family is making a sizable contribution to this ministry. I know money as never the object for your help, but I believe a grateful man does not come empty-handed."

He looked around the room then turned to his wife, and told her (speaking in French), "This is the office where Charlotta made the last video. Do you see the background area?"

She answered, "I noticed that too. Everyone here has been so helpful to our daughter."

Your majesty, Pastor Frank interjected, "Your daughter, Her Royal Highness, was such a blessing to everyone here. No-one else knew who she was, but she served everyone with love and was a bright presence for all of us every day. We are all going to be heartbroken that she is leaving. But, I think you will be pleasantly surprised this morning. I am told she is playing a song for you both today. Something that she wrote herself."

Pastor Frank escorted the king and queen on a tour of their facilities. They were impressed by the sheer size of the church, and the sanctuary which seated over 3,000 people. This was a large church indeed thought the king as there were more than three services each Sunday morning.

They were shown to their seats as the front two rows were roped off just for their entourage. The media was already filing into the church and setting up cameras in the back of the building. They were escorted to the rear of the church sanctuary but would still have full access to the live video feed from the church service as well.

The king couldn't believe that Charlotta played music before such large crowds every week. Each day of this trip continued to reveal the impressive factor of Charlotta's role here in the new home she created for herself. He beamed with pride.

One of the assistant pastors entered the stage to give the announcements. He didn't say anything about the media or the people sitting in the two front rows. It was no longer a secret who Cindy was. Every news station on cable news as well as the local channels had continuing coverage about the visit of the royal family in Northern California.

The announcer then invited the church body to stand as the members of the worship team walked up onto the stage to lead the church in worship.

The whole crowd stood up when they entered and you could hear several gasps and whispering as Charlotta filed up onto the stage in single file along with the rest of the worship team. There was also noticeable stirring among the entire media delegation in the back of the church. The whole music group led the church in worship including Charlotta at the piano where she played every Sunday with the band for months. The worship group played very professionally as usual.

It was fitting, Charlotta thought, that no-one should take any attention away from God as the people drew near to him. Nothing has changed anyway, Charlotta was playing with the group just the same as she did every Sunday. Charlotta was honored that they did not say anything special about her before they started.

She is still a humble servant just like all the others on the stage with her, giving an offering, to a holy and mightier King than any other king.

After the worship service, Paige made a simple announcement. “As you all know Cindy is not Cindy. She is the Crown Princess of Sweden, Princess Charlotta. Paige cried as she continued. Like all of you, I never knew who she was. But she always gave the impression to me and to all of us in the worship team that there was something special about her, a light. She served with all of us with such humility and always made each of us feel more important than herself. I will tell you, that many of us will be heartbroken to see her go. She is family to all of us here at Victory Church. Now Cindy, I mean the Princess, has written a special song about her family that she wanted to share with all of you this morning.”

The worship team departed the stage leaving Charlotta alone at the piano. She began playing the most beautiful classical style melody, and then sang the first verse and the chorus in Swedish, she sang the second verse in French, but the chorus in Swedish. The crowd was mesmerized as she sang her first solo before them. She sang with the most beautiful voice that she captured everyone’s heart that morning.

The high pitched chorus' in Swedish was the most beautiful thing anyone had heard. Then she sang the entire song in English (although the English version did not rhyme as well when translated):

Dearest father, you are my protector.
You cared for me and taught me how to live right
You were always there for me
Even when I failed you
You never gave up on me
You always made me feel accepted and safe

Dearest mother, you are my comforter.
You never withheld love to me
You taught me how to be a woman
you were always my best friend
You never tired to listen to me when I needed you
You always made me feel loved

(chorus)
You are the king and the queen so royal and majestic
You rule a nation and lead our people
you are my mommy and my daddy

Her mother and father, the king and queen stood, and both cried as she sang. Again, they broke royal protocol, but no-one would judge them this time either. The media would leave them alone, even the media was mesmerized by the beauty and the loving emotion of the song. Several TV stations cut their regular programming to show the church service in its entirety.

The entire audience including many in the media clapped and cheered after Charlotta finished her song. She bowed and walked off the stage straight to her parents and hugged them both and sat down next to them with Scott sitting on the other side of her.

Pastor Frank entered the stage and stood at the podium. "Wow, I didn't expect that. You can see, we were graced with Princess Charlotta every Sunday. She has meant so much to all of us. I can only say to the people of Sweden you are so lucky. I believe God sent her here to all of us. But also, to one family. I want to show you all a video clip from an earlier service not long ago."

The lights darkened slightly as the video started playing on the screens and various monitors inside the church of the baby dedication service so many months ago with Scott and the children. The crowd wowed again when the video showed them as they first walked up onto the stage with Annabelle and Maryanne holding on the back of Scotts belt loop. It was deeply moving still to see the footage. The king and queen also cried when Pastor Frank interviewed each of the children on stage and prayed for the family. They couldn't believe how scared and vulnerable Scott and the children looked. Yet it was impressive how Scott tried to be brave and declared to the whole church how he named Naomi. It also was amazing how prophetic Pastor Franks comments were at the dedication service.

Seeing this video for the first time really struck the king hard at how important it was for Charlotte to come to America when she did. He turned and looked at Scott admiringly for the first time as a father would to a son.

The queen, on the other hand, was in awe at everything she saw. She couldn't believe her daughter played music in a band, and then to play and sing a solo song before the world. She sang to everyone about how much she loves her parents.

She watched the video of Scott declaring to the world that he would take care of his family no matter what. The queen knew how Charlotta was influenced so much and inspired to value her parents so much. The queen also realized how miraculous it was for Charlotta to meet such a young man.

Pastor Frank began his sermon with the book of Ruth. He spoke again of Naomi's struggle after losing her whole family. One of the two surviving relatives in her family still left her. There was just Ruth by her side, her daughter in law Ruth, a foreigner. Naomi is a woman in this story who struggled with grief, she was alone. She had no chance of regaining the family she lost and was doomed to live out her life as a lonely widow.

She was a woman that knew the sounds of many voices and laughter in her home. The years of celebrating holidays with a house full of people of loved ones. Then in just a short time. They are gone, and only the silence in her home now. Yet, there was Ruth, this foreigner, who came into Naomi's family. She brought love and loyalty to this family.

She fought together alongside Naomi against the darkness of grief to grow her family, and soon, she re-married a man named Boaz.

Boaz was the father of Jesse, the father of David. King David. Through this foreign woman, Naomi's family became a family in a line of magnificent royalty. A family with many kings and princes. Eventually, this family line brought us the Messiah.

Pastor Frank continued, "There are too many similarities here today not to believe this is not just a coincidence that the Crown Princess of another nation came here to America to Scott Mann.

She fought together with him to keep his family together, and now they are to become a family. A Forever Family!" As soon as he said those words the audience cheered loudly interrupting the service.

Pastor Frank waiting for the cheering to subside then continued the service and thanked God for bringing Princess Charlotta to bless all of them. He thanked God for the privilege of witnessing first hand the power in the moving hand of God.

Chapter 31

Scott took Monday morning off from work. Ludvig asked Scott to accompany him for his meeting today. The King had Linda Maxwell make the next appointment in advance. Ludvig asked Scott if they could drive together in his truck to spend time alone with him. Two of the Swedish security agents were to follow them in their SUV.

As soon as they climbed up into the cab of the truck, the king asked Scott, how he taught Charlotta to drive his big truck.

Scott answered, “It was nothing really. She already knew how to drive. We practiced in the parking lot at the church and drove around the neighborhood a few times, and she was pretty much ready for her test. The only thing difficult for me was simply when she changed the seat and the mirrors.”

“Why is that wrong son?”

“You see this is my dad’s truck. When I started driving this truck, I noticed the position of the seats and the mirrors were last set by him. My dad sat in this truck and set the seats for himself, and I didn’t want to ever change them. I wanted to remember my dad by sitting in his seat as it was. I felt close to him that way. But she got in and moved them right away.”

“It must have been so hard for you to lose your father, I cannot imagine what you went through.”

“Sir it was hard, but It was then at that moment, that I knew I was going to be ok. Your daughter came into my life and brought so much love and care for all of us. She wanted to learn to drive so she could help us more and we could spend more time as a family together. She came into my life and began to erase the grief that followed me. It was time to change the seats and mirrors of my heart too. I realized on that very day that I could begin to let go of the loss of my parents, and move forward to the joy of a new life.”

“So, in a way”, the king asked, “She was motivated to get this license then?”

“Yes, she was not going to let anything get in her way.”

They followed the GPS directions to the address given to them by Linda Maxwell. King Ludvig did not tell Scott where they were going, just that he needed to say thanks to some special men. Although Scott became increasingly nervous as they entered a very rough neighborhood in West Sacramento.

They arrived at a large building in an industrial neighborhood bordering a residential neighborhood. The first thing Scott noticed that there were hundreds of Harley Davidson motorcycles parked on the street, and dozens more parked inside the parking lot area.

The king asked Scott to park in the parking lot at a designated area. The SUV with the security agents parked on the street and stood by their vehicle. They did not walk inside the compound apparently confident the king's security would be fine.

There were hundreds of bikers standing in a long line in front of the building. The king and Scott exited the truck and were warmly greeted by several men, one of whom was the president of the club, Hank Jones. Scott remembered the chance meeting he had with Hank and his club several months ago in the restaurant that night they paid for his dinner. But he wondered why they were here today.

The Sgt at Arms explained to the king and to Scott a highly embellished story of how Charlotta rescued Hank Jones at a traffic accident and singlehandedly, loaded his motorcycle into her truck, and took him to the doctor against his wishes. She made sure he was treated and brought him back to their club.

Scott listened in awe...

They ended their tour in the Clubhouse office. The king then opened his briefcase and presented a large antique golden carving of a coat of arms. He stated to the men present, "This is my family's coat of arms. This particular piece has been in my family for four hundred years. I am presenting this to Hank Jones and your club in extreme appreciation, simply a gift from a father of his lost little girl.

No-one knew what to say, the king continued, "Sir, I cannot tell you how many tears my wife and I shed over this great fear of harm coming to our daughter. Even after the FBI found her whereabouts in this country. I could still not sleep at night worrying about her safety as she lived in a strange country so far from home. It wasn't until I heard from the FBI, that you sir, made a declaration that no-one would harm her here. If anyone did they would face extreme violent punishment at your hands. I knew at that time that my daughter was finally safe. It's not that I don't trust the FBI to protect her, oh well, let's just say I don't trust the government (everyone laughed). I actually slept in peace for the first time that night since she left my home, our country. This coat of arms represents our family. You, sir, are forever an ally to my family. I will never forget the peace you gave us."

Hank humbly answered the King, "Sir I don't deserve your gift, but thank you this is an honor. I now know why your daughter was so respectful and helpful to me, to us. She was raised to give honor and respect. Interesting, before we knew who, she was, she stood up for me, a complete stranger, and made sure I was ok. But when I realized she was the princess. I knew she wanted to be left alone. I respected that and decided to help her obtain what she wanted, to be left alone. We would make sure she was safe. It was the least we could do for her."

Scott and King Ludvig then spent the rest of the day together. They drove to Scotts martial arts school where he trained with his dad. Scott gave him a tour and introduced him to the instructors. Scott appreciated this time spent with Ludvig today.

The following morning, the royal family had a politically important event planned for the day. They all drove in a caravan to the Mexican consulate in San Francisco. The Mexican government planned a formal reception on the front grounds of the consulate property to honor the Head of State of Sweden. There were a military band and a small Mexican military honor guard. This event was also covered by a large media presence. This was big news today.

Scott and Charlotta and the rest of their entourage stood nearby while the King was formally greeted by the Consul General. Scott was amazed when he saw the king and the Consul General walk in front of the group of soldiers as they stood at attention. They saluted the officer in charge of the soldiers and then walked through the ranks of the honor guard inspecting the soldiers in their sharp dress uniforms. There is so much protocol he was just not used to seeing.

The king and his party were then escorted inside the building. They were to hold a public press conference inside the lobby of the consulate. The king spoke in Spanish during the entirety of their time there as well as the Press Conference. He whispered to Scott, "Yes you will need to learn Spanish as well as Swedish."

Scott said he understood.

He knew that being with the Princess he would now be involved in many future events that he would need to learn all the proper protocols and decorum. Yes, that included learning Spanish and of course Swedish.

The Mexican Consul General (whom the Princess met with earlier), along with the Mexican Ambassador to the United States, the Royal family, and Scott Mann stood near the podium together.

The King of Sweden began his statement, “My daughter, the Crown Princess of Sweden, walked into the doors of your consulate so many months ago. She came as a lost foreign traveler seeking help. The Mexican government showed great hospitality and received her with respect and dignity. They helped her and offered every further assistance possible. For this my country is grateful. I am grateful. To show my gratitude I want to return to your country some of your heritage.”

He motioned to his security men standing nearby they retrieved several cases containing three solid gold statuettes from the Aztec era. They brought the treasures forward placing them on a table near the podium.

The king continued with his speech, “The king of Spain gave these artifacts to my great grandfather as a wedding gift. These items were removed from your country by Spanish explorers long ago. However, I realize that I cannot keep them as they rightfully belong to you. I also want to say that at this time our governments are working together on several projects of economic cooperation between our countries that would benefit us all in the future.” The crowd cheered.

The Mexican Consul General spoke next and explained the manner of Princess Charlotta’s visit several months ago and how she revealed herself to them.

The Mexican Ambassador also spoke briefly and thanked the King for returning the Aztec treasures. He promised they would be brought to a museum in Mexico City.

They each answered several questions and concluded their visit. This was the third time the King saw Scott conduct himself during interviews with the media. He was quite confident by now that he would be able to handle any issues that the pressures of being married to a royal could present.

Chapter 32

After the visit to the Mexican consulate, the king and queen volunteered to stay at home with the children and watch the news coverage on TV about their time in America. It seems the whole world could not get enough of the Royal family and the modern fairytale romance.

Scott and Charlotta took a bike ride through the bark. And stopped at their favorite spot at the wooden bridge. They talked together about the events that happened this week.

"Cindy I can't believe you helped those Bikers and befriended them to the point that they swore a blood oath to keep you safe."

"I know. I saw the bike crash and recognized the injured man as the one who bought our dinner the night you hired me. I was so grateful for the kindness they showed you that night. After looking back at what you went through, I realized that it was the simple kindness of strangers that were sometimes the only lifeboat for you in a sea of sadness. It was all I could think of was to give back the same kindness"

"Did you really say to him, 'Young man I decidedly outrank you'?"

"Yes, I just reacted to his stubbornness."

"Wow, you never cease to amaze me, Cindy."

"I amaze myself sometimes, I never realized how dangerous they really were."

"No Cindy, you amaze me. Ever since I first met you. I had butterflies in my stomach that first time and I still get them. I can't believe you love me."

"No Scott it's the other way around, I can't believe you love me"

They kissed...

The following morning, the family took a short flight to Southern California for their next visit. Linda Maxwell scheduled an interview for Scott and the Princess on the "Nighttime Talk", a famous late-night TV comedy variety show. The Princess was finally going to get a chance to go to Hollywood. The King and Queen, and the girls came along so they could sit in the studio audience and watch. After all, this is Hollywood now. No-one wants to miss out on possibly meeting a celebrity. They thought it odd that Princess Charlotta was requested to come to the studio a couple of hours before everyone else. She told her family she was supposed to pre-record something at the studio, but it was a surprise.

"Good evening America, this is Davey Talon, on your favorite nighttime talk show. Our special guests tonight will be her Royal Highness, Princess Charlotta Bergfalk of Sweden, and of course California's favorite son, Scott Mann." The audience cheered loudly and exuberantly.

After the monologue, Davey Talon invited his guests to come out. Charlotta entered the stage first followed by Scott Mann with loud cheering from the studio audience. Davey Talon stood and bowed as she walked past his desk to sit down.

"Welcome. Welcome, your Highness!, and to you too, Scott Mann, wow I can't believe we have both of you on our show tonight."

"Thank you, Mr. Talon", The princess answered.

Davey Talon continued, "We are also privileged to have in our studio audience, the Majesties King Ludvig Bergfalk of Sweden and Queen Amelie along with The Mann children".

The camera panned to the audience as they stood in the front row. Everyone cheered loudly.

"Now I heard your alter ego, when you came to America was, 'Cindy Mason'. What do I call you, Cindy or Charlotta?"

Looking very stern and authoritative she answered, "You can call me 'Your Royal Highness.'", The entire audience erupted in laughter as Davey seemed embarrassed.

"Now please tell me, Your Royal Highness, how was it when you first came to America? Was it very hard to adjust? I'm sure it must have been a huge shock not only coming from Europe to a different country but also coming from a different social class to find yourself immersed in our American middle class."

"The adjustment was not as hard as you would think. Everyone I met welcomed me with huge open hearts and kindness."

"Well Your Royal Highness, I heard you also had a part to play in that. It seems you helped and touched so many people's lives here in California."

"I decided, I could fit in easier and disappear into American society if I served and gave of myself to others. It was very fulfilling to me, it changed my life. I don't ever want to stop looking at people, no matter who they are, as precious souls more important than who I am. I learned it is better to see how I could serve people rather than seeking to be served."

The audience clapped heartily.

"Now according to some viral pictures, you got your California Driver's license so you could help out with your family's needs. But you're not actually driving around in a little sports car, but rather a big 4WD truck. Look at our screen we have some video footage of you and your California commuter car."

The audience looked at the large monitor screen of a pre-recorded video. Charlotta walked into the parking lot wearing a racing uniform and placed a racing helmet on her head. She walked over to a large Monster Truck titled "Slamdownage". This truck had the largest tires ever recorded on a regular pick-up truck. It was famous across America at many car shows, and truck events. Slamdownage currently holds the record for smashing or driving over the most wrecked cars in a stadium.

The princess was assisted by the owner of the vehicle as they climbed a rope ladder to get into the driver seat. The owner of the truck sat in the passenger seat.

There were cameras inside the cab of the vehicle as well as the parking lot. He instructed the princess at the controls as she gunned the powerful engine of the truck and edged it across the parking lot with the loud rumbled growl of the idling engine toward several junk cars. The cars were staged in the parking lot amidst several traffic cones staged as a sort of mini driving course. She gunned the gas and drove right up on top of, and over the three parked vehicles. Scott, as well as the King and Queen, gasped in surprise while the audience cheered exceedingly loud and long.

Charlotta laughed and said “Surprise” to her parents in the front row. The camera panned to the front row showing the king and queen sitting smiling with the three children.

The show host continued, “Now Princess, you have become America’s darling too. I must say I have never seen anything like it. Most Americans don’t really follow European royalty except for the Brit’s. You're more famous here than anyone in the entire British Royal family. Now, the reason we asked you both on the show tonight was that I do have a special guest and a special surprise for your Royal Highness. I would like to invite Michelle Johnson, Governor of the State of California out.”

The entire crowd cheered very loud and long to greet the governor. There was an excitement to see the first American political official meet Princess Charlotta.

The Governor walked out on stage, and out of respect, curtsied to the Princess as she shook her hand.

The Governor then said, "I too am a huge fan of Your Royal Highness and to both of you. Scott were all so very proud of you. I remember sitting next to you, your mom, and your sisters at your father's funeral. You are a very special young man. You both deserve each other". Scott humbly thanked the Governor.

She continued, "Now I must say, The Royal Princess came to my state as 'Cindy Mason', a regular girl from Minnesota. Yet she wasn't so regular at all. She touched so many lives around her. Cindy Mason became a 'hero of kindness' in her own community of Rockville, not just to Scott and the children, but to her church, their school, neighbors and friends alike. It is my pleasure to announce, that the California State Legislature held a special session recently and unanimously voted her Royal Highness Charlotta Dorothea Katarina Maria Bergfalk as the honorary Queen of California."

She held out a framed certificate showing the declaration and then handed it to Charlotta. The entire crowd cheered and screamed in delight as she was handed the framed certificate.

"Now I would like to also add, as the Governor of California, I am told you fraudulently obtained a California Driver's license in the name of Cindy Mason. I am here to rectify that. I am hereby issuing you the proper license in your correct name. I am told you are the only royal princess in the world holding a valid California Driver's License. You earned it your Royal Highness."

The crowd again cheered in delight.

"I must say, I wish I could keep you here with us forever." The whole crowd cheered and clapped again.

Scott and Charlotta answered many questions from the host Davey Talon along with the Governor of California. This episode of nighttime talk had the highest TV ratings of any TV show daytime or nighttime. The ratings were second only to the Superbowl.

Chapter 33

This was the family's last week in America before they returned to Sweden. Amanda Peters worked secretly with Linda Maxwell for the next big event, some type of recognition award to be presented to Scott.

Amanda and Linda tried to make Scott understand this was something mandatory that he needed to come to. This was not something he had a choice if he wanted to attend or not.

Everyone in the Royal family was highly urged to attend, and they were all required to travel to San Francisco for the award presentation. The annual FCWC (Family and Children Welfare and Care) Conference is held in San Francisco every year for social workers, therapists, pediatricians, district attorneys, and police detectives all relating to CPS. This conference is a five-day event with several keynote speakers. Several classes and workshops also provided for thousands of attendees. On the last day of the event, awards are presented to individuals in each discipline who have impacted the care and welfare of children.

Scott and his siblings, as well as Charlotta and her parents, were ushered into the large auditorium at the convention center, there were several thousand people in the auditorium as well as a large media presence.

Scott wondered what he was in for.

Moments later, Dr. Joan Spencer was invited to come up to the stage. Dr. Spencer began, "This next award is our most prestigious award given at this conference. The Beatrix Lansford Foster Parent of the Year award. This honor is awarded to the Foster parents who have overcome great sacrifices, difficulty, and challenges in the effort to provide a loving, safe, and stable environment for children in order to nurture and prepare them for their forever family. At this time, I would like to invite Amanda Peters up to the Stage to assist in the presentation of this award."

Amanda Peters walked up on the stage next to the podium and was visibly moved.

Dr. Spencer then said, "This years Beatrix Lansford Foster Parent of the Year award goes to Scott Mann."

The entire Crowd stood in a standing ovation and heartily cheered for several minutes. Amanda Peters cried on stage. Princess Charlotta also cried. The king and queen were also both visibly moved.

Scott walked up to receive his award from Dr. Spencer and Amanda Peters. The crowd continued in their standing ovation.

Amanda Peters gave a short introductory speech regarding how she received the Mann case as well as how Scott endured many hardships and challenges and still grew as a caregiver for all three of his children. Amanda cried often during her speech.

Later, Amanda privately told Scott that the entire CPS community across the state kept a close watch on him with great interest. This award was long in the works even before Cindy was revealed as the Crown Princess of Sweden.

Hank Jones, along with millions of other Americans, watched the TV coverage of the Royal Family and their highly publicized activities while they were in America.

Hank asked his Sergeant at Arms, "So they are all leaving California, the day after tomorrow? Now I am led to believe whenever a royal in Europe pulls up stakes and leaves, there is always some sort of military escort. I don't think anyone in our government is going to give any type of escort for this family as they head to the airport. They deserve one I believe. Hey, after all, she also the Queen of California, right?"

The Sergeant at Arms agreed.

"Ok, I want you to call up all of our California Chapters I want everyone here now. Our organization is going to provide the escort whether the government wants us to give one or not. We will provide the sendoff that family deserves. They will get the respect they deserve."

The Sergeant at Arms made numerous phone calls within the hour. He advised Hank Jones." All of our chapters from across the state are sending as many as they can. They are leaving tonight and some head our direction on tomorrow. We should have about 1200 bikes, that's got to be a record."

Hank Jones responded in pride, "We're going to make a statement to the world who we are and who we stand for."

The day came for the royal family to return to Sweden. This would be Scott's first trip outside of America. King Ludvig and Queen Amelie arrived at Scott's house with three SUV's which included their security escorts as well as another SUV with Sandra Boyd and two other FBI agents were in the other vehicle.

Scott and the children loaded their suitcases into the first SUV and the family prepared to leave. Moments later, they all heard an exceedingly loud thunder in the distance it grew louder as it approached their neighborhood. Soon, long dual columns of bikers arrived on Scotts street. Hank Jones was the first rider in the front of the pack. He climbed off his bike and contacted Sandra Boyd along with several members of the Swedish security team. They advised them they were providing the escort for the royal family.

Agent Boyd tried to talk him out of it but after seeing the hundreds of bikes on their street alone (Not counting the sound of hundreds of other bikes reverberated from the other nearby streets in the neighborhood). She realized this was something that was not going to go away.

She quickly contacted her superiors as well as the CHP to provide traffic breaks for the entire parade.

The King walked outside to meet with Hank Jones and shook his hand. "Sir, I see you and your friends are out for a pleasure ride."

"Yes, your majesty. I realized there was no military escort for you or your family. You deserve respect. So, we decided we will be your escort to the airport sir."

The king smiled with respect and appreciation.

Soon, several news helicopters appeared in the sky. Several CHP patrol cars arrived as well. They met with Hank Jones and advised they would provide traffic breaks at all major intersections for the entire parade. It was quite a spectacle, this time it was broadcast worldwide, with over a thousand Harley's escorting the royal family. The entourage was almost a mile long.

The motorcycle entourage escorted them all the way to the Sacramento Airport. Hank Jones saluted goodbye as soon as they exited the Freeway. He led the motorcycles back onto the freeway on-ramp and departed ways with the royal family.

Their plane lifted off for Washington DC for one last important event. The Royal Family was invited to a State Dinner at the White House in their honor.

As the plane started down the runway Cindy held Scott's hand tightly and cried. She told Scott she was sad to leave. She had made so many good friends here. She admitted she was very happy with the life they had in California.

Cindy looked outside of her window as the plane continued to gain altitude over the suburbs of Sacramento. She tried to locate Scott's home and neighborhood. She wanted to see one last time the park she rode their bikes in, their church, and the local grocery stores. She hoped to get one more glimpse of the house and everything else she knew she was going to miss. This had been her home these last months. Cindy, the Crown Princess of Sweden, knew she was forever changed by this experience.

Princess Charlotta meditated the rest of the flight about all the people she met and the things she did. How she made friends with people that didn't know who she was or anything about her wealth and title. She was accepted and befriended by so many good people.

Chapter 34

The Royal Family arrived in Washington for the State Dinner. They met the Swedish Ambassador at the Swedish embassy prior to the dinner.

Scott Mann was awestruck at the pomp and ceremony when the king arrived. The royal family was treated like heroes. The Swedish honor guard provided the proper military and official welcome similar to the event at the Mexican consulate in San Francisco. The Swedish Women's Association Choir also sang for the Royal family immediately following the honor guard ceremony at the embassy.

It seemed that every single embassy employee was outside standing in an organized formation to greet their Monarch's.

After the greeting ceremony, they were all escorted inside a private office to meet alone with the ambassador. Scott noticed immediately that the ambassador was very cold on his initial greeting. He avoided eye contact with Scott and only spoke with members of the Royal family.

As soon as he could, Scott spoke quietly with Charlotta, "Cindy, did you notice that the ambassador would not speak with me. I wonder if he is angry with me for something."

"Scott I wouldn't worry about it, he is a political appointee, you can never figure people out who are career politicians."

"Do you think he doesn't like me because I am an American?"

"No Scott, I wouldn't worry about him. Let's have fun we're going to meet your President pretty soon.

Scott took the girls aside before their night at the state dinner to talk to them about all of the public appearances and to see how they were feeling about all the attention. Annabelle and Maryanne both didn't seem to care about all of the media attention. They knew that Cindy (The girls have both opted to refer to her as "Cindy" as well.) would not be leaving them and that comforted them greatly. They were both so proud that she is a Princess and a leader of a whole country.

The Swedish embassy provided childcare for the children so Scott could attend the State dinner with the Royal family. The ambassador along with a few Swedish actors and musicians along with a few well-known Swedish athletes working in America were also invited to the State dinner.

All eyes were on the Princess as she entered the white house, she was obviously the most beautiful woman in attendance. Even Scott was amazed at her beauty and had never seen her in a formal dinner dress before. The President of the United States was very gracious to the Swedish Royal family he even joked about Princess Charlotta carving off a piece of America by conquering the state of California and becoming the first official monarch of a US territory. It was very moving to see the President of the United States admit she is the true queen of California. He also lamented Sweden was going to take one of the best young men our country ever produced as he looked over at Scott Mann. The president then told Scott that he would be hearing from him soon, Scott wondered what he meant, but didn't think much about it.

The following morning after the widely publicized state dinner, Agent Sandra Boyd sat in her office in Washington. She enjoyed every minute of being back in her familiar surroundings once again. This is the first time in months she was finally back home in Washington. She felt a huge sense of relief that this case is officially over. Her superiors congratulated her on a good job and for carefully and with great finesse navigating through such a hot potato of an assignment.

Sandra sat in her private office when she heard a loud commotion in the main floor outside. Agent Boyd looked out of her small office and saw everyone in their cubicles standing on their feet. Then she saw the SAC (Special Agent in Charge) of the Washington Bureau was escorting Princess Charlotta along with two of her security men straight to her office.

Agent Boyd stood at her feet and curtsied when the Princess entered her office. Everyone else including the Swedish security detail waited outside of the office. The Princess closed the door.

"Special Agent Boyd, I wanted to thank you for your hard work and for looking after me this whole time. I know how carefully you managed each of the people I came into contact with and how sensitive you were to keep my secret."

"It was a joy your highness, this will be a case that I will remember for the rest of my life. I wouldn't trade my experience in doing this and the privilege of getting to know Scott Mann and yourself for nothing."

"Agent Boyd, that is why I am here today. You see we're leaving America this afternoon. But I thought about it and realized I have committed a crime in your country. I obtained a false passport and entered your country. I also obtained false drivers' license in that name. I know this is illegal. I cannot keep these documents. I would like to turn them over to you now."

The Princess then handed the US passport and the California Driver's License in the name of Cindy Mason and laid them on Agent Boyd's desk.

"Agent Boyd, you are a professional and your superiors did well in assigning you to my case. I am honored. Now I need to return to the hotel and prepare for my return to Sweden."

Agent Boyd thanked her as well. After she left, Agent Boyd smiled looked at the passport and license. She realized this was indeed a very valuable souvenir. She had the items framed in a shadow box and hung on her wall in the office.

Agent Boyd laughed to herself, "…And I thought she was going to be the typical spoiled brat. What a class act she was."

The whole royal entourage boarded their plane and lifted off from the airport. Scott Mann looked out the window and thought to himself. "Wow, what a surreal couple of weeks". He wondered how things were going to go for his family in Sweden. Scott knew there was going to be huge public events at first. He hoped however that they could settle down into being a normal family for a while. He also wondered how normal their lives would be with Cindy being the Crown Princess.

Would her public duties interfere with them being a family, or would the Cindy Mason he knew in Rockville be gone forever? He decided that no matter what he would stick by her, and no matter what, with faith on God he would be able to keep his family together.

As soon as the plane lifted off Scott watched the excitement on Cindy's face as she talked with her mother and father about their return to Sweden. They were engrossed in an animated discussion in Swedish and French. Scott knew that if he joined the conversation, they would immediately speak English with him. Nevertheless, Scott still wondered how cultural differences would affect him and his sisters. He hoped he wouldn't feel out of place.

He asked the girls what they thought about going to Sweden. Annabelle said they were going to real fairytale land. Scott had to admit that he too thought of this as a fairytale. He had never been to Europe or traveled anywhere. This was very exciting and adventurous do doubt.

Chapter 35

The parade through Stockholm began as soon as they arrived at the airport. There were over a million people lining the parade route through the city.

Hundreds of soldiers on horseback wearing blue and white uniforms and wearing chrome helmets with white buffalo hair plumes escorted the royal family through the city streets. The sound of hundreds of horse hooves trotting on cobblestone streets could be heard echoing between the buildings. Scott, Charlotta, and the children sat in one carriage. The King and Queen sat in a separate horse-drawn carriage. The two carriages were followed by vehicles containing the security team which consisted of police officers on horseback along with police officers on motorcycles. The huge entourage was quite a spectacle indeed.

Scott and the children were awestruck as they rode through the streets of Stockholm. This was nothing like anything he had seen in California. The architecture of the buildings was nothing like he had seen in America. He was sure some of the buildings were hundreds of years old. There were waterways and bridges throughout the city. It seemed there was a medieval style giant cathedral on every other block as they rode past the narrow streets of the town. The sound of the horse's hooves and the feel of the carriage wheels running over cobblestones added to the quaint feeling you perceived while riding by the old European shops and businesses. Scott was fascinated by how clean everything was, it seemed like the Cobblestone streets were immaculately clean. He didn't see even a single gum wrapper or cigarette butt anywhere on the roadway.

He couldn't believe this is his life now. The girls thought this was a real-life fairytale, better than any ride at an amusement park. If only mom and dad could see them now.

Scott felt very intimidated watching the throngs of people along the roadside as they stood cheering in front of the shops and businesses of Stockholm. Scott marveled as he watched the soldiers in their dress uniforms also lining the parade route. He couldn't believe his eyes. Cindy is the leader of this country! They rode into the gates of the palace. Greeting them were hundreds of soldiers standing in formation wearing the same blue uniforms as the men on horseback. Scott also watched in awe as their horse-drawn carriage cleared the palace gates with this most amazing palace in the background. The Swedish military band began playing to greet the royal family, along with hundreds of soldiers in dress uniforms standing in formation on the palace grounds.

Later that night, after their tour of the palace and getting settled into their rooms, the whole royal family (including Cindy's other siblings) was scheduled to meet for dinner in the palace dining room. Scott tried encouraging himself to get past this strong feeling of nervousness and insecurity. He thought to himself that he shouldn't be so intimidated because he already participated in the White House State dinner. Tonight's dinner is nothing compared to that right?

This was just Cindy's simple family gathering. He still wondered why he was so nervous. Maybe he just wanted all of them to like him because he loved their oldest sister.

Cindy met him at his bedroom to walk with him into the dining hall together. "Hi Scott, I'm sorry all of my brothers and sisters were not home together when we arrived. So, we decided to have us all meet at dinner. what do you think so far of my home?"

"Well, where do I begin? You have an amazing life, Cindy."

"It's nothing Scott, I thought you had an amazing life. Please don't worry about all this fluff, that's all it is, is fluff. Scott you know, nothing in life matters to me now but you. Well, you and the girls."

"Cindy I will tread through a world of 'weird fluff' just to be with you. You are my everything too, I mean it. You are my wonderful everything, Cindy. I love you."

"I love you too Scott", she said as she leaned over and kissed him on the lips gently and slowly. "I can't believe I get to kiss you, Scott. Now would you like to meet my brothers and sisters?"

The Princess smiled, held his hand and led him into the dining room. Each of her siblings stood and either bowed or curtsied in respect to her rank as she entered the room. Cindy introduced Scott to each of her six brothers and sisters. Moments later, the King and Queen entered the dining room. Everyone stood and bowed again. They remained standing until the King and Queen took their seats and sat down.

Scott enjoyed Cindy's brothers and sisters, they seemed quite jovial. Her family was awestruck by her recent fame and popularity.

Cindy's youngest sister, Louisa, was 10-years old. She sat next to Annabelle and Maryanne and just couldn't stop smiling and joking with both of Scott's little sisters. Louisa thought they were darling little girls, but at the same time, she couldn't fathom what they went through to lose both of their parents. Louisa decided that Scott was her knight in shining armor because he kept all of these children together. She promised the girls they could all play with her toys after dinner.

The other siblings stared in awe as baby Naomi would not let anyone hold her except the Princess. They definitely were not used to seeing her with a baby. Naomi's high chair was placed next to Charlotta so she could help Naomi with her dinner. The Queen also seemed very proud of her daughter. It was so surreal to see The Princess in this role as a mother especially when Naomi called her "Mama".

However, Reinhold, the oldest male amongst her siblings seemed jealous of her popularity. He was also jealous of Scott Mann as well. This kid was a year younger than Reinhold and yet it seemed the whole world is falling over backward for him. Reinhold also did not agree with Sweden's new modern laws regarding the succession of the monarchy. Now the eldest child period, either male or female, is to inherit the crown. Reinhold believed he should have the right since he is the eldest male. He envied his sister Princess Charlotta.

Reinhold believed perhaps the key to get the Crown Princess out of the way for his succession and to inherit the throne himself would be to either disqualify his sister or to get her to abdicate her title and status.

Perhaps her fiancé, this common American, was the key for him. Reinhold decided he would talk to some of his friends for advice as well as some members of their government.

The servers began bringing out the food to the family. Reinhold reached out his foot and tripped one of the servers as she brought out a tray of food. She fell almost on top of Scott striking her chin very hard on his knee as she went down. The whole tray on his food spilled on both of them.

Scott immediately got up and leaned over to assist the female server. "Are you ok?" he helped her up, and also helped her gather up the tray of food. He led her into the kitchen to make sure she was ok. Scott cleaned the spilled food from his own clothes and walked back into the dining hall and took his seat. The serving staff all took notice of Scott's concern and his willingness to do the right thing and make sure she was ok.

No-one said anything for a moment after Scott returned and assumed his seat at the table. Then Scott broke the silence, "That's funny", Scott said turning to Reinhold, "I like a good joke to test out some one's character. But, it's not cool to hurt or embarrass someone innocent in the process (referring to the server)."

Again, no-one commented on the incident and continued eating. It appeared to Scott that Reinhold's attitude has created a controversial family issue that everyone was afraid to address. He was quite surprised that even Cindy kept to herself and did not stand up to him either.

During dinner, the king mentioned to Scott, that they were going to have to award him a title of some sort because their constitution required the heir apparent could only be married to a person of title. This is not an unusual custom as even Prince Phillip had his official title bestowed upon him after marrying Queen Elizabeth. The title would help Scott fit into society much easier. Reinhold paid special attention to this announcement. Perhaps this is something that might help his cause.

After dinner, Scott felt insecure about the matter and requested to speak with the king and Cindy alone.

“I thought about it, but I do not feel this is for me. I mean the title. I am not a Lord or a Duke, neither am I landowner here nor was I born in a special family.”

Cindy replied, “But you have to go along with this request. It's part of our society, its law.”

The king also added, “Yes Scott our constitution requires this. We can make up a position to grant you. When you get married, you will become a Prince.”

“I understand becoming a Prince once I marry the Princess. But I cannot claim some other title now it's only a façade. I feel like I'm becoming something I'm not, just to satisfy some society rules. Besides, I need to set an example to my sisters, my children to be true to yourself. This is important to me.”

“I understand Scott” Cindy replied, she continued, “But you have to do it this way. I can't protect you if you fight against this. There are some things we have to follow just because we are the royal family.”

"Can't we ask to change it? I mean could we go to the parliament or something to ask them to change the law?"

Cindy looked horrified. The king also looked very disappointed. Scott continued, "But doesn't family come first? I mean isn't it important for a man to make his own decisions for what he thinks is best for the health and well being for his own children?"

"Yes Scott", the king answered, "But we cannot do anything to change how we govern our own family. We belong to the people, there are a very strict set of rules for the royal family and we must abide by them."

Scott looked at Cindy, "You understand, don't you? I can't become something I'm not just to impress people. I mean my sisters need to know that we stand for what we believe in. That was true to ourselves. That character means everything."

Cindy was afraid to agree and pleaded with Scott to compromise in just this one thing. Scott however, thought this was a bigger issue. It involved having leadership over one's own family to make your own moral and ethical decisions on how to be a family. No government or constitution should interfere with family.

Scott said he wouldn't make any rash decisions right now, but he told the king and the princess that he would do the right thing for all of them. Cindy and Scott both worried that this could cause a rift between them.

They had been in Sweden for two weeks now and Cindy noticed that Scott was more distant from her since this issue with him receiving a title arose. He seemed distracted. She had never seen him in this emotional state before. The Princess feared that Scott was getting tired of the "new her" (her other identity as the Princess), and just wanted things to go back to the way they were when she was just "Cindy" in California.

He was gone most of the day and night for a couple of days, Cindy worried about him and inquired from her security staff where he had been spending his time.

Agent Wilbrink then informed the Princess that Scott was in the royal archives conducting research of some sort. Princess Charlotta went to the royal archives to talk to Scott.

“I have been missing you, honey.”

“I'm missing you too.”

“What are you doing here that is taking so much of your time away from me?”

Cindy enjoyed the first week when they arrived in her country. They went out sightseeing with the girls every day together. They toured Gamla Stan (Old Town) Stockholm to give Scott a chance to see the traditional architecture of the city. The girls loved visiting the Vasa Museum located on the island of Djurgården near central Stockholm. The museum was a 64-gun wooden warship that sank on her maiden voyage and sat at the bottom for over 300 years. The boat had been salvaged and painstakingly restored. The Vasa is now one of the most visited museums in all of Scandinavia.

Scott even visited a martial arts kickboxing gym in Stockholm so he could start planning out a normal life for himself once again. The whole gym stopped what they were doing within seconds of Scott and the princess walking in the door. Everyone was so attentive and explained each of the classes they offered throughout the week.

But now Scott seemed consumed and unavailable. Scott answered Cindy's question about what he had been so distracted with and tried to explain what he was doing and that he was not upset with her for anything.

“I’m doing some research for a way how I can work this out with your government. I need to work this title thing out for my own conscience. It bothers me that they can dictate so much of our lives. We need to be our own family. It’s worth fighting for.”

“Scott, you can’t. Please, you can’t do this fight. It would be so embarrassing for me and my family. Please, you can’t fight and win this one. I know you have overcome so much. But this one thing you have to let go.”

Scott could see the fear in her eyes and wondered why she didn’t want to back him up on this. This was the first time Cindy opposed him so overtly. But, he knew it was worth the fight. Scott decided he would do the right thing even if it caused her to struggle for a time. She needed to see him fight for their family.

Cindy left him in the library and went to tell her father. This could cause a royal scandal. She worried that for the first time this could cause some very negative publicity.

Scott resumed his searching after Cindy left. He found this dusty old book, in a dark corner of the basement. Scott thought to himself that the book must not have been too important since no-one has read it since it was published. The book seemed like it was going to fall apart when he opened it. Scott then asked one of the palace domestic staff to interpret the book for him since it was written solely in Swedish. The staff was only too glad to help since Scott had stuck up for one of their own on the night of Reinhold’s bullying at the dinner table.

They did find something that might help. He decided to go forward in the fight…

The following morning Scott stood in the parliament building just outside the meeting chamber of the Riksdag (the Swedish governing legislature). After a few hours, several members of Riksdag saw him standing there and sent a staffer to inquire why he stood outside the meeting chamber.

Scott informed the intern, that he wanted an audience before the parliament. He found an old law dated from 1728, that stated if any member of the public waited until after the general session of parliament ended.

Then that member of the public could be invited in to speak before parliament and bring his case before them if there was still time left on the schedule.

Chapter 36

Word quickly spread through the parliament that Scott Mann was seeking an audience with them. Many wondered why he would want to speak with them. Many others were offended that he, an American, would demand to speak to them. It was enough that he was engaged to their own beloved crown princess!

They waited until the very end of the day, making Scott stand in the foyer before the parliament doors for almost eight hours.

Just before the end of the session, they decided to allow Scott inside to present his case, but they also invited the media inside as well. Scott Mann could make whatever case he wanted to present before everyone. But now he could possibly face the scrutiny of the public, and of course a serious grilling from the Riksdag members themselves. This would be a great embarrassment to him and the royal family as well if he bungled this. They waited for the public access channel to move their camera feed in place before inviting Scott to speak.

Scott began: "Honorable members of parliament, I am grateful and humbled for the privilege to be here before you. I am grateful for the wonderful hospitality and kindness all of Sweden has shown my family. However, I am here today to seek your assistance in regard to an old law setting the boundaries of marriage and family for the royal family. It is stated, that 'The heir apparent may marry anyone of title, of genteel background'.

I've been informed that a special title will be granted for me in order to marry the Crown Princess. However, I believe every man should have the right to choose for himself the priorities and standards for his own family. Written laws can sometimes generalize a righteous need, especially for the nation of Sweden. But these laws cannot foresee the unique circumstances faced by each individual family."

"I cannot accept a title of a gentleman especially when I have never lived such a life. I mean no disrespect at the generous notion that your government proposes. This title, however, is a wrong fit for me and my children. They have been taught from birth to live lives of integrity and honor. If they were to see me claim this title, a façade so to speak, to represent myself in public as something I am not. This would conflict with everything, I and my father before me, has tried to instill in these children. Honorable members of parliament, I respectfully request that you change the law (immediately many of the members started interrupting Scott, booing, and hissing) as lawmakers you can assist me in this noble request."

At that, the speaker of parliament began angrily challenging Scott. "How dare you disrespect us after you have been lucky enough in life to marry far above your means. Furthermore, you have been offered a title of respect to save your family honor and keep you from embarrassment in future public events. How dare you present yourself to us so arrogantly and in such an ungrateful manner!"

Scott rebutted, "Sir I assure you, I mean no disrespect or ingratitude. I am only seeking to preserve my own family moral values and standards."

Scott was interrupted by another member of parliament, "What values and standards do you represent young man? How can you know values coming from your own meager social background, or your American ways, the so-called rich national cultural offerings that your people give to the world, like reality TV or every other foolish notion Hollywood produces? The Swedish people are very insulted by your request today. You demean our royal family."

Princess Charlotta was in the palace going over wedding plans with her personal assistant and her publicist. When her father quickly ran into the room and turned on the TV. They watched as Scott debated with the entire parliament on live TV. Each of the local channels quickly picked up the feed to televise the event nationally on every Swedish channel.

The princess became angry, and then embarrassed. She asked her father, “Why doesn’t Scott understand there are some things that we must accept in our lives here? He doesn’t realize that he is making a public mockery of us all.”

Charlotta started crying, and both of her assistants quickly left the room. The king was shocked at his daughter’s response. She had never voiced any frustration in Scott to him or anyone else.

Her father didn’t realize how much pressure she felt from her own government, and the structure of this system governing every aspect of her life. He thought to himself, no wonder why she ran away. She must have felt like a piece of state property and that her very life is not even her own. There are so many behavioral protocols that govern a royal’s life and that alone can be stifling. But of course, there are also legal statutes that govern and structure how Royals must live. That is unless they want to abdicate. He felt a certain sense of compassion for his daughter.

He turned up the TV and said they should see what is being said and will try to cope with the fallout later.

Scott continued to give a very polite explanation for his request, as he ignored growing insults hurled at him from various members of parliament. He rebutted their refusals in a complete respectful tone and demeanor. His bearing and humility had a very gripping effect on the listener.

As the princess and her father continued watching, they too became sold on Scott’s point of view. The king noticed he even felt a tinge of guilt for never standing up for his own family earlier. His own daughter now feels that same stress and pressure that he only knew too well. Why didn’t he stand up to his own government earlier? The king felt so proud of Scott as he seemed like an angel before a crowd of vicious angry men.

But somehow Scott still continued to bring a strong and clear point from a position of strength that no-one could really disagree with. Scott's demeanor made him seem even more likable.

Then something happened during the televised proceedings, the Princess screamed in horror as she watched!

~~~~~~~

Scott continued debating with the whole group of determined opponents and noticed that they increasingly grew angry at him. Scott started his next sentence, "I cannot yield..." Then he felt dizzy for a moment and then collapsed to the floor, passing out...

Several of the members of parliament rushed up to assist Scott. They immediately called for medical help, and helped him back to his feet and sat him down in a bench nearby. Scott was simply exhausted from a combination of standing all day, jet lag, and lack of sleep from staying up all night for his own research. Perhaps the whole culture shock of being in a strange country also added to the fatigue of stress. The camera's continued to broadcast this very emotionally charged event, and large crowds immediately started forming up in the grassy garden areas and bridges behind the parliament house. The Parliament house is located on an island on the outskirts of the center of Stockholm. Immediately, thousands of people from Stockholm flooded to the parliament house.

This was quickly turning into a spectacle so big, that the Riksdag members could not, and would not continue to engage in. It's as if Scott has somehow become an innocent martyr in the public's eyes. The politicians quickly realized that they faced huge public embarrassment, shame, and worse, possible defeat in future elections for their own sad behavior.
~~~~~~~

Scott seemed fine but as a precaution, he was taken to a local hospital via ambulance. The entire Royal family quickly raced to the hospital to check on Scott. Scott was not in any danger but no-one wanted to take any chances at this point. Scott would get a full and complete medical check before being allowed to leave.

Everyone in Scott's hospital room watched on the TV monitor as the Riksdag continued the meeting, this time humanely, debating on how to reconcile the law with Scott's needs.

One of the members brought up a point that seemed to please everyone. Scott would be granted the title of 'Knight of the Royal Order of Seraphim' if the King approved. They could not change the law but crafted a good compromise that should solve this dilemma. They decided that they would still grant him a title, but a true title of chivalry.

The King sat so proudly with Scott in his room as they watched the TV. He couldn't believe how Scott debated valiantly, and as a gentleman, to keep his family honor and stand to true to his values and the values of his parents. The King realized that the Riksdag and any other members of the Swedish government would not challenge Scott in the public arena anymore.

Scott was all of his family's hero, including Reinhold. Reinhold made it a point to apologize to Scott and the rest of the family for his poor behavior during dinner last week.

Charlotta held Scott's hand tightly, she confessed to him that she was angry at first that he had argued with her government in a public forum. "Scott", she continued, "I was embarrassed, honestly. I have never seen any royal figure challenge their government it's just not done in these days. I guess I feel part of the machinery too. That's why I ran away to America. I am humbled though because your presentation to our people was well informed, proper, legal in every manner, and carried out so honorable. You proved to all of my people that you are a true gentleman. I'm sure this is going to have shock waves everywhere in Europe."

Scott answered, "I'm so sorry for carrying out my plan discreetly and not informing you of what I was going to do. I should have. There should never be this kind of secrets from either of us. I'm learning too in our relationship. But I just didn't want to be distracted. I knew this was going to be important for our family in the future for our kids. I also needed to let your own government, and anyone else for that matter, know that I am not the kind of man that takes up a title and this bolstered up false image of myself if it's not true. This goes against everything I stand for."

Charlotta listened and felt so comforted in his choices. She also felt this admiration of respect for him. She knew without a doubt that he would be a gentleman in their marriage. She felt just as if she had won a lottery prize when she looked at him.

In the days to come, several royal families across Europe invited Scott and Princess Charlotta to come for official State business and unofficial business in their respective countries. It seemed Scott had inspired many of the Royal families in Europe to realize that their families are more important and more precious than holding fast to old and stiff royal protocols.

Princess Charlotta and Scott were the power couple in Sweden and in all of Europe for that matter. Every working-class family in Sweden felt close to their princess as well. They rejoiced in the fact she could identify with their lives and the struggles of being a normal citizen having experienced the mundane problems of raising a family. No politician wanted to challenge that dynamic.

Scott joined a martial arts School in Stockholm and also began his next semester of college classes online. The Princess began to fulfill her role in earnest and made several public appearances for various events. Life started to get somewhat routine for them as they began their wedding preparation.

Chapter 37

King Bergfalk summoned Scott and Princess Charlotta to his business office in the Royal Palace in Stockholm. The summons was immediate and seemed important. Scott and Charlotta arrived to see a well-dressed businessman in the office with the King.

The King introduced John Williams as an attorney for the Manchester family. The king seemed very shaken but remained silent. They shook hands and sat down.

Mr. Williams began. “Scott I am honored to meet you. My clients are one of the most prominent families in the world. We have followed you very closely once news of your family circumstances became known in America, especially when the viral videos took us all by storm. We were very intrigued by your story. My clients and I give you great condolences to your family. For your mother, and my client's nephew, your father.”

Everyone in the room stared in disbelief. “Yes sir, my primary client is Reginald Manchester. I believe he is your father's namesake. You see your grandfather Jack was Reginald's older brother.”

Scott interrupted, “You must be mistaken”.

“Actually Scott, we are 100% quite certain. You see they were very close as brothers growing up. ‘We're all of us there are' was originally the special mantra they used together as children. Reginald was crushed when Jack left to the Marines. Then when Jack disappeared, left to California, the family lost track of him. Reginald never stopped looking for his older brother. Once your story became known, we knew where to look. Jacks military records revealed who he was, and then it was a matter of time when we found his public records with the county clerk in Sacramento County. We found the original documents for his name change from Manchester to Mann.

Then we hired a private detective to follow you. He collected a discarded coffee cup from you. The DNA test proves it without a doubt. You are Jack Manchester's heir. At this time, you are now one of the richest young men on the planet. More importantly, you have a whole family desperate to see you. My Client Reginald is very old and requests to meet with you before he dies. You must return with me to Connecticut as soon as possible."

The King added, "Scott he is telling the truth, I had my attorney look over the documents. It appears you do have a bigger family than you thought. The King smiled, "Scott you are not all of you there are! I still can't believe God brought my daughter to you. It seems He has such a big plan. None of this was a mistake or coincidence of fate. I must say, Charlotta, told me that the closer we get to you, we will continually become overwhelmed by you, by the kind of man you are. I am humbled in your presence young man. I think your new family, the Manchester's, will also find you quite special as I have. Therefore, I decree, you and Charlotta must go at once."

Scott turned to Mr. Williams, "I am stunned, I don't know what to say. I will go to see my great uncle. However, I am not interested in money. Why would they save my grandfather Jacks money for me anyway?

Isn't there going to be some big family fight over me being this surprise upstart trying to take their family inheritance away? Honestly, I don't want to bring Princess Charlotta into this kind of battle and drama."

"Sir" Mr. Williams answered, "There is no family squabble over Jacks money. Jacks father, knew after he lost track of his son that he made a grave mistake. He split his estate into two equal halves in his will. Reginald managed all of the family's assets, all of the businesses, and the investments. But my firm has managed to keep them very separated into the two halves. Reginald was very clear to all of his children not to give up the fight but to find Jack or his surviving children to welcome them back to their equal part of the family. Scott, there is no debate in this matter. The whole family wants to meet you, to see you and your sisters. They are so honored it's you, Scott. They are all quite decent people, all of them Scott."

Scott and Princess Charlotta had a private discussion with the King and Queen. The King felt this was a strong priority for Scott to meet with his long-lost family. Charlotta agreed.

Scott wanted to speak with them in private before they jumped to a rash decision. He was worried that the Princess was already gone from the country long enough. What would people think if their princess went back to America once again so soon?

The King laughed and warmly looked at Scott, "Son you have already set a great example for all of us. You set a new precedent when you stood up for your family in front of all of the Riksdag. We do need to put our family first before any public relations business or rules of the royalty. The Princess' public events will always be here for her. But you need to meet your family. The Princess should go with you."

Scott smiled, "I guess we have a family to meet."

Scott and the princess, along with Annabelle, Maryanne, Naomi, and their Swedish security detail arrived at the JFK airport. Agent Sandra Boyd met them at the airport with some of her handpicked colleagues to assist in the security detail. The US government insisted on providing extra security. Which of course, they personally requested Agent Boyd.

The convoy of vehicles drove straight to the Manchester estate in Greenwich Connecticut. Scott was ushered into Reginald Manchester's room to meet with him alone for a moment. Scott brought with him the family photo albums that he kept with him since leaving California.

Reginald sat up in his hospital bed in his bedroom. There were several monitors near the bed along with an IV bag stand. Reginald was so excited the nurses tried to calm him. He held Scott's hand and then wept.

He continued to weep as he looked over each of the photographs in the albums. Scott shared many wonderful stories of his grandfather growing up. Scott also shared other stories about his mother and father and how much he (Reginald) would have loved them.

Reginald then invited the princess and the children inside the room. Reginald cried again when he saw each of the girls and insisted on holding little Naomi even with his frail health.

He asked for his own children to also come inside the room. He introduced each of his sons and daughters to Scott, the children, and the Princess.

Surprisingly, Reginald's children were gracious and did not seem threatened by Scott or the princess in any way. They gave Scott a tour of the mansion and advised him that the mansion was his. Each of Reginald's children had their own estates and did not want to keep up on the older Manchester mansion.

A team of attorneys completed several legal documents and volumes of paperwork during the course of the week and Scott Mann was now officially part of the Manchester clan and assumed his share of his grandfather's inheritance. Scott's net worth now exceeded that of the royal family. Scott and Charlotta discovered that his new family was very large indeed. He was no longer alone in this world.

They enjoyed meeting each of Scott's uncles and aunts. There is no doubt that being with Princess Charlotta definitely helped Scott and the children blend into elite society here in America.

The couple decided that they would return to Sweden for their wedding and then they will move back into their California home. Scott wanted to finish college at the school where he is currently enrolled. The girls will get to continue with their school where they attended last year. More importantly, Scott and Charlotta would have the privilege of finishing the legal adoption of Annabelle and Maryanne in the county where they all grew up. Then they will move back to Sweden after his graduation from college.

Chapter 38

"...weeping may remain for a night, but rejoicing comes in the morning."

Psalm 30:5 (NIV)

Crown Princess Charlotta Dorothea Katarina Maria Bergfalk arrived at the Stockholm Cathedral, a church built in the 13th century. She stepped out of her horse-drawn carriage and listened to the bells that could be heard ringing and echoing throughout the city of Stockholm. The whole nation was in a great festive mood for the wedding of their Crown Princess and Scott Mann from America.

The pews were lined with dignitaries, politician's, including the president of the United States, and royals from all over Europe. But more importantly among the guests were Sgt John and Sandy Weathers, Amanda Peters, Linda Maxwell, Cheryl Adams, Pastor Frank Billings, and of course Hank Jones. It's important to note that there was several Manchester's in attendance as well. Cindy's dream had become a reality. She was marrying her true love. Scott, as in her dream, was not alone, but surrounded by numerous loving family and friends including his new long-lost family. He appeared as the happiest man ever to walk into that church.

King Ludvig Berfalk was handsomely dressed in his naval uniform, as he escorted his daughter the Crown Princess down the aisle toward her waiting for true love. She wore the most beautiful white wedding gown with a train at least 25 feet long.

Yes, even though she was a princess her whole life, this day far surpassed her wildest dreams of a most beautiful and perfect wedding day. The King escorted her down the aisle of the cathedral between the rows of pews. The King stopped to hand over his daughter to her groom. Of course, Scott wasn't standing alone. He was honored to have Sgt Weathers as the best man at his side. His father would have been honored.

After the service, Paige Wilson sang two romantic wedding songs that filled the halls of the cathedral with the sound of an angel. This truly was a wedding that would make any scene in heaven envious.

Scott had suffered through the darkest and scariest times in his life. But in the midst of his darkest pain and deepest fear. Cindy Mason showed up. She brought life, love, warmth, patience, and peace into his life. Scott found relatives too, a family he could have never dreamed of.

Yes, though there were many tears shed in the night, but Joy came in the morning.

The End